W9-BYG-134

DOING HARD TIME

STUART WOODS

LARGE PRINT PRESS

A part of Gale, Cengage Learning

GALE
CENGAGE Learning·

Farmington Hills, Mich • San Francisco • New York • Waterville, Maine
Meriden, Conn • Mason, Ohio • Chicago

GALE
CENGAGE Learning

Copyright © 2013 by Stuart Woods.
A Stone Barrington Novel.
Large Print Press, a part of Gale, Cengage Learning.

ALL RIGHTS RESERVED
This is a work of fiction. Names, characters, places, and incidents either
are the product of the author's imagination or are used fictitiously, and
any resemblance to actual persons, living or dead, businesses,
companies, events, or locales is entirely coincidental.
The text of this Large Print edition is unabridged.
Other aspects of the book may vary from the original edition.
Set in 16 pt. Plantin.

LIBRARY OF CONGRESS CATALOGING-IN-PUBLICATION DATA

Woods, Stuart.
    Doing hard time / by Stuart Woods. — Large print edition.
      pages ; cm. — (Thorndike Press large print basic) (A Stone Barrington
    novel series)
    ISBN-13: 978-1-4104-6123-0 (hardcover)
    ISBN-10: 1-4104-6123-8 (hardcover)
      1. Barrington, Stone (Fictitious character)—Fiction. 2. Private
    investigators—Fiction. 3. Bel Air (Los Angeles, Calif.)—Fiction. 4. Large type
    books. I. Title.
    PS3573.O642D65 2013b
    813'.54—dc23   2013020389

ISBN 13: 978-1-59413-695-5 (pbk. : alk. paper)
ISBN 10: 1-59413-695-5 (pbk. : alk. paper)

Published in 2014 by arrangement with G. P. Putnam's Sons, a member
of Penguin Group (USA) LLC, a Penguin Random House Company.

Printed in the United States of America
2 3 4 5 6   18 17 16 15 14

Doing Hard Time

Somerset Public Library
1464 County Street
Somerset, MA 02726-5234

SOMERSET FICTION
32040002402137
WOODS STUART
Woods, Stuart.
Doing hard time /

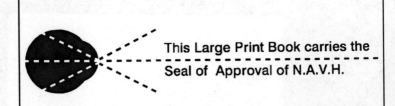

This Large Print Book carries the
Seal of Approval of N.A.V.H.

DOING HARD TIME

1

Teddy Fay didn't like the way the man was looking at him. He pushed his cart around a bend, then trotted halfway down the next aisle in the supermarket and stopped. The man appeared behind him and glanced at Teddy in what he perceived to be a furtive manner. Teddy didn't like it. He especially didn't like that the man was uniformed as a deputy sheriff.

Teddy didn't think of himself as an unnaturally paranoid person; still, after years as a fugitive, albeit now a forgotten one, his sense of self-preservation had become honed to a fine point, and he could not ignore that. He ducked around the next corner, abandoned his shopping cart, and moved quickly toward the rear exit of the big store. He passed through a stockroom and out into the alley behind the store, then he broke into a trot. Before the deputy had had time to miss him and start looking,

Teddy had arrived back in the parking lot in front of the store, started his car, and driven away.

He drove away from the store in the opposite direction from his house, then started to work a pattern of turns that took him in a circle, back to his neighborhood, always checking his rearview mirror and occasionally stopping for a minute or so to see if a sheriff's cruiser would pass him. He took forty minutes to make the ten-minute trip to his house, and he had the garage door open with the remote as he turned into the driveway, so that he didn't have to slow down until the car was inside and the door down. He had enjoyed living in the North Carolina mountain town, but the time had come to move on.

Once inside, Teddy checked the living room window to be sure he had not been followed, then he went to his laptop, entered the eighteen-digit password, found his departure checklist, and printed it. He went to the kitchen, looked under the sink and found the box of surgical gloves he kept there. He donned a pair then went to his bedroom and packed his two duffels with the clothing and belongings he did not want to leave behind. That done, he put all his remaining clothing into a big plastic leaf bag, then vacuumed the house and furniture thoroughly and put the vacuum bag into another leaf bag, followed by every remaining item that he owned, including the used sheets and towels and everything in the refrigerator and freezer. The house had now taken on a bare look, containing only the furnishings that had come with the rental.

When he was satisfied that he had packed everything he was going to take with him he put his belongings and the two leaf bags into the back of the old station wagon he had been driving for the past ten months, then he returned to the house, found a spray bottle of alcohol-based window cleaning fluid, and spent nearly four hours wiping down every door and door handle, piece of furniture, kitchen cabinet, and surface in the house that could retain a fingerprint.

He spent half an hour at his computer, first logging onto the CIA mainframe, then finding his way to the FAA website and creating a new registration for his airplane, using a tail number from a list he had already reserved and had had stick-on numbers made for.

He then packed his laptop and the contents of his safe, including some $400,000 in cash, into a hard suitcase, then he counted out three months' rent, put it into an envelope addressed to the real estate agent, along with a note in childish block capitals explaining his departure, and left it on the kitchen table. Since he didn't have a cleaning lady, it might be weeks before someone found it.

He made a final sweep of the house, then put the suitcase into the rear of the station wagon and, using a yard rake, broke the lightbulb that automatically came on when the garage door was opened. It was past one in the morning, now, and as he closed the garage door with the remote, he checked the block once again for any threat. That done, he tossed the remote into a rosebush in front of the house and left the neighborhood.

He drove several miles across town then tossed the leaf bag containing the useful items he no longer wanted into a Salvation Army collection bin, then, a couple of blocks away, he threw the other leaf bag into a building-site dumpster.

Now clear of the town, he drove to the Asheville Regional Airport and tapped in the code that opened a gate on the back side of the field. He drove to his hangar, opened it, and drove inside. He packed the Cessna 182 RG with his belongings, wiped down the station wagon thoroughly, and left

10

another envelope with three months' hangar rental and a note under a windshield wiper.

He stripped off the plastic, stick-on tail numbers on the airplane and replaced them with the new number. Finally, using the tow bar, he moved the airplane out of the hangar and closed the hangar door. He stripped off the surgical gloves and ran quickly through his checklist, then started the airplane and turned off the master switch, darkening the instrument panel and the interior lights. With only a quarter of a moon and the runway lights to show him the way, he taxied to runway 34 and, without slowing, started his takeoff roll. He thought it likely that, at this time of night, the controller on duty in the tower was probably occupied with some task or reading a magazine and would not notice the small, unlit airplane leaving the airport.

Teddy kept the airplane as low as was safely possible until he was a good twenty miles from the airport, then he turned west and began his climb. Not until he had reached 8,500 feet did he turn on the master switch, the exterior lights, the instrument panel switch, and, finally, the autopilot. He had no specific destination in mind; he would think about that after daylight.

He set his traffic avoidance equipment to a range of twenty miles; an alarm would alert him to other aircraft at or near his altitude. He inclined his seat a few notches, pulled a light blanket over himself, and sought sleep.

Teddy woke with the dawn and looked around him. The American mid-South lay before him, and so did the Mississippi River. He checked his fuel supply and figured he could make Fort Smith, Arkansas, in an hour or so. He landed there, refueled, paid in cash, and had breakfast from a vending machine, washing it down with the free coffee. In half an hour he was back in the air.

Then a wonderful thing happened: the light headwind he had been bucking all night changed, first to a stiff breeze off his beam, then to a fifty-knot tailwind. He began to put real distance behind him.

He was west of Albuquerque near Gallup when he saw it ahead of him. He started a descent until the object revealed itself in the clear, desert air: a Stearman biplane, parked at one end of a dirt strip nestled against a collection of buildings — a motel, a store or two, and a gas station backed up against the landing strip. He circled the little town once and saw what he was looking for: a fuel tank sitting on a wooden cradle near the Stearman. He checked the windsock and put the Cessna down on the dirt.

A man came strolling out the rear door of what appeared to be a garage adjoining the gas station, and he stood by until Teddy had turned everything off and shut down the engine. "Good day to you," the man said, as Teddy got out of the airplane and stretched. "My name's Tom Fields. What can I do you for?"

"You can top me off," Teddy said, offering his hand. "I'm Billy Burnett. Is there someplace where I can get a hamburger?"

"Sure thing," Fields said. "Right across Main Street at the motel." A teenaged boy came out of the garage wiping his hands on a rag. "This is my grandson, Bobby."

"What's this place called?" Billy asked. "I didn't see it on the chart."

"No, you wouldn't. This is Mesa Grande, New Mexico. The world pretty much passed us by when they opened up I-40."

Billy followed Tom Fields into his auto shop and looked around: clean, everything in good order, well equipped — all he required in a workshop. "Nice place you've got here," he said.

"Thanks. Right through that door there is my equipment-rental business. I've got a

13

forklift and a backhoe and some pneumatic drills, plus a lot of smaller stuff. I'll pass both businesses on to Bobby, if I can live until he grows some more. Right now, he's just changing oil and fixing flats. I'm going to send him to mechanic's school when he graduates from high school." He pointed out the front door. "There's your hamburger," he said.

"Thanks, Tom," Billy replied. "Will you join me?"

Tom looked at his watch: "I reckon I will."

Billy was introduced to Sally, a handsome woman of fifty who owned the motel and kept the lunch counter, and the two men had a leisurely lunch, while Teddy shot an occasional appraising glance at Sally, who frankly returned his interest.

"What brings you out our way?" Tom asked over coffee.

"Oh, I just sold my business back in upper New York State, and I thought I'd see some of the country. I lost my wife a year and a half ago, so there was nothing holding me back." Teddy had already adopted Tom's manner of speaking and a little of his accent. It was the natural actor in him.

"What kind of business?"

"Machine shop. Tom, do you reckon I

could borrow enough tools from you to change my alternator? It's been erratic, and I've got a spare aboard."

"Sure you can. I'll help you."

"Thanks."

The two men changed the alternator, then Tom looked at his watch. "I've got to run home," he said. "My wife, Nell, had a little stroke last week, and she's coming home from the hospital in Albuquerque in an ambulance. Due in half an hour."

"You go ahead," Billy said. "Anything I can help you with while you're gone?"

Tom scratched his head. "That's good of you to offer. I've got a Ford over there needs a new water pump. You reckon you could handle that during my absence? I'll pay you for your time."

"I'm glad to help," Billy said. "Don't worry about paying me, I'm right well off these days."

Tom left, and Teddy changed the water pump, teaching Bobby what he was doing. Twice they paused to sell some gasoline to passing cars and clean the windscreens.

It was close to six o'clock before Tom came back. He glanced at the Ford. "Nice job," he said. "Billy, it's too late in the day to start off somewhere. Why don't you come stay with us tonight? My daughter, Bobby's mother, is fixing supper, and we've got a big old house."

"I'd like to have dinner, Tom, but if you don't mind, I'll get a room over at the motel." Before dinner was over, he had offered to stay on for a week or two, until Tom felt comfortable about coming back to work full-time.

After dinner he accepted a drink, then excused himself and drove back to the motel. As he walked through the diner door, Sally was ringing up the check of her last customer of the day.

"It's Billy, right?"

"That's right," Teddy said, sliding into a booth.

"Can I get you something?"

"I'll take a cup of coffee if you'll have a drink with me," he said, placing half a bottle of bourbon on the table before him.

"I'll get us some ice," Sally said. She did that, then slid into the booth with him and watched as he poured.

"I could also use a nice room for a week or two," Teddy said, lifting his glass to her.

Sally clinked glasses and took a deep pull on her whiskey. "I reckon I can find you a place to sleep," she said.

It was as easy as that: he had a job, a bed, and someone to share the latter with. Once again, Teddy Fay had effectively vanished in a puff of smoke.

2

Stone Barrington sat in the fourth row of the University Theater for the winter graduation ceremony of the Yale School of Drama. On one side of him sat Dino and Vivian Bacchetti; on the other side, as far as possible from Viv, sat Mary Ann Bianci Bacchetti, Dino's former wife and the mother of his son, Ben.

Peter Barrington and Benito Bacchetti, the graduating sons, stood on either side of Hattie Patrick, Peter's girlfriend, and, as their names were called, each stepped forward to accept their diplomas from the dean of the School of Drama.

There followed a slightly overlong address to the graduates by a Famous Broadway Director, himself an alumnus, then the ceremony was ended, and everyone involved made for the exits.

As the crowd shuffled toward the doors, Stone saw a familiar face just before it disappeared through the exit. He couldn't place it, but the face had somehow induced a small trickle of anxiety in his guts. Troubled by the feeling, he dismissed it, filed away the face in his mind, and resolved to pull it up later, when he was not so occupied with the matters at hand.

Half an hour later, Stone, Dino, and Viv, but not Mary Ann, who could not tolerate sharing any social occasion, even this one, with her husband's new wife, had said good-bye to her son and vanished. Nobody said "good riddance," but the words were written on the faces of both Dino and Viv, and Ben looked decidedly relieved.

Hattie sat at the concert grand Steinway, playing Chopin waltzes for background music, as Peter's entire graduation class, an even dozen, and their parents and friends sipped champagne, a Veuve Cliquot Grande Dame, supplied by Stone, who now sidled up to his son.

"That went well, I thought," Stone said.

"I know what you want to know," Peter said. "What are my plans?"

"Are you coming back to New York for a while?" Stone asked his son.

"We're leaving for California at dawn," Peter said. "We decided to drive."

"You're going to drive your Prius all the way across America?" Stone asked, incredulously.

"Nope, I traded it for a Porsche Cayenne Turbo," Peter replied. "And we've rented a U-Haul trailer."

"You can't get all this," Stone said, indicating the well-furnished apartment, "into a trailer."

"You're right, Dad. That's why the movers are coming tomorrow and packing and shipping everything to L.A., where it will be stored while we look for a place to live. The U-Haul will hold the stuff we absolutely have to have with us for a couple of weeks."

"That makes sense," Stone said. "Where will you stay when you arrive?"

"Our cottage, Vance's old one on the Centurion Studios lot, is being renovated for us. We can camp out there."

"At the risk of intruding into your personal life," Stone said, "may I point out that we have a perfectly good, five-bedroom house on the grounds of The Arrington, your mother's namesake hotel? You might be a great deal more comfortable there, and there's room service for more than pizza. I'd be happy to give them a call and let them know you're coming."

"Thanks, Dad," Peter said, as if this

alternative had never occurred to him, "we'll take you up on that."

"When will you be arriving?"

"Next Friday. We start at the studio the following Monday. Our script has already been approved for production."

"So you're jumping in at the deep end, then?"

"You could put it that way, I guess. Having a shooting script already approved gives us a head start."

So did the ownership of forty-five percent of the studio's stock by himself and Peter's trust, Stone mused. "I expect you'll get a warm reception from Leo Goldman Jr.," he said.

"Leo told me he's going to treat us just like everybody else at the studio," Peter said. "No favoritism."

"Okay," Stone said, "and if he fails to do that, we can always muster enough votes on the board to fire him." Stone and his friend, Mike Freeman, CEO of Strategic Services, Stone's principal law client, both served on the board and together voted a majority of the shares.

Peter laughed heartily. "I hope it won't come to that, Dad."

"You never know what can happen when you're doing hard time in Hollywood,"

Stone said.

"What do you mean by that?" Peter asked, sounding genuinely curious.

"After a few weeks at Centurion Studios, you won't need to ask," Stone said. "By the way, I know this will sound odd, but I'd like for you to call me if you meet anyone out there who is Russian."

"I don't understand."

"I know. I just saw someone at your graduation ceremony who looked familiar, and, on reflection, I somehow think he's Russian."

"Dad, I know you've recently had some serious troubles with a Russian Mob, but why would any of them be at my graduation ceremony?"

"I don't know, but I want you to be alert to the possibility that, if you meet someone who is Russian, he may not be a friend. Please, just call me."

"All right, I will."

Dino wandered over, Viv in tow. "Now that we've outlasted Mary Ann, why don't we get out of here and leave these kids to get drunk and have a good time?" Dino always worried when his ex-wife had too much access to his son. He said she had a way of eating people's brains.

"The car's parked out front," Stone said.

"Let's say our goodbyes."

There was a round of hugs, kisses, and standard advice, then they were in Stone's car, headed from New Haven back to New York.

It was very quiet for a while, then Dino finally spoke. "I don't know why," he said, "but I feel like crying."

"Oh, Dino," Viv said, "get a grip."

"I feel like crying, too," Stone said.

But neither of them did.

3

Stone pulled into his garage, which had been enlarged into the basement space of the house next door. He had recently purchased and remodeled the house, and it now contained a duplex flat for guests and three other apartments, into which he had moved his secretary, Joan, his cook and housekeeper, Helene, and his newly acquired houseman or butler, Frederick Flicker, known as Fred. Stone had received a year of Fred's service as a gift from his Parisian friend, Marcel duBois, and the man had quickly made himself indispensable.

Fred greeted them and took their coats as they let themselves into Stone's house from the garage. "Good evening, Mr. Barrington, Chief, and Mrs. Bacchetti. Dinner will be served in about an hour. May I fix you all a drink?"

"You may, Fred," Stone said, following him into the study. They sank into comfortable chairs and received their usuals from Fred's silver tray. Fred inquired if they required anything else, was told no, then vanished.

"I want one of those," Dino said, raising his scotch in Fred's general direction.

"I don't think there *is* another one of those," Stone replied.

"Dino," his wife said, "we have two unoccupied maid's rooms in our new apartment. Why don't you find yourself a nice retired cop and install him there?"

"I don't think retired Irish or Italian cops fall into the employment category of butler," Dino said. "I can just see one now, stumbling around the apartment, spilling drinks."

"All right, I'll look into it then," Viv said.

Stone laughed. When Viv said she'd look into something, that meant it was practically done. "I predict you'll have a houseman inside of a week," Stone said.

"Now, wait a minute, Viv," Dino said. "I don't know if I can afford a houseman on my salary."

"You forget, my darling, that we have two salaries now. We can't afford a Rolls-Royce, but we can afford a houseman."

"Dino," Stone said, "shut up and leave this to Viv. Haven't you learned to do that yet?"

"Awright, awright," Dino said. "Don't the two of you gang up on me."

"Dino," Stone said, changing the subject, "did you see anybody at the graduation ceremony that you made as Russian?"

Dino frowned. "Gimme a hint."

"Tallish, pale hair and skin, hefty, decent suit."

"Got him," Dino said. "I didn't read him as Russian, but you're right, he could be. You worrying about Russians?"

"After the past few weeks," Stone said, "I'll worry about Russians for the rest of my life."

"What would one of that mob be doing at Peter's and Ben's graduation?"

"That's what worries me," Stone said.

"Excuse me for a moment," Viv said, rising. "I'll be right back."

"Dino," Stone said when she had gone, "you don't know how lucky you were to find that woman."

"Oh, yes I do," Dino replied, "and if I forget for a moment, she'll remind me."

"How's the city's new chief of detectives doing?" Stone asked, referring to Dino's new job.

"He's scared shitless that he's going to make some big mistake and embarrass the commissioner when the guy's about to an-

26

nounce his run for mayor."

"You'll do fine," Stone said, "because you have good instincts — both cop instincts and political instincts."

"There are a lot of unhappy captains who didn't get the job," Dino pointed out.

"You're going to have enemies no matter what job you're in," Stone said. "You had enemies when you were running the detective squad at the Nineteenth Precinct, and you always handled them with aplomb."

"Aplomb? That's a word I've never associated with myself," Dino said. "I like it."

"It comes naturally to Italians."

Viv returned to the study and sat down. "We have an interview tomorrow at six PM," she said.

"Who's interviewing us?" Dino asked, looking mystified.

"We're doing the interviewing: I spoke to Eduardo Bianci, and he spoke to his man, Peter, who recommended a nice couple."

"If I wanted to find a guy to slip a knife into somebody's liver, then I'd ask Peter's advice."

"Can't a person have more than one talent?" Viv asked.

"Eduardo is in love with you," Dino said. He had introduced her to his former father-in-law at their wedding.

"Maybe a little," she admitted.

"Hey, wait a minute! You said 'couple'?"

"We need a housekeeper," Viv said. "That daily cleaning lady isn't cutting it — nothing gets really clean. And anyway, we have two maid's rooms — they can use one for a sitting room and the other for a bedroom."

"You've got this whole thing worked out already?"

"Dino," Stone said, "I told you: shut up and get out of her way."

Fred appeared. "Dinner is served in the kitchen, as requested," he said.

They polished off their drinks and went downstairs.

"I'll see what I can learn about the Russian guy at graduation," he said to Stone as they started down the stairs.

After a first course of smoked salmon, Fred set three plates in front of them, each covered with a slab of meat that hung over the edges.

Dino cut off a chunk and ate it. "Interesting," he said.

Viv tried it, too. "A little gamy, but nice, even tender. What is it?"

"Moose," Stone replied.

The Bacchettis set down their knives and forks and stared at Stone. "What?" Dino said. "Did you find that at Grace's Market?" he asked, referring to a tony East Side grocery.

"Bill Eggers shot it. He sent me fifteen pounds of it."

"And you thought you'd feed it to us?" Dino asked incredulously.

"What have you got against moose?" Stone asked.

"Nothing that would make me want to kill it and eat it."

"It's like when you're eating venison you're eating Bambi," Viv said.

"There is no moose equivalent of Bambi," Stone said. "At least I don't think there is. Anyway, Bambi is a baby deer. Eggers shoots only grown-up moose. Or meese. What is the plural of moose, anyway?"

"Mice?" Dino offered.

"Dino," his wife said, "you're just making it worse."

Reluctantly they re-attacked their moose. Finally, Dino had had enough and dropped his utensils. "Maybe it's more like horse," he said.

"A moose is almost as big as a horse," Stone said. "And the French eat horse."

"I give up," Viv said, putting down her fork. "Too many comparisons. Next time you serve us moose, Stone, disguise it in a stew or something."

"I've still got twelve pounds of it," Stone said.

"Is that a threat?" Dino asked.

"Just information."

"I didn't want to know that."

4

Hattie was driving. "Look, a hill," she said, pointing ahead.

"I don't believe it," Peter said from the backseat.

"No," she replied. "Upon reconsideration, it's not a hill, it's a landfill. There was a sign back there."

"Where are we?"

"Somewhere in western Kansas, according to the GPS map."

"How can people live here?" Ben asked from the front passenger seat. "There are no hills and no trees."

"I saw a tree about an hour ago," Hattie said.

"That one doesn't count," Peter said. "It was in somebody's front yard. They probably imported it from someplace with a surfeit of trees."

"Like North Carolina," Ben said. "They have a surfeit of trees."

"Can't you guys think of anything to talk about?" Hattie asked.

"We're talking about trees," Ben said.

"And very earnestly," Peter added.

"Talk about ideas, not plants."

"Yeah," Ben said. "Anybody got an idea for a movie we can make?"

"We've already got a movie to make," Peter said.

"But what do we make after that?" Ben asked.

"How about a musical?" Hattie suggested. "I love musicals."

"Leo Goldman Junior says musicals lose money," Ben said.

"Okay, then let's make a moneymaking musical."

"A musical with old music or new music?" Peter asked.

"Old music," Hattie replied. "It's a lot better than new music."

"With dancing?" Ben asked. "I mean with real dancing, like Fred Astaire, not dancing like boogieing."

"Real dancing."

"Then we'll have to discover a new Fred Astaire," Peter pointed out. "The old one died." He looked over his shoulder. "Is there a car following us? All I can see is the U-Haul trailer."

Hattie checked the rented mirror that was clipped onto their SUV. "There's a dot in my mirror. I don't know if it's a car."

"What else could it be?" Peter asked.

"A truck."

"Then it would be a bigger dot. Anyway, it's been following us all day."

"Maybe it's the only other car in Kansas besides ours," Ben said.

"But why is it following us?"

"Maybe it wants to mate with our car," Ben offered.

"Oh, come on, guys," Hattie said. "When are you going to stop talking about a car following us? You're just being paranoid."

"We're not paranoid if there's an actual car following us," Peter said.

"Well, I'll give you this," Hattie said. "It never seems to catch up, and it never drops out of sight."

"It's following us," Peter said.

Back in New York, Stone called Mike Freeman, CEO of Strategic Services, the second-largest security company in the United States, and a partner in The Arrington. "You feel like a trip to L.A. to see how the hotel is doing?" Stone asked.

"You just want to check up on Peter," Mike said.

"It could be like spring break," Stone said.

"You forget I'm British. What's spring break?"

"It's a week or two of vacation, when college kids go somewhere and get drunk."

"You make it sound like such fun," Mike said. "When do you want to go?"

"We can go anytime we like," Stone said. "You have a big, fast airplane."

"That's true," Mike said. "It does kind of sound like fun, and we can check up on our movie studio and see how it's doing. How about tomorrow morning?"

"Perfect," Stone said. "That'll give me a chance to clean up my desk before we go. And we'll get there right after Peter."

"You sure you don't want to take your airplane?" Mike asked.

"It's a lot slower than your airplane," Stone pointed out. "And we'd need to stop at least twice for fuel. We could overnight in Santa Fe and check up on how Ed Eagle is doing."

"Let's take my airplane," Mike said. "Two days of traveling is too long."

"Especially when you've got a Gulfstream Five," Stone said.

"All right, pick me up at nine tomorrow morning."

"Where, home or office?"

"It's the same place. Call me when you're five minutes away."

"Done." Stone hung up and buzzed Joan. "Mike and I are going to L.A. tomorrow morning."

"To work or play?"

"Some of both. We have to find a way to make the trip tax-deductible."

"You're just going to check on Peter and Ben and Hattie, aren't you?"

"What, you think I'm an overprotective father?"

"Of course."

"Let's clean up any work I have left, so I won't have to worry about it."

"You never worry about work. Hang on, call coming in." She put him on hold, then came back. "Dino on two for you."

Stone pressed the button. "Hey."

"I was just thinking," Dino said, "I've got some vacation time coming. Why don't we go out to L.A. and have some fun?"

"What about Viv?"

"She's running a protection detail for some business guy who's headed to Miami for a few days."

"That's convenient. Actually, I was about to call you. Mike and I just talked about going to L.A. You want to go to check up on Ben, don't you?"

"Well, as long as we're out there, we can check up on the kids."

"Yeah, okay, as long as we're going to be out there anyway, why not?"

"When?"

"Be here at eight-thirty tomorrow morning. We'll pick up Mike on the way."

"We taking your airplane or his?"

"His."

"Right, you're on." Dino hung up.

5

Hattie checked her rearview mirror for the thirtieth time in the past two hours, and the dot was still there. Abruptly, she turned off at the next exit.

"Where are you going?" Peter asked, waking from his doze.

"Route 66," she replied.

"Like the jazz tune?"

"Right. We'll pick it up somewhere around Amarillo."

"Then Gallup, New Mexico," Peter said, remembering the lyric. "But wouldn't we make better time on the interstate?"

"No doubt, but the dot in the mirror has been there all morning, and I'm tired of looking at it. If it's a semi it will stick to the interstate, and we'll be rid of it."

"And if it isn't?"

"A car would probably still stick to the interstate, too," she said, "but if it follows us I'm going to stop and buy a gun."

"Where would you buy a gun?"

"How about at a gun store?"

"Isn't there a waiting period?"

"Then we'll look for a gun show, where the waiting period doesn't apply, according to every news report I hear."

"Hattie, aren't you being just a tiny bit paranoid?"

"More than a tiny bit."

"Okay," Peter said, and tried to go back to sleep.

In the late afternoon, Ben was driving and Hattie was asleep in the backseat. Peter awoke from a doze. "Where are we?"

"Almost to Gallup," Ben said. "I got off Route 66 a couple of miles back and turned south, to see if the dot follows us."

"The dot is still there?"

"It turned up an hour ago, as if it had been waiting just over the horizon."

"I'm beginning to think that Hattie's idea of buying a gun isn't such a bad one."

"I've got my dad's old .38 Special in my bag," Ben said.

They hit a bad pothole in the old two-lane highway, and there was a *pop,* followed by a fluttering noise.

"Shit!" Ben spat. "I didn't have time to avoid that one. Now we've got a blowout."

He pulled over at a wide place on the shoulder, and they got out of the car.

Hattie sat up. "What's going on?" she asked.

"We've got to change a tire," Peter answered. "Go back to sleep."

"Gladly," she said, and sank back into the seat.

They had to unload their suitcases to get at the spare, which turned out to be a strange-looking emergency tire.

"How far do you think we can get on that thing?" Ben asked.

"I don't know. I'll look it up in the manual when we're done," Peter replied.

They changed the tire and put the old one in the U-Haul, then returned their luggage, but not before Ben had taken a long look down the highway behind them, then retrieved the .38 from his suitcase and tucked it into his belt. "The dot is still back there," he said, "but it stopped when we did."

Peter was looking in the driver's manual.

"How far is the tire good for?" Ben asked, starting the car.

"A hundred miles," Peter replied, "at fifty miles per hour."

Ben sighed and pulled back onto the highway. "We'll try to replace the tire at the first place we come to. We need gas, too," he said.

"We just passed a sign for an Esso station."

"An *Esso* station?"

"Yep. We should be able to get some very old gasoline there. It's five miles ahead."

Shortly they passed a sign announcing their entry into Mesa Grande, New Mexico. The Kiwanis Club met at Sally's Diner on Tuesday evenings, it said.

"Up ahead, on the right," Peter said.

Ben pulled into the service station, which had a sign on the pumps saying, "Independent." A wiry-looking man in his fifties strode out of the office and walked around to the driver's window.

"Yessir?" he said.

"Fill 'er up," Ben told him, and they got out of the Cayenne to stretch their legs. Hattie woke up and went to the ladies' room. The tank full, the man began to clean the bugs off the windshield.

"You had a flat, did you? We can fix that for you," he said as he worked.

"A blowout," Peter replied. "Can you fix that?"

"I guess not," the man said. "Let's take a look at it."

Peter opened the U-Haul and took out

40

the wheel with its ruined tire.

The man looked at it closely. "That would be from that pothole about five miles back," he said.

Peter and Ben laughed aloud. "Must be good for business," Peter said.

"I've hit it myself," the man said. "I reported it to the county, but they're slow to move." The man pointed across the road. "I suggest you go over to the diner and speak to Sally, who can fix you up with some rooms."

"Can you replace the tire?" Peter asked.

"No, and neither can most tire dealers in the state," the man replied. "It's a high-performance Pirelli." He glanced at his watch. "If I hurry, I can get the Porsche dealer in Albuquerque on the phone before they close at six, and they can put a tire on the Greyhound bus to us tomorrow morning. I can have you out of here by noon."

"Sounds good," Peter said, eyeing the motel across the road with doubt. "Tell me about the motel," he said.

"It's the cleanest, homiest, most comfortable motel in town," the man said. "It's also the *only* motel in town, but don't be put off by that. Sally will take care of you, and she's a good cook, too."

"Great," Peter said. "You order the tire,

and we'll walk across the road."

He followed the man's directions to pull the car over and unhook the U-Haul, then handed him the keys. "My name is Peter Barrington," he said, offering his hand.

The man wiped his palm on his coveralls and shook Peter's. "My name's Billy," he said.

The three young people each grabbed a suitcase and walked across the road, while Billy phoned the Porsche dealer and ordered the tire.

The call made, Billy drove the Cayenne into the garage and onto the hydraulic lift. *Might as well get that wheel taken care of now,* he thought. He hosed it down to wash the dust away, then spun off the studs and set the wheel on the shop floor. There was some mud and dirt caked in the wheel well, and he turned his hose on that, too, dissolving it to run down the drain.

Then Teddy saw something he didn't expect. Way forward in the wheel well, the hose had revealed a black box, perhaps one inch by two and an inch thick. A two-inch antenna sprouted from the upper end of the box.

He knew what that was, because he had invented a GPS transmitter very much like it in his time at the CIA and installed many of them. The question was: Where and in whose hands was the receiver?

6

Stone sat in the jump seat of the Gulfstream jet and watched the two pilots join the VOR A instrument approach for runway 21 at Santa Monica Airport. He knew from experience that the controllers usually vectored you onto final approach a couple of thousand feet high, and he wanted to see how the two pros would get the airplane down to final approach altitude while, at the same time, slowing it to final approach speed. He always had a hard time with that in his own airplane, but the Gulfstream pilots did it brilliantly, and they touched down exactly where they were supposed to at the exact speed they were supposed to.

A quick turn into Atlantic Aviation, and they were there. As the engines shut down, one of the Arrington's fleet of Bentley Mulsannes eased to a stop near the foot of the airplane's airstair door, and the trunk lid silently opened.

With their baggage unloaded into the car, the three men piled into the Bentley, and they started for the hotel. They had not reckoned on what the widening of I-405 would do to the afternoon traffic, and they crept along the few miles to the Sunset Boulevard exit. Once there, they were on Stone Canyon Road in a flash, then turning through the gates of the splendid new hotel. An Arrington security guard was there to identify them and wave them through without the usual stringent procedures, and they arrived at Stone's house five minutes later.

The grounds were laid out among gardens, and no building was more than two stories high. The effect was more of a luxurious neighborhood than a hotel, and it was more inviting.

The Arrington was built on a large tract of land that had been assembled over several decades by the late movie star Vance Calder, to whom Arrington had been married before his death. Stone had helped Arrington turn what had been her home and property into America's premier super-luxury hotel, and one of the provisions in the initial contract was that the hotel company would build her a new house on the property. After their marriage and her death, Stone had inherited the house.

The butler quickly directed the three hotel bellmen in distributing their luggage. In his suite, Stone unpacked and hung up his suits, then changed into cotton trousers and a short-sleeved shirt and took a glass of iced tea out to poolside behind the house.

He read the day's L.A. *Times* while sipping his iced tea and soon fell into a doze in the comfortable high-backed wicker armchair. A moment later he was half-awakened by a splash behind him, then by the sound of someone doing laps in the pool. That would not be Dino, he thought, and probably not Mike Freeman, either. He swiveled the chair slowly around to face the pool and was greeted by the sight of a woman's legs disappearing under the water. There had been a flash of her body above the legs, and it wasn't wearing a swimsuit.

He watched until she surfaced and began breaststroking toward him, apparently not noticing his presence.

"Good afternoon," he said finally.

She stopped dead in the water and her gaze found him in his chair. "Who are you?" she demanded. "And what are you doing here?"

"I am Stone Barrington, and I am sitting, drinking iced tea, and reading the newspaper. It's clear what you are doing, but not who you are or why you are swimming in my pool."

"*Your* pool?" she asked, with the withering certainty of someone who knows herself to be in the right.

"All right, I'll repeat myself: *my* pool." He nodded toward the house. "Right behind *my* house."

"Well then," she said, "I will get out of *your* water, if you will be kind enough to turn your back."

Stone smiled. "Certainly not. I intend to enjoy all the fruits of *my* property."

"Swine!" she said, then turned, swam to the steps, and regally climbed them, displaying broad shoulders and slim hips in all their glory. She walked to a chair where she had left her things, dried herself and her blonde hair slowly with a small towel, then slipped into a terry robe. Ignoring him, she turned to go.

"As long as you're decent, you may as well join me for a drink," Stone said.

She stopped and turned toward him "Oh, now I understand. You're Arrington Barrington's husband."

"Widower," Stone corrected her.

"All right," she said, and began to walk around the pool toward him. "I'll have a piña colada."

Stone picked up the phone beside him and said, "Two piña coladas," then hung up and rose to greet her, offering his hand. "And your name?"

"Emma Tweed," she said, and her accent was British.

"Please sit down. Your drink will be here shortly. What brings you to The Arrington, Emma?" he asked. "And all the way from London?"

"I was tired of the London winter, and I was reliably informed that this is now the best hotel in the United States."

"I like to think of it as the best hotel in the world," Stone said, "but thank you."

"How modest," she said. "One would think that you had invented the place."

"Well, it was my idea, but a large group of talented people invented it. I just offered guidelines."

The butler appeared with their drinks on a silver tray and served them, then vanished.

She raised her glass. "To your guidelines," she said.

"Tell me, why are you able to leave London at the drop of a hat? Do you not have to earn a living?"

"I earn a very nice living as a fashion designer," she said, "but since I own my company, I am able to come and go as I please. Actually, I can work anywhere. You might say my work is portable."

"How nice for you. What do you design?"

"Everything from underwear to clothes to home furnishings. By the way, I'm not really trespassing: I'm staying right over there." She pointed at a house mostly screened by plantings.

"Ah, yes, that was Vance Calder's guest-house. I stayed there a couple of times when he was alive. This was his pool, too, so it's easy to understand how you could think it belonged to your quarters. How long have you been here?"

"Since yesterday."

"And what do you think of The Arrington so far?"

"I cannot fault it on any count," she replied. "It is everything I was told it would be."

"I'm pleased that you are pleased."

"How is it that you are able to drop everything and come to Los Angeles? You're a New Yorker, aren't you?"

"Yes, and I'm an attorney there. The hotel is one of my clients, and I serve on its board, so you might say this is a business trip — at least, that's what I would say if I thought you were an agent of the Internal Revenue Service."

She smiled for the first time. "That's something like what I'll be saying to our Inland Revenue in the UK," she said. She drained her glass. "Well, if you'll excuse me, I'm due at the spa for a little work." She stood up.

Stone stood, too. "Would you like to join some friends and me for dinner here this evening?"

"Thank you, that sounds very nice. What time?"

"Drinks at seven," Stone replied.

"See you then," she said, then turned and sauntered down the path toward her accommodations.

"It was my pleasure, believe me," Stone called after her.

She seemed to laugh, then, without turning around, gave him a little wave.

"Wear something you designed," he called out to her disappearing back. She gave the little wave again.

Stone went back into the house, and the butler materialized. "Mr. Barrington, your son just called but said not to disturb you. He's stopping overnight in New Mexico to get a tire changed, and he will be a couple of more days before arriving."

"Thank you," Stone said. "We'll be four

for dinner, then." *Unless I can get rid of Dino and Mike,* he thought.

7

It was nearly six o'clock, and Teddy was about ready to close up and go to Sally's for dinner, when a black Lincoln Navigator with blackened windows came to a stop beside the gas pumps. He walked out to the car and stood by the driver's window, which was impenetrable to his gaze. He rapped on the window with a knuckle. "Can I help you?" he shouted.

The window slid down. The first thing Teddy saw was a GPS antenna stuck to the inside of the windshield and a screen mounted on the dashboard. "You can fill this tank," the man said. "With the premium." He was large, bald, and his companion in the front passenger seat was on the beefy side, too.

"Yessir," Teddy said, and as he turned away toward the car's fuel filler he heard the driver speak to his companion in Russian. One of the many skills Teddy had picked up in his time at the CIA was languages. He had a gift, not so much for speaking but for understanding them.

"You see the rented trailer over there?" he said. "It appears our prey have stopped for the night at the motel, there. This little burg is a good place to deal with them," the driver said. "We'll get a room for the night, then tomorrow morning we'll wait for them on the road, kill them, and bury them in the desert. No one will ever hear from them again."

Teddy stopped in his tracks. "You fellas Croatian?" he asked. "That what you're speaking?"

"We are Italian," the driver said.

Teddy turned on the pump, unscrewed the fuel filler cap, stuck the nozzle in, squeezed the trigger, and locked it. Fuel began to flow. Teddy walked back past the driver's window. "Scuse me, gotta take a leak," he said to the man. "Your tank is filling up." As he walked away from the car he heard the door open and the driver say in Russian, "He may have heard something. Take care of him."

Teddy walked into the garage and found his duffel. He removed a small .380 semi-automatic pistol and screwed the silencer he had built into the barrel, then stuck it in his rear waistband, under his shirttail. He went into the john and waited, the pistol in his hand, facing the door, and after a minute he flushed the toilet. The door flew open, and the Russian passenger began raising his weapon. Teddy shot him once in the forehead and watched him collapse in a heap. He picked up the man's pistol and fired it once into the wooden floor, then waited.

Another minute passed, and Teddy heard the other Russian. "Yevgeny!" he yelled.

"Come help me!" Teddy called back, in Russian.

"Can't you do anything yourself?" the man yelled back, and Teddy could hear his footsteps. He aimed the pistol at a spot just inside the outside door and waited. A moment later the driver appeared, and Teddy shot him in the head. The man had been holding a pistol, too.

Teddy walked outside, returned the gas nozzle to its pump, got into the Navigator, and drove it into the garage. He got out, closed the garage door, and switched on the neon sign that said CLOSED over the pumps.

He was thinking fast now. With considerable effort, he hauled the two bodies to the rear of the Navigator, opened the rear door, and tossed the men's luggage over the rear seat, then he muscled the corpses into the luggage compartment, tossing their weapons in behind them, and closed the door. Then he turned on the hose and washed their blood down the drain in the men's room floor. He already had his plan worked out.

Teddy went next door to where the rental equipment was stored and started the backhoe. He had had some experience with the machinery when, back in Virginia, he had dug his own swimming pool behind his house. He drove the machine out the rear door of the building and into the piñon trees that grew wild behind the property, found a clear spot, and began to dig. After a couple of minutes' work he had established a rhythm, and in about an hour, he dug the equivalent of his Virginia swimming pool in the sandy soil.

He left the backhoe idling, went back into the garage, started the Navigator, and drove it out to the hole. It was a little awkward among the piñons, but he maneuvered the SUV alongside his hole, then he switched off the ignition. He got back onto the backhoe and drove it toward the Navigator at a ninety-degree angle, then stopped eighteen inches from the vehicle.

He got the backhoe's blade under the SUV and began to lift it from the side. Soon, the Navigator toppled over onto its side into the waiting hole. The noise of it hitting bottom was muffled by the vertical sides of the hole and the surrounding piñons.

Teddy turned the backhoe around and used the earthmoving blade to push the soil back into the hole, taking another half hour to fill it, then he drove the backhoe over it a few times to pack down the soil. After he had used a piñon branch to smooth the earth, there was nothing left to see.

He returned the backhoe to the building and hosed off the dirt and dust, then locked up for the night. He freshened up and changed his clothes in the men's room, then walked across the road to Sally's Diner.

The three young people were sitting in a booth, finishing their dinner. He waved to them. "Your tire will get in on the eleven-o'clock bus tomorrow morning," he said to them, "and I'll get it right on your vehicle."

He sat down on a stool at the counter. "Evening, Sally," he said.

"Evening, Billy."

"You got any meat loaf left?"

"Sure, I do."

"Any bourbon left in that bottle?"

"Enough for two," she said, filling a pair of glasses with ice and pouring some. They both took a swig, and then Sally served both of them some meat loaf.

The three young people walked over with some cash for their check and left it on the counter. "Thanks, Sally," Peter said.

"You kids may as well sleep late," Billy said. "I'll have your car ready by noon."

"Okay, thanks," Peter said. "Good night."

"Good night, then," Billy said, and the three of them left for their rooms.

"Who was in the Navigator?" Sally asked.

"A couple of guys. I filled them up and they drove on. I tried to sell them one of your rooms, but they seemed to be in a hurry."

8

Stone came down before dinner to find Dino and Mike already having a drink. He sat down, and the butler brought him a Knob Creek on the rocks.

"We're having a guest for dinner," he said to his friends.

"Anybody we know?" Dino asked.

"No, someone newly arrived from London. Her name is Emma Tweed, a fashion designer. She's staying in the old guesthouse behind the bushes, and I found her in our pool this afternoon."

"Typical," Dino said to Mike. "He finds them everywhere."

The doorbell rang, and the butler ushered in Emma Tweed. She was wearing a multi-colored silk dress with a low neckline and a short skirt. Stone made the introductions, and the butler brought her a martini. "I had hoped that my son, his girl, and Dino's son would join us this evening, but they're somewhere in New Mexico with a flat tire."

"I'm sorry to miss them," Emma said. "I have a twenty-three-year-old daughter who has left school. She arrives tomorrow."

"My son, Ben, will be delighted to hear that," Dino said.

"Beautiful dress," Stone said. "One of yours?"

"Indeed," Emma said. "I hardly ever wear anything else." Her blonde hair was swept straight back and fell nearly to her shoulders; she had a light tan and seemed to be wearing hardly any makeup.

"Were you a competitive swimmer in your school days?" Stone asked.

"I was. I'm surprised you could tell."

"Something about your proportions," he replied.

"Ah, yes, my shoulders. I can't hide them."

"And you shouldn't."

"Well, gentlemen, I know why Mr. Barrington is here, what's your excuse for getting away from winter in New York?"

"Getting away from winter in New York," Mike said. "Who needs an excuse?"

"Mike is also on the board of the hotel," Stone said. "He also runs the world's second-largest security company."

"And you, Mr. Bacchetti?"

"Please, let's do this on a first-name

59

basis," Stone said. "Dino is shy, so I'll tell you that he is the chief of detectives for the New York City Police Department."

"I feel safer already," Emma said, "in safe and well-qualified hands."

"What is your daughter's name?" Dino asked.

"Tessa. How tall is your son?"

"Six feet."

"Is he intimidated by tall women? Tessa is six-two."

"Ben is not intimidated by anything — certainly not tall women. How does Tessa feel about men shorter than she is?"

"She has learned not to use height as a measurement of character," Emma said. "After a few mistakes. I think she actually prefers looking down at men."

"Then they should get along well."

"Why are the children in New Mexico?"

"They insisted on driving from New Haven, Connecticut, where they have all three just graduated from Yale, to their new work in L.A."

"Which is?"

"They are a team: Peter, my son, writes and directs films. Ben produces them, and Hattie, Peter's girl, writes their scores."

"Such creativity!"

"It spills out of them. Has Tessa chosen a

career?"

"It has been her dream since childhood to be an actress. She's fresh out of RADA — the Royal Academy of Dramatic Arts."

"And she's seeking her fortune in L.A.?"

"She's having a look at it. She's never spent a winter in a warm place, and I'm afraid she may like it here too much."

"Everybody falls for the weather," Stone said. "It's a pity she's not here this evening. We're expecting one of Hollywood's most famous actresses, Charlene Joiner, for dinner. She said she'd be a little late."

"Uh-oh," Dino said. "Stone has fixed you up, Mike."

"I wanted it to be a surprise," Stone said.

"Okay, I'm surprised," Mike replied. "Charlene Joiner! Imagine!"

The doorbell rang, and Charlene swept into the room, all smiles. Big kisses for Stone and Dino and firm handshakes with Mike and Emma. "I'm so sorry to be late, but we wrapped a film an hour ago. I changed in my trailer."

"I've seen your two most recent films with my daughter, who's an aspiring actor," Emma said. "We both thought you were splendid."

"Thank you so much," Charlene said,

61

beaming. "I've had a good run of luck with directors and scripts lately. Is your daughter in town?"

"Arriving tomorrow."

"Then you must let me arrange a tour of Centurion Studios for her."

"She would love that."

"I'm sure Ben would be delighted to conduct the tour," Dino said. "Charlene, our boys, Peter and Ben, are arriving in a couple of days, along with Peter's girl, Hattie Patrick."

"Yes, I met them at the grand opening of the hotel, and I heard Hattie perform at the piano, too."

"Yes, I had forgotten."

The butler came into the room. "Dinner is served," he said, and they all went in.

After dinner and brandy, Stone walked Emma back to her cottage. "I do like the dress," he said. "You look almost as good in it as you do out of it."

She laughed. "You're not going to let me forget this afternoon, are you?"

"Why should I? I'll never forget it."

They stopped at her door, and she opened it. "It sounds like we're both going to be pretty busy after tonight," she said. "Would you like to come in?"

"I'd like that very much," Stone said, and went in. Things progressed very quickly after that.

After breakfast, Peter, Hattie, and Ben walked across the highway with their bags and put them into the rear of the Cayenne, then Peter went into the office to pay his bill.

Teddy took his credit card and ran it, then Peter signed it.

"Thanks for making this go so smoothly," Peter said to him.

"There's something you should know," Teddy said. He held up the little GPS transmitter. "I found this in the wheel well of your car. You were being tracked by someone."

Peter looked at it closely. "So we're not crazy. We were all sure that we were being followed, and for a long time, too."

"You won't be followed anymore," Teddy said. "I had a brief conversation with two Russian gentlemen in a big black SUV, and they turned around and went back the way they came. You have any idea who they might be?"

"My father had a problem with some Russians recently," Peter said. "He told me to watch out for them."

"Your father was right — they were not nice people. Who is your father?"

"His name is Stone Barrington. He's a lawyer in New York."

Teddy knew that name; he had met the man on the island of St. Marks a few years back, and he had been in the company of Holly Barker, who was with the CIA. "Well, he's a smart guy. Tell him about this, and listen to his advice."

Peter wrote down his cell number. "Billy, if you should find yourself in L.A., this is my number. We're all going to be working at Centurion Studios. You seem like a very capable man, so if you're ever looking for work out there, call me."

Teddy tucked the card into his pocket. "You never know," he said.

The two shook hands, and the young people got into the Cayenne and drove away.

Once on their way, Peter said, "You're not going to believe what Billy Burnett just told me." And he told them.

9

Teddy Fay waved off the kids in the Cayenne, then he went back inside and began to put the office and shops in good order, pending the return of Tom Fields after a few days off to see to his wife during her recovery. He was interrupted only a few times by cars stopping for gas, and by the arrival of Bobby after school. Teddy had already managed to broaden the range of the boy's skills with cars, and he could see him becoming more confident in his judgments.

Teddy found a few minutes to walk the few hundred feet to where he had buried the black SUV containing the bodies of its Russian operators. It had been windy during the night, and the site was not only undisturbed, but now invisible.

He was walking back to the filling station when he heard the whistling of a turbine engine overhead. He looked up to see a single-engine airplane circling the filling station's airstrip, much as he himself had done a couple of weeks before. Shortly, the aircraft turned on a final approach to the strip, but the pilot seemed to be having problems with setting the power for landing. He abandoned his first approach and went around, but continued to have problems with airspeed, rising and falling on approach. His landing was hard and barely controlled.

Teddy waved him over to a parking spot and waited while the pilot took five minutes to get everything shut down as per the checklist. The airplane, he knew, was a late-model Piper Malibu Mirage that had been converted to a turboprop with the installation of a Pratt & Whitney jet engine turning a propeller. Teddy had read articles about it and had even ordered a brochure from the engine converters, JetPROP Aviation, in Spokane, Washington. He had considered buying one, but had never managed to make the decision.

Finally, the pilot exited the airplane via the little airstair door, mopping his face with a handkerchief. "Shit!" he said, as he approached Teddy, his hand out. "That was a really shitty landing, wasn't it?"

"I've seen worse," Teddy said, "but not

much worse."

The man laughed. I'm Howard Strunk," he said. "I just bought this goddamned thing, and I miss my old 182 bad."

"Have you had any instruction in it?" Teddy asked.

"I had one day with a guy," Strunk said, "then he got the flu, then I got the flu, and by the time I was out of bed, he was long gone. I reckoned I just needed some time in the left seat and I could do it alone. I'm starting to believe I was wrong. You got any jet fuel here?"

"I'm afraid not," Teddy said, "but from what I've read about that airplane, you can add enough 100 Low Lead aviation fuel to your tanks for a flight over to Gallup, where they've got Jet A."

"Have you got a cold drink around here?" Strunk asked.

"Sure, come on inside, and we'll find you a Coke."

Strunk stopped at Teddy's 182 RG and walked around it. "Can I have a look inside?" he asked.

"It's unlocked."

Teddy waited while Strunk had a good look at the avionics, then he took the man inside and put a cold Coke in his hand. Strunk collapsed into the old leather armchair in the office. He downed the Coke in one long swig. "Gotta get my blood sugar back up," he said. "Haven't eaten all day."

Teddy got him some cheese and crackers from the vending machine and another Coke, and he gradually stopped looking so shaky.

"Where you from?" Teddy asked.

"Las Vegas, New Mexico, east of Santa Fe. I been flying around all day, trying to get a handle on that airplane, and I haven't made it."

"There's a motel over there, if you want to get a night's rest," Teddy said. "If you don't want to add the 100LL to your tanks, I'll drive over to Gallup and get you fifty gallons of Jet A in jerry cans."

Strunk thought about that. "Is that your 182 out back?"

"Sure is. It's a retractable."

"Nice one."

"Thanks. I do all my own maintenance, and I put a Garmin glass panel in it."

"I saw that."

An idea was forming in Teddy's mind, and he thought that all he had to do to make it work was nothing.

"Now, that is my kind of airplane," he said, "and you've made it beautiful. How old is it?"

68

"One of the last dozen manufactured, before they shut down, then started up again," Teddy said.

Strunk asked some questions about the avionics and seemed satisfied with the answers. "Would you consider a trade?" he asked.

"You mean a swap? Mine for yours?"

"That's exactly right. I'll give you the deal of a lifetime."

"You mean you want to take a bath on that like-new turboprop, just to get back into an airplane you feel comfortable in?"

"I can afford the bath," Strunk said. "I'm an impatient man, and I'm what you might call a highly motivated seller. Can I see your logbooks?"

Teddy went to the office closet and retrieved a nylon briefcase. "All the records are in there," he said, handing it over.

"Mine are in a leather bag on the rear seat," Strunk said. "You go have a look, then we'll talk."

The two men perused each other's logbooks, and Teddy began to get excited. The Mirage had had only a hundred hours on it when the conversion to turboprop took place, and only twenty-two hours since. He put down the bag and walked back to the 182.

"Satisfied?" Strunk asked.

"It's a very nice airplane," he said.

"Let me make you an offer," Strunk said, scratching his head. "You give me your airplane and half a million dollars cash, and you've got yourself a brand-new, almost, JetPROP."

"Any liens on it?" Teddy asked.

"None. I pay cash for everything. Tell you what, if you haven't got the half million in cash, I'll give you a short-term loan with a balloon in a year — give you time to arrange financing."

"I pay cash for everything, too," Teddy said, "but I've only got four hundred grand on me."

Strunk laughed loudly. "On you?"

"In a deposit box not half a mile from here," Teddy said.

"I hadn't reckoned on that big a bath," Strunk replied.

"It's the best I can do," Teddy said. "Or you can take a bus back to Las Vegas and send somebody over here to fly your Jet-PROP back to you. After seeing that landing, I don't think you ought to do it yourself."

Strunk held out his hand. "You go get your four hundred grand," he said, "and we'll download some paperwork from the

Internet and make it official."

And so the deal was done. Two hours later, after a title search and the signing of a bill of sale and the relevant FAA documents, Strunk started the engine of the 182 RG, raced down the airstrip, and headed west.

Teddy climbed into his new JetPROP and looked at the panel. It had the latest Garmin 1000, three-screen system; it was just beautiful.

Teddy found the operator's and avionics manuals in the rear of the airplane, went back into the filling station, settled into the leather armchair, and turned his photographic memory to the memorization of everything. He paused once, to close the filling station, then went back to reading. As darkness arrived, he closed the manuals, locked up, and walked across the road to where Sally was waiting with his dinner and a bottle of bourbon.

"I bought me a new airplane," he said to her as he took the first bite of her meat loaf.

Sally sighed. "Well," she said, "I guess that means you'll be moving on, Billy."

He nodded silently and sipped his bourbon.

"You know," she said, "you've never talked about your past, but I think it must be one hell of a past."

"You won't get an argument from me about that," Teddy said.

"And I expect that's all you'll say about it."

Teddy nodded.

"I sort of thought you might be on the run from somebody or something. Maybe robbed a bank."

"We're all on the run from something," Teddy said. "But I've never robbed anybody."

Sally put the dishes away. "Well, come on to bed, honey, and I'll give you a real send-off."

And she did.

10

Stone and Dino were having a late-afternoon drink on the terrace beside the pool when they heard the beeping of a car horn, and a moment later, Peter, Ben, and Hattie appeared, looking mildly disheveled. Hugs, kisses, and greetings were exchanged by all, and the kids took a seat.

The butler appeared. "May I get you all something to drink?"

The kids ordered beers.

"And what luggage do you wish unloaded?" the butler asked.

"Everything in the boot of the car," Peter replied. "We'll sort out which rooms later. Don't even open the trailer. We'll have to figure that out later."

The butler disappeared and a steward materialized with the beers, which were quickly depleted and replaced.

"So," said Stone, when they had quenched their initial thirst, "tell us about the trip."

"It was fabulous," Hattie said.

"It was long," Ben interjected.

"It was very interesting," Peter said.

His father knew from experience that Peter's use of "very" was not hyperbole. The young man used the language precisely, not like a student. "Tell me about the interesting part," Stone said.

Peter took another swig of the beer and burped. "We were followed," he said.

"By what? Gangs of teenaged girls?"

"Well, of course, but more than that — by Russians."

Stone and Dino both sat up straight.

Peter told them about the dot in the rearview mirror and their attempts to lose it. "Finally," he said, "when we had the blowout and made it into this wide place in the road called Mesa Grande, the guy changing the tire made a discovery." He rooted around in a pocket, came up with the device, and handed it to Stone, who handed it to Dino.

"GPS tracker," Dino said. "That explains why you couldn't lose them."

"How did you find out they were Russian?" Stone asked.

"We left the car with this guy at the filling station, who had to call the Porsche dealer In Albuquerque to order a replacement tire, then we took our bags across the road to the motel and checked in. We had dinner at the diner at the motel and went to bed, and the next morning, when we were loading our luggage back in the car, the filling station guy showed me that, said he found it in the wheel well when he changed the tire."

"Then why didn't you see it when you put the temporary wheel on?"

"He said it was covered in mud and dust from the road. That would have made us miss it. Then he told us that two Russian guys showed up in a black Lincoln Navigator, and they had the GPS tracking equipment and an antenna on their dashboard. They were talking about us in Russian."

"How would some pump jockey in a Podunk New Mexico town know what they were saying in Russian?" Stone asked. He was now getting concerned.

Peter shrugged. "I don't know, but this guy was no ordinary pump jockey, he was very smart. He told me his name was Billy Burnett, asked me your name, and said he had heard of you from somewhere."

"From where?" Stone asked.

"He didn't say, he just seemed familiar with you."

"Describe him."

"Late forties, five-nine or -ten, one seventy, unlined face, nice smile, short, thick, dark hair going gray, fit-looking, wiry, sort of. He had what I guess you'd call a desert tan, though he wasn't all leathery like people get who are exposed to that kind of sun for a long time."

"Accent?"

"Sort of local, I guess. He sounded like the other people we talked to in New Mexico."

"He was a local and he had a desert tan, but not for very long? And he knew me?"

"Not knew you, exactly, but knew who you were."

"What did he say, exactly, about me?"

"I don't remember exactly what he said, I just got the impression that he knew who you were, not necessarily that he'd met you."

"Let's get back to the Russians," Dino said. "What happened to them?"

"That's the weirdest thing," Peter said. "Billy Burnett said he'd had a word with them, and they turned around and headed back in the direction they came from, and that we wouldn't be bothered by them again." Peter shrugged. "And we weren't bothered by them again."

"Okay, let's summarize," Stone said. "You're tracked more than halfway across the country by two Russians in an SUV with pretty sophisticated equipment. They follow you to this Mesa Grande place, where they caught up with you, then this pump jockey has a word with them, and they turn around and go home. Is that it in a nutshell?"

"In a nutshell," Peter said.

"Well, I don't buy that," Dino said.

"Neither do I," Stone echoed.

"I'm not trying to sell it to you," Peter said. "It's just all I know."

"That doesn't make any sense at all," Dino said.

"Did I say that it made sense?" Peter asked.

Stone spoke up. "I'd like to meet this guy, this . . ."

"Billy Burnett."

"Well, maybe you'll get to. He said he might get to L.A. and I gave him my cell number."

"Peter," Stone said, "if you hear from this guy, I want to know about it *immediately.*"

"Okay, Dad, but don't get the idea that he's some kind of threat to us. He was extremely helpful, didn't overcharge us, helped us out with the Russians, and I'm glad I met him."

"Nevertheless," Stone said. He looked up to see Emma Tweed and an extremely tall, extremely beautiful young woman coming up the path from the old guesthouse. "Ah, here are our dinner guests," he said. "Ben, you're on deck."

"Huh?" Ben asked.

"Look sharp, kid," Dino said. "You're about to meet somebody."

"None of us looks very sharp right now," Peter said. "May we be excused to shower and change?"

"Run before they get here," Stone said, "and don't be long."

The kids fled before Emma and Tessa reached the terrace.

"Who was that?" Emma asked, as she pecked Stone on the cheek, "and why are they running?"

"That's Peter, Ben, and Hattie, and they've been driving all day and requested permission to freshen up before meeting you two. This must be Tessa," Stone said, offering a hand.

Emma made the introductions, and the two sat down and ordered drinks. "You all looked so intense as we approached," she said. "What was that about?"

"A great mystery," Stone replied.

11

Teddy, after exhausting himself with Sally, slept dreamlessly, then awoke early and began to think.

His first problem was to restore his cash liquidity, and he didn't have a bank account to wire to from his Cayman Islands bank, where much of his tidy fortune resided. And he could hardly ask Tom Fields or Sally to receive it for him; that could get very messy.

He asked himself where he wanted to go next; that was easy: Los Angeles. But where else? He wanted to fly his new airplane and master the avionics before he flew into busy airspace, like L.A., and he wanted to see more of the West. He thought about it as he had breakfast and walked across the road to open the filling station, then he had it: Las Vegas. Easy come, easy go attitude about money, good hotels and restaurants, and poker. Teddy loved poker. He called one of the big splashy hotels and told the operator he wanted to speak to someone about opening an account.

"A charge account?" the woman asked.

"A cash account." He waited until the phone was answered by a man with a New York accent.

"What can I do for you?"

"I'm coming to Vegas, I want to play some poker, and I don't want to carry a lot of cash with me. Can I send it ahead of me?"

"Your name?"

"William J. Burnett."

"Phone number?"

Teddy gave him his current cell number.

"How much would you like to send us?"

"Two hundred and fifty thousand dollars." Teddy could hear the man smiling as he gave him a bank account number and a personal account ID.

"You'll have it before two o'clock today," Teddy said.

"How long will you be staying with us, Mr. Burnett?"

"Maybe four or five days."

"Have you made a room reservation yet?"

"No, I wanted to see if you'd take my money first."

The man laughed. "Mr. Burnett, the hotel would like to comp you a suite for your stay with us."

"Thank you very much."

"Don't mention it. Can I arrange any, ah, entertainment for you while you're here?"

"I'll decide after I arrive."

"Good. When will that be?"

"Two or three days?"

"And how will you arrive?"

"Private aircraft. Let's say three pm, the day after tomorrow."

"Excellent. We'll have you met at Atlantic Aviation at that time. Your greeter will be Charmaine, and she will be at your disposal as a personal assistant during your stay with us, making any restaurant or entertainment arrangements you wish. If she's not to your liking, call me and I'll assign a replacement. My name is Pete Genaro, and I'm the hotel's comptroller."

"Thank you, Pete. See you in a couple of days."

Teddy hung up, then sent a coded e-mail to his bank in the Caymans.

Tom Fields arrived about eleven o'clock, and by then Teddy had all his things in the airplane and had put the office in order.

Tom looked around. "Awful neat," he said. "You going somewhere?"

"Time for me to move on, Tom. I've got a lot of country to see."

Tom sighed. "I sort of felt it coming, I guess. I'd hoped I could persuade you to stay longer, Billy, maybe permanently."

"That's awful flattering, Tom, but I've been working too hard for too long, and I want to stretch my wings."

"Bobby said you traded for a new airplane."

"I had to — the guy practically landed on top of me."

"Can I see it?"

"Sure, c'mon." Teddy walked him out back and showed him the airplane and the cockpit.

"That's a sweet pair of wings," he said. "You got fuel?"

"I called the airport at Gallup and got them to send a truck over. All it took was money."

"That's usually all it takes," Tom replied.

They said their goodbyes, and Teddy got in and walked himself through the startup checklist. The airplane started immediately with that turbine whine that Teddy liked so much. He worked slowly through the taxi and takeoff checklists, and when he was ready, he rolled onto the dirt strip and eased the throttle forward. The airplane pressed him back into his seat and got off the ground sooner than he would have believed possible. He set an altitude, turned on the autopilot, and tapped the identifier for Sedona, Arizona, into the flight computer, then he sat back and let the airplane do its work.

Teddy spent the night in Sedona, enjoying the town and a good restaurant, then he took off for Vegas, touching down a minute before three PM. As he taxied up to the FBO, Atlantic Aviation, a Rolls-Royce pulled out to the ramp, and when he shut the engine down it glided to a stop at the airplane's door. As he stepped down, a petite, very blonde young woman in a very tight business suit and very high heels got out of the car and offered her hand.

"I'm Charmaine, Mr. Burnett," she said, "and I'm here to make your stay in Las Vegas as pleasurable as possible."

"It's Billy," he said, shaking her hand, then he handed his leather duffel to the chauffeur, who introduced himself as James, and followed Charmaine into the rear seat. The door closed with an impressive *thunk,* and cool air enveloped him.

Charmaine handed him a champagne flute and filled it from a bottle of Dom Pérignon, which was in an ice bucket built into the car. "What's your pleasure, Billy?"

"Well," Teddy said, "it occurs to me that if I'm going to drive around in a Rolls-Royce with a beautiful woman, I need some new clothes."

"What are your tastes?"

"Traditional."

"We have a very handsome Ralph Lauren store on our property."

"Mr. Lauren sounds just perfect."

The Rolls floated away, and Teddy sank into the soft seat and sipped Dom Pérignon.

Charmaine took charge at the Ralph Lauren store, picking out suits and jackets for him to try. Since Teddy was a perfect 42 Regular in the Lauren cut, alterations were limited to hemming the trousers, and Charmaine pressed them for a quick delivery.

Four hours later, Teddy's masseuse finished her work, and he showered away the oil, then opened his closet to view his freshly delivered wardrobe. He chose a dark blue Purple Label suit with a chalk stripe, a blue-and-white-striped shirt, a becoming necktie, and a pair of shiny black alligator loafers. He had never spent so much money on clothes before, but he was in a celebratory mood.

He and Charmaine had a very fine dinner in the hotel's Wolfgang Puck restaurant, and when he asked the headwaiter for a check, the man said, "Just tip the waiter, Mr. Burnett." Teddy tipped both him and the waiter lavishly.

"What next, Billy?" Charmaine asked.

"Is the game of poker played in this establishment?"

"Oh, yes," she replied.

Teddy stood up. "Show me."

12

At dinner, Ben Bacchetti and Tessa Tweed sat next to each other and quickly seemed to bond, a fact that did not go unnoticed by the rest of the group, particularly Tessa's mother, who monitored their conversation closely.

After dinner, over brandy, Emma Tweed sat on a sofa with Stone.

"You look worried," Stone said.

"I am, I suppose. You saw what happened at dinner with Tessa and Ben."

"I saw them enjoying each other's company," Stone said.

"It was more than that, I'm afraid. I have a feeling this is going to turn into something. They have far too much in common and are far too attracted to each other. I had visions of Tessa working in the West End theater for a few years before forming a real relationship, and now it seems to have happened too quickly."

"I didn't raise my son — he came to me in his teens, and he met Hattie at school almost immediately. They've been together ever since, and it's been wonderful for both of them. My advice is to relax and let nature take its course. It will work or it won't."

"I know that's what I should do, but I'm a mother — what else can I say?"

"You and I connected rather quickly," Stone said. "You can't deny that sort of luck to Tessa."

"She's going to the studio tomorrow morning, and I'm going, too."

"Why don't I take you to the studio a little later, after they've had time to see their new bungalow and Tessa has seen the studio?"

"I guess I can wait that long," she said. "What bungalow?"

"Peter's stepfather, Vance Calder, had the bungalow as his office and dressing room for decades, and the studio has given Peter the place. The kids worked with an architect and one of the studio's set designers to make some improvements and enlarge the space, and they haven't seen the finished product yet."

"This I want to see," Tessa said.

"So do I," Stone replied.

Teddy played four hours of deliberately

sloppy poker, dropping $22,000, while watching the other players carefully. He figured he could get the money back and more, and tonight would make him a favorite of the casino.

Charmaine walked him back to his suite, but stopped at the door. "Would you like me to send up someone for you?" she asked.

"Thank you, no," Teddy said. "I prefer to make that sort of arrangement for myself, and not with a pro."

"As you wish," Charmaine said. "Shall I let you sleep late and pick you up for lunch?"

"That sounds perfect, then I want to play some more poker."

"Careful, Billy, the losses can add up."

"I can stand them," Teddy said. He shook her hand and let himself into his suite.

The following morning Peter hooked up the U-Haul trailer to the Cayenne and drove Hattie, Ben, and Tessa to Centurion Studios. The guard at the gate had a parking sticker and a map of the lot waiting for them. Peter drove to the bungalow and found six reserved parking places in front with their names on them, plus three for guests. He parked the U-Haul in the parking lot across the street, and they crossed to the bungalow.

There were some rocking chairs and a swing on the front porch; it looked like a 1930s California home. They went inside and found the place perfectly decorated with the things they had picked out from photographs. Hattie's piano was waiting in her studio, and a tuner was working on it.

Tessa had a look around and finally said, "You lot must be very important people around here."

"They certainly are," a man's voice boomed from behind them.

Peter turned to find Leo Goldman Jr. standing in their sitting room. He pumped their hands and was introduced to Tessa.

"Tessa is from London," Ben said. "She's just finished at RADA and wanted to have a look at L.A."

"An actress?"

"And someday, a director," Tessa said.

Leo nodded. "You kids get settled in. There'll be a couple of men to bring your stuff in from the trailer, and I'll have that returned to U-Haul for you. There are three electric carts in the parking lot with your names on them, keys in them. I'm also assigning a very smart lady to you as your office manager. See how it goes, and decide if you want to make her permanent. Her name is Ruth Pearl, and she knows this studio like the palm of her hand. She worked for our head of production for twelve years, until he retired, and his replacement brought his own people with him, so we're looking for a new berth for her."

"We'll look forward to meeting her," Peter said.

Leo indicated that he wanted to speak to Peter on the front porch. When they were out of earshot of the others, he said, "That girl Tessa is gorgeous. I want to test her."

"I'm sure she'd like that," Peter said, "but I'll let Ben put it to her. Let's let it be his idea."

"Gotcha," Leo said. "Have Ben call me, and I'll set it up." They shook hands, and Leo got into a golf cart and drove away.

Stone and Emma arrived shortly before noon and found a tall, slim woman in her mid-thirties putting office supplies into her desk drawers and a storage closet. She moved the pencil between her teeth to her bun. "I expect you're Mr. Barrington and Mrs. Tweed," she said, with a soft, Southern accent. "I'm Ruth Pearl, the new office manager around here. The kids — that's how I think of them — are out on a studio tour, but they should be back soon, and they want to take you to lunch at the studio commissary. A table is already booked. May I show you around the bungalow?"

"Thank you, yes," Stone said. They followed her into Peter's office and editing suite, then Ben's office, then Hattie's studio, which was soundproofed and contained some professional recording equipment.

"This is astonishing," Emma said.

The kids returned to the bungalow, excited, then they all went to lunch in the golf carts.

Teddy finished his lunch with Charmaine, then she escorted him to the poker table, where three of last night's players were just sitting down. Teddy ordered $50,000 in chips and took his seat. This time he would be paying attention.

13

Teddy sent his new luggage down with a bellman, then he went to the casino, to the cashier's cage. He had played poker for three days and had come out sixty thousand dollars ahead. He asked the cashier for the money and his earlier deposit in cash, and handed her an empty briefcase. She made a phone call, then left with Teddy's briefcase.

After a moment's wait a beefy man in a black suit appeared in the cage and stuck his hand between the bars. "Mr. Burnett, I'm Pete Genaro. We spoke on the phone."

"Of course," Teddy said, shaking the man's hand.

"The cashier is getting your cash now, but I'm concerned about your leaving the hotel with it. I'd like to send a security man to the airport with you and see you safely off."

"That's very kind of you," Teddy replied.

"I don't want to pry unnecessarily," Genaro said, "but we ran a little check on you, and although we came up with a couple of dozen William Burnetts, I don't think any of them is you."

"Probably not," Teddy said. "I keep a low profile."

"Where are you from? Originally, I mean."

"I was a military brat," Teddy replied. "I was born on a base and lived all over the place on other posts."

Genaro sighed. "I see. The casino is, naturally, concerned with dealing with folks who might not be on the up-and-up."

"I didn't know that playing poker was a crime," Teddy said. "Or is it just winning?"

"We're happy for our players who win," Genaro said. "It's good advertising for us when somebody walks away with a lot of money, but can you give me a Social Security number?"

Teddy recited from memory the account number he had set up, and Genaro wrote it down. He sat down at a computer and ran it, then he turned back to Teddy.

"Well, you exist, and you don't have a criminal record. That's good enough for us."

"Thank you, Mr. Genaro."

The cashier appeared with Teddy's briefcase and let him peek inside. "It's been machine-counted," she said. "Would you like to count it again?"

"You have an honest face," Teddy said. "I'll trust you."

He shook hands with Genaro again.

"We look forward to having you back soon, Mr. Burnett," the man said. "Just call me, and I'll comp another suite for you."

"Thank you." He turned to go and found Charmaine standing there with a large man in a dark suit.

"We'll accompany you to the airport," she said.

They left the casino and got into the Rolls that had met him when he arrived. The security man sat in the front seat.

"Well," Charmaine said, "you had quite a run at the poker table."

"I did all right," Teddy said. He took an envelope from an inside pocket. "This is just a little expression of gratitude from me, for all your help and your company."

The envelope disappeared into an inside pocket of her suit. "You're very kind. I hope I'll see you back sometime soon."

"Funny, that's what Pete Genaro said. I think he wants to get some of his money back."

She laughed. "Probably. I'd like to see you again on a personal basis, too."

"Do you ever come to L.A.?"

"Frequently," she said. "Is that where you live?"

"Not exactly, but I'll be spending some time there." He gave her his cell number. "I'd like to hear from you."

"Then you will," she said, tucking the number into her bra.

The Rolls pulled up to his airplane. "We had it washed and refueled," Charmaine said.

Teddy leaned over and kissed her lightly on the lips. "You think of everything. When you come to L.A., it'll be my turn."

He loaded his luggage, said his goodbyes, and started the engine. "Vegas ground, N123TF," he said into the radio, "requesting a VFR departure." He taxied to the active runway, was cleared for takeoff, then turned southwest toward the Palmdale VOR. As he approached it he called SO-CAL approach and requested a VFR clearance for the Kimmo Two arrival, which terminated at Santa Monica, and in less than an hour he was setting down at the little airport by the sea.

The airplane secured, he rented a car at Atlantic Aviation and asked for a recommendation for a hotel on the beach.

"How much do you want to spend?" the woman at the desk asked.

"I'd like something high-end," he said. Teddy had always been a little tight with his money, but he had enjoyed the hotel in Las Vegas, and he thought he'd spring for something comfortable in Santa Monica before he found a rental.

She made a reservation for him at a hotel called Shutters, on the beach, then pulled out a map. "It's right here where Pico Boulevard meets the beach."

Teddy drove to the hotel, which was beautiful and across the road from the beach. He checked into a suite, unpacked, and called the concierge to arrange a massage.

Pete Genaro's phone rang. "Genaro."

"It's Vinnie," a man's voice said.

"Where did he go?"

"I checked, but he didn't file a flight plan — just took off. He could be anywhere."

"Okay," Genaro said. He hung up and tapped in a number.

"This is Charmaine."

"Did you find out where Mr. Burnett was headed?"

"I asked him where he lived, but he avoided answering. He did say he would be in and out of L.A. for a while. I asked him for a phone number, but he gave me the

96

same cell number you have."

"Yeah, I ran that. It was a throwaway."

"I didn't feel that I could push him any further."

"You got any plans for one of your L.A. trips?"

"I could go whenever you like."

"Give him a couple of days, then call him and tell him you're coming into town. I want to know more about this guy. I watched him on the cameras, and he's one hell of a poker player. I had the impression that he could have walked away with a lot more of our money if he'd put his mind to it."

"I'll give him a call, then."

The following morning in Paris a phone rang in an office building, and Majorov answered. "Yes?"

"It's Andrei. I've been through all the GPS tracking tapes."

"And what did you learn?"

"We lost Ivan and Yevgeny at a little town called Mesa Grande, in New Mexico," the man said.

"What do you mean, 'lost them'?"

"I mean that, as far as GPS is concerned, they vanished into thin air."

"You mean they removed the tracker from

their car?"

"I don't know, maybe it failed. They stopped in the town, maybe for petrol, then the recording shows they left the main road and drove into the desert a few hundred feet, then the signal was lost. I had a look at the satellite map, and there is nothing there."

"What do you mean, 'nothing there'?"

"The town has maybe half a dozen buildings, mostly on the highway. Where the signal disappeared, there is nothing but desert."

"What about the Cayenne?"

"It was in Mesa Grande overnight, then continued to Los Angeles. It has been on the grounds of The Arrington for two days, hasn't moved, but I can't find the car by satellite."

"Could they have removed the tracker from the car?"

"It's possible, but it's unlikely that they would find it, unless they were looking for it. It would have been placed in a wheel well."

"I want Ivan and Yevgeny found," Majorov said. "What's the nearest place we have somebody?"

"Phoenix, Arizona. We could have somebody there tomorrow morning. He could fly into Gallup, which is only a few kilometers from Mesa Grande."

"Do it," Majorov said. "I want to get to the bottom of this."

"It will be done."

14

Stone, Mike, and Dino played golf at the Bel-Air Country Club, where Mike was a member, and later, at the bar, Stone raised the subject of Billy Burnett.

"Peter told me this story about losing a tire in New Mexico, and the guy who replaced it for him." He related the whole event to Mike, who had not been present at the time.

"So what troubles you about that?" Mike asked.

"It troubles me that some very smart gas pump jockey in New Mexico knows me, or at least knows who I am."

"You're a famous guy, Stone," Dino said, with more than a tinge of irony. "Or maybe infamous is a better word."

"Okay, there are a few square blocks of New York City where my name might be familiar, but . . ."

"Maybe they read *Vanity Fair* in New

Mexico," Dino said. There had been an article about Arrington's death in that magazine. "Or maybe he read that journalist's book about you and Arrington."

"I'm sorry, but that just doesn't make any sense," Stone said.

"What are you thinking, Stone?" Mike asked. "Do you have a hypothesis?"

"A very shaky one," Stone replied. "I'm wondering if the guy could be Teddy Fay."

The other two men regarded him silently for a moment.

"So," Mike said slowly, "you think that the CIA's number one fugitive, who hasn't been heard of for a couple of years, moved to New Mexico, just in time to change Peter's tire for him? Or do you think that Teddy Fay is following Peter?"

"Neither of those options is a sane possibility. If it's Teddy, it's just an enormous coincidence."

"I don't believe in coincidence," Dino said. "I believe in evidence."

"Dino, your whole life is a long series of coincidences, going back all the way to your conception."

"Let's not talk about my parents' sex life, okay?"

"If they had conceived you on a different night, everything could have been different

— you could have been a girl. Then think about the rest of your life, right up to meeting Viv. If the department had assigned her to a different precinct, you might never have met her."

"He has a point, Dino," Mike said. "Stone, I know a little about Teddy Fay, but fill in the blanks for me, and from the beginning."

"All right: Teddy worked at the Agency for more than twenty years, nearly all of them in Technical Services. For at least fifteen of those years, he was the deputy director of the department, which meant that, when an agent was sent out on a mission, Teddy supplied all the background and equipment for him — passports, visas, clothing, weapons, secret fountain pens that do amazing things, et cetera."

"Well, fifteen years of that would give him all the tools he needs to disappear in America."

"Exactly."

"He killed a couple of people, didn't he?"

"There are rumors that he shot the speaker of the house at the time — Eft Efton. The evidence was by no means conclusive, though."

"How does this guy finance himself? Doing odd jobs like working at a filling station?"

"Holly says he's an inventor — he designed a lot of those household gadgets that you see in TV infomercials, and some of them made millions. She thinks he's set up a way to collect the royalties into one or more offshore bank accounts."

"I guess that's doable," Mike said.

"I actually met him once. So did Dino."

"Tell me about that."

"Holly Barker got sent down to an island in the Caribbean, St. Marks, where a retired CIA agent lived. I forget her name, but she and Teddy had reportedly had an affair. Dino and I went along to provide her some cover, and when we got there we met the woman's boyfriend, a fairly elderly guy who may have been heavily disguised, but I couldn't spot a toupee or anything else. Holly believed him to be Teddy, and she had been sent there to be sure that he never left the island alive. When he finally ran, she got off a couple of shots at him and may have wounded him, but we never knew. A couple of years ago, Holly told me that he called her at the Agency. There was a CIA officer who had become obsessed with finding him, and Teddy told her to call the guy off or he would kill him. Teddy proposed a kind of truce.

"Holly called the man off, but he persisted, and he was found a few days later in his own bathtub, with his wrists slit. Holly got another call from Teddy, saying he was done, and that was it. Nobody heard from him again."

"There's a novel in that story," Mike said.

"Well," Stone said, "I'm not going to write it. I want nothing further to do with Teddy Fay. I consider him extremely dangerous, and I certainly don't like the idea that he may now have made my son's acquaintance."

"He's not dangerous to anybody except people who are trying to hunt him down and kill him," Dino pointed out.

"Nevertheless," Stone said.

"I'm trying to think of ways to help," Mike said, "but if this guy is as good as you say he is, we're not going to find him. If he contacts Peter, though, then we might have a good chance."

"That's what I don't want to happen," Stone said.

"Well, you're not in charge of that. Just tell Peter to let you know if he contacts him."

"I've already done that."

"One final question: Suppose he is Teddy Fay, and you find him — what then?"

Stone stared at the ceiling.

"I want to hear this, Stone," Dino said. "Answer the man."

"All right, I don't know."

"How about this," Mike said. "If you meet him, just tell him you know who he is and you don't want him around your son."

"You think that might work?"

"He obviously doesn't want to be identified."

"He might take umbrage," Dino said. "I wouldn't want Teddy Fay taking umbrage at me."

"Good point," Mike said. "Tell you what, Stone. If this guy turns up, say nothing to him out of the ordinary — just tell me. I'll take are of scaring him off."

"How are you going to do that?" Stone asked.

"It's better if you don't know, but I'll tell you this: he will never know that you identified him. He'll just think that he blew his cover accidentally."

"All right," Stone said. "If I meet this Billy Burnett, and I think he's Teddy Fay, then I'll give you a call. I don't want to do that unless I'm certain he's the guy. I don't want to turn some innocent into a victim."

"I understand your scruples, but if you think he *might* be Teddy Fay, please let me know, and I'll handle it."

"You're not going to hurt him, are you?"

"Stone, my people are not thugs, but they have ways of warning people off. The threat of exposure should be enough, if he's Teddy Fay."

"If he's Teddy Fay," Dino said, "I don't think I'd threaten him."

15

Igor landed the rented Cirrus at Gallup Airport, then hired a car and drove south. Mesa Grande was just where it was supposed to be and looked just as it was supposed to look: dusty and a little forlorn.

Igor had received the call from Paris and the GPS surveillance tapes that had been e-mailed to him. He had printed enough stills to help orient himself in the search for Ivan and Yevgeny in their Lincoln Navigator, but first, he thought that speaking to a few human beings might be useful. He started at the gas station.

A teenaged boy ran out of the building and asked what would be his pleasure.

"Actually, I just rented the car, so I don't need any gas yet," Igor replied. "What I could use is a little information."

"What kind of information, sir?"

"A couple of friends of mine passed through here last week, and I'm trying to find them. They were driving a black Lincoln Navigator. Have you seen anybody like that?"

"No, sir, but I only work after school. If they came by here before that, I wouldn't have seen them."

"Who would have been working here while you were in school?"

"Last week? That would be Billy Burnett."

"May I speak with him?"

"I'm afraid he moved on at the end of last week. He was only here for, I don't know, two or three weeks. He was helping us out while my uncle, Tom Fields, the owner of the place, was taking care of his wife."

"Do you know where Billy Burnett moved on to?"

"I don't know. Uncle Tom said he just got in his airplane and flew away."

"What kind of airplane did he fly?"

"When he got here he had a nice Cessna 182 RG, but he swapped it with a feller for a like-new Piper Malibu that had a turbo-prop conversion."

"You remember his tail number?"

"November one, two, three, tango, fox-trot."

"What's your name, son?"

"Bobby."

"You're a bright boy, Bobby, and I appreciate your help. Where'd Billy take off from? Gallup?"

"No, sir, we got an airstrip behind the buildings, here."

"Do you mind showing me?"

"No, sir. Come on." The boy led him through a workshop, and Igor saw a backhoe and a forklift through a door leading to the next building.

Out back there was, in fact, an airstrip, with a windsock and a fuel tank marked 100LL. An old Stearman biplane was tied down at one end. "You mind if I take a stroll around?" Igor asked the boy.

"No, sir, but I gotta get back out front, in case somebody wants gas."

"You go ahead," Igor said. "I won't get lost." The boy ran back through the shop, and Igor unfolded the printouts of the GPS tracking. He located his position behind the buildings, then he began walking, checking the printout now and then, following the dotted line that led, first east, then north into what appeared to be a solid forest of piñon trees, none of them more than about six or eight feet high. But they weren't all that close together, and there was room for a big car to drive among them.

He checked his bearings and walked into the trees on a path approximating the dotted line, and a couple hundred yards later, he came to a clearing. He looked around for tire tracks but saw none. There had been a big line of thunderstorms through here last week, he remembered, because they had come through Phoenix, too, then gone on into Texas. A hard rain would have obliterated tire tracks. Then he saw something that interested him.

A few yards into the clearing he came to a slight indentation in the earth, and it was rectangular — about eight feet wide and twenty feet long. It was as if a large hole had been dug, then filled in again, then the dirt had settled. He thought about what that might mean, and he wished he had a metal detector.

"Something I can help you with?" a voice behind him said. Igor turned to find a man of about sixty standing behind him.

"Good day to you," Igor said. "You must be Mr. Tom Fields."

"I am."

"Your nephew was showing me your airstrip, and I just took a little stroll."

Fields nodded at the papers in his hand. "You looking for something out here?"

"I'm looking for a couple of friends of mine who passed through here last week, driving a black Lincoln Navigator. Did you by any chance see or talk to them?"

Fields shook his head. "No, I was home with my sick wife most of last week. If my nephew Bobby didn't see them, Billy Burnett might have."

"That's what Bobby told me. He also said that Billy moved on late last week. Do you have any idea where he went? I'd like to talk to him."

"No, he just said he had a lot of country to see. He had recently sold his business in New York State and retired. He happened to land here, looking for fuel, and we got to talking, had lunch together. He knew his way around cars and machinery, and I invited him home for supper and asked if he'd like to work for me for a while. He did, but he never would take any money."

"Do you have his address or a phone number?"

"I don't think he has an address anymore, but I think I have his cell phone number in the office. Come on, and I'll see if I can find it."

"Mr. Fields, before we go, can you tell me what that is?" He pointed to the big indentation in the desert soil.

"Never seen that before," Fields replied. "Looks like something heavy must have made it."

"Or maybe there was a hole dug, then refilled."

"Could be that, too," Fields agreed.

"Is that your backhoe in the building next to your shop?"

"Yes, I've got a little equipment-rental business."

"Did Billy Burnett know how to operate a backhoe?"

"Might've. He was handy with machinery."

"Do you think he might have used your backhoe to bury something out here?"

Fields looked at the indentation, then back at Igor. "What, exactly, are you getting at?"

Igor didn't speak for a moment.

"You mean, like a Lincoln Navigator?"

"It seems like a possibility."

"That's the craziest thing I ever heard," Fields said. "Why would Billy do a thing like that?"

"I don't know," Igor said honestly. "Do you, by any chance, have a metal detector?"

"No, I don't, and I don't know where you'd find a thing like that. I mean, this area isn't exactly a Civil War battlefield. You're not going to find any old bayonets out here."

"Mr. Fields, you say you rent equipment. Could I rent your backhoe for an hour or two?"

"Do you know how to operate a back-hoe?"

"No, sir, but I expect you do."

Fields looked at the indentation, then back at Igor. "It's a hundred dollars an hour, plus operator," he said.

Igor produced some bills, peeled off five hundred dollars, and offered it to Fields. "Will that do it?"

"Yessir, it will," Fields said, pocketing the money. "Hang on a minute, I'll go crank up the backhoe. You've got me interested, now. I'll get Billy's number for you, too."

"Thank you, sir." Igor stood and stared at the indentation. Ten minutes later, he heard the backhoe coming.

Fields stopped and handed him a slip of paper. "There's Billy Burnett's cell number. You want this whole area dug up?"

"I think just a trench down the middle would do it," Igor replied.

A little under an hour later, the scoop of the backhoe struck something hard, making a noise.

"Sounds like metal," Fields said, climbing down from the backhoe and taking a shovel out of the toolbox bolted to the side. He walked into the trench and started digging.

Igor followed him. "Here, let me do that,"

he said. He took the shovel from the older man and started a new trench within the old one. Soon, he had a hole two feet by three. "What do you make of that?" he asked Fields, nodding at the hole.

Fields got down on his knees and brushed away some soil with his hands. "Well, I'll be damned," he said. "I reckon that's the underside of a car or truck," he said. "Or maybe a Lincoln Navigator." He got back on the backhoe and started to enlarge the trench he had dug.

After another fifteen minutes of digging, he had exposed the entire bottom of the vehicle. He switched off the backhoe. "Take a look at this," he shouted to the man behind him. He didn't get a reply, so Fields turned and looked. The man was gone. Fields walked back to the filling station and checked out front. The man's car was gone, too.

Fields went to the office and dialed Billy Burnett's number.

"Is that you, Tom?" Billy said.

"That's right, Billy."

"What's up? You and the wife and Bobby okay?"

"Yeah, we're okay. I found something pretty weird out behind the airstrip, though."

A moment's silence. "What did you find, Tom?"

"Well, this feller came by here looking for a couple of friends of his driving a Lincoln Navigator. He found this indentation in the ground out back, so I got the backhoe out and did some digging, and sure enough, there's a car buried out there, upside down."

"I see," Billy said. "Can you describe the man for me?"

"I'd say about thirty-five, six-two, well built, sandy hair. Had an accent of some kind — I couldn't place it, but his English was good."

"I see."

"You want to tell me about this, Billy?"

"Tom, to tell you the truth, I don't think you want to know."

"What do you think I ought to do? Should I call the sheriff or the state police?"

"Anybody in the car you found?"

"I haven't looked."

"Tom, you could call the police, but if you do, your life and your business are going to be disrupted for weeks, maybe months to come. My best advice is to fill up the hole, walk away, and put it out of your mind."

"Who were those two fellers, Billy?"

"They were very bad people who followed that boy and his friends I ordered the tire

115

for. They were going to hurt them. They tried to kill me."

Fields thought about it for a minute. "Well," he said, finally, "I don't reckon they're worth digging up, then."

"Thank you, Tom. My best to your wife and Bobby."

Fields hung up, went outside, and started up the backhoe.

Teddy had no sooner hung up than his phone rang again. The caller ID said PRIVATE NUMBER. "Hello?"

"Is this Billy Burnett?" An accented man's voice.

"I'm sorry, you've got a wrong number." He broke the connection, but the phone immediately rang again.

"Hello?"

"Billy? It's Charmaine."

"Hey, there. Can I call you right back?"

"Sure." She gave him the number.

Teddy hung up, opened the cell phone, and removed the SIM card, then he broke the card in half, stomped on the phone several times, and put the pieces in the wastebasket. He got another throwaway phone from his briefcase and called Charmaine back.

"I thought I might come down to L.A.

tomorrow," she said. "Would you like that?"

"I certainly would. What time will you arrive?"

"Let's see, I guess around six-thirty or seven."

"Well, meet me at a restaurant called Michael's, on Third Street, in Santa Monica. You can Google it for the exact address."

"I'll do that," she said. "Can you put me up for a night or two?"

"You betcha," Teddy said. "Oh, let me give you a new phone number, the old phone broke."

16

Igor sat in the parking lot of the Gallup airport. He got out his cell phone and called the Albuquerque Flight Service Station. He was connected to a briefer by an automated system.

"Gallup Flight Service."

Igor filed an IFR flight plan to Phoenix Sky Harbor, and when he was done, the briefer said, "Anything else I can do for you?"

"Tell me, is there any way you can look up a tail number and tell me if there was a flight plan filed, say, a week ago, for that number?"

"What's the number?"

"November one, two, three, tango, foxtrot. A JetPROP."

"Hang on a second." The sound of typing could be heard. "Where from?"

"Probably a VFR takeoff and he opened his flight plan in the air."

"I've got a couple of flight plans for that number: one from Las Vegas, New Mexico, to Albuquerque Golden Eagle, then another one from there to Santa Fe, then one from Santa Fe to Gallup, but he canceled in the air short of Gallup. That's it."

"Thanks so much," Igor said, then hung up. He got on his laptop, went online and to a program called FlightAware. He typed in the tail number, and a message said that no aircraft with that number was currently in the air. He started at the end of the week before and worked backward, but found no trace of the airplane leaving the Mesa Grande area. Billy Burnett had not turned on his transponder: smart. He did, however, catch the airplane two days later, landing at Las Vegas International, and three days after that, departing. Burnett turned off his transponder after leaving Las Vegas airspace, though, and he could have gone anywhere, so Igor didn't know where to look next.

Igor checked his watch: just after two PM. He calculated the time in Paris, then dialed a number.

"Who is this?" an annoyed man asked.

"It's Igor, in New Mexico."

"Ah, Igor," Majorov said. "Did you find Ivan and Yevgeny?"

"Yes. They're buried in the desert at Mesa

Grande, inside the Navigator."

A baffled silence. "You're not making any sense."

"Someone killed both of them, then put them in their car, dug a large hole with a backhoe, and pushed the car into it. Then he filled up the hole again. I had a man dig down until we found the car."

"Holy shit. What did you do then?"

"I got the hell out of there. I expect the man called the police."

"Do you have any idea who did this?"

"I think it was probably a man called Billy Burnett."

"Who is he?"

"He was working at a filling station in Mesa Grande when Ivan and Yevgeny stopped there. They had followed the Barrington boy and his friends into the town, where they had stopped for the night. Something happened, some sort of disagreement, I guess, and there was a fight. Ivan and Yevgeny lost."

"I want you to find this Billy Barnett," Majorov said.

"Burnett."

"Whatever. Find him."

"And take him out?"

"Maybe not. I think I want to talk to him myself, if he took on two of my best men

120

and killed them."

"I warn you, he's not going to be easy to find. He has no fixed address, and when he left Mesa Grande I traced him on the FlightAware program flying into Las Vegas, but he left three days later and I couldn't tell where he went. He has a cell number, and I called it, but he said I had a wrong number. I called back, and the number was engaged, and when I called back again, I got a recorded message from the phone company saying that the number didn't exist. He probably destroyed the phone."

"Igor, I want him found. Think of something."

"I've got one chance. If I keep a watch every day on the computer, I might catch him in the air again and be able to trace him."

"I have some business in Las Vegas, and I will be there the day after tomorrow, at the usual hotel. I'll call you when I get there."

"Good. In the meantime, I'll keep watch for the tail number." Igor hung up, turned in his rental car, and flew back to Phoenix.

The following morning he went to his office, set his laptop on the conference table, turned it on, and logged onto FlightAware. N123TF was not in the air. He called in an assistant and sat him down at the computer.

"I want you to sit here for as long as you can and watch for this tail number." He wrote it down. "When you get tired or hungry or have to go to the toilet, get someone to replace you, all day, every day. We're going to watch the skies for that airplane. Got it?"

The man sat down, nodded, and stared at the screen.

17

Teddy sat at the bar, nursing a drink for nearly an hour before Charmaine showed up. She came in looking very un-Vegas, in a pretty cotton dress, her hair in a ponytail.

"Hey, there," he said, getting down from his stool and hugging her. "Let's get our table." He left some money on the bar for his drink and signaled to the headwaiter that they were ready to sit down. A moment later they were at a good table in the garden, taking in the night air.

"I didn't think I'd get down to L.A. this soon," she said. "But fortunately, something came up that gave me an excuse."

Teddy waited for the waiter to set down her martini and some menus before he spoke again. "Let me guess what came up," he said.

"I don't think you can guess."

"My guess is Pete Genaro suggested you come see me."

She blushed a little and stared into her drink. "Why would you think that?"

"Pete was having a little trouble categorizing me when I checked out, and my guess is, he wants to know more."

She took a sip of her martini. "Pete said you were one hell of a poker player."

"Maybe so, but rusty. I hadn't played in years. That's why I lost the first night."

"Pete said he thought you could have won a lot more, if you'd put your mind to it. I think you were down the first night because you wanted to be."

"You're a smart girl," Teddy said. "Tell you what, before you go back to Vegas, we'll work up a little story about me for you to tell Pete."

"I wouldn't like to lie to Pete," she said. "That could have repercussions."

"You won't be lying, you'll be telling him what I said when you asked me some questions."

"Well, maybe in that case . . ."

"All right, let's get that out of the way, so we can concentrate on each other. Ask me some questions."

"Is Billy Burnett your real name?"

"Burnett was my birth name, but I used my stepfather's name all the way through school and in the army. After that, after my stepfather died, I changed it back to the original. And Pete has already seen proof that I exist when he ran me through his computer."

"How old are you?"

"How old do you think I am?"

She cocked her head and looked closely at him. "Forty-eight," she said.

Teddy laughed. "That's a very good guess." Teddy was in his early sixties, but during his ten months in Asheville he had had some work done: he cured his baldness with hair transplants; he had dental veneers attached to his teeth; and he had his face and neck lifted and implants inserted that firmed up his jawline and changed the character of his face. No one who had seen him a year ago would ever recognize him.

"You look very fit," she said. "Do you go to a gym?"

"No, but I exercise every day using an old book called the *Royal Canadian Air Force Exercise Plans.* I've worked my way slowly up to the upper levels, where it's very strenuous, but it doesn't require any weights or other equipment. I run a couple of miles once or twice a week, too — less than I used to. It's not good for the knees."

"Where did you go to school?"

"At military bases all over the world. I was

born on one. My father was a colonel in the army, and a couple of years after he died, when I was three, my mother was remarried to one of his friends, also an army man."

"Did you go to college?"

"I graduated from the United States Military Academy, which I attended because all I knew was army, and because I was entitled to admission, because my father had won the Medal of Honor in World War Two." Teddy had chosen his alias after reading an account of the events leading to his chosen father's medal. If Pete Genaro looked there, he would learn only what Teddy wanted him to know.

"How long did you serve in the army?"

"Eight years, in military intelligence, which some people say is a contradiction in terms."

She laughed. "What did you do after the army?"

"I stayed in intelligence, but with another arm of the government."

"Now, let me guess: you won't tell me which arm or anything about what you did."

"You're partly right, I won't — rather, can't — tell you what arm, but I can tell you that my work was equipping other intelligence officers for their missions."

"What kind of equipment?"

"Every kind you've ever read about in spy novels or seen at the movies."

"When did you stop doing that?"

"A few years ago."

"So you live on a government pension?"

"Not entirely. The technical skills I acquired in the army later helped me invent a lot of ordinary household items. A few of them made a lot of money — still make a lot of money — so I have no financial worries."

"Where do you live?"

"Right now, in a very nice hotel on the beach, where I'm going to take you after dinner and ravish you."

She laughed merrily and finished her martini. He ordered another drink for them both, then they ordered dinner.

"Now it's my turn," he said. "How old are you?"

"How old do you think I am?"

"Thirty-two."

"Close enough."

"Now, so I won't wear myself out asking a lot of questions, give me a brief autobiography."

"I was born in a little town in Georgia called Delano, and I went to the public schools there and later got a degree in English Lit from the University of Georgia.

I married a guy I met in school — charming, but a gambler, and that got us to Las Vegas, where he went to dealer school and then got a job in a casino. He ran up a gambling debt and then got fired when he tried to run a scam against the casino with a friend of his who was a card counter. Then I divorced him and got a job at the casino and paid off his debt. They liked me and promoted me, and now I handle the VIP guests. Is that enough for you?"

"That's enough basics," Teddy said. "I'll learn the rest a little at a time."

Their dinner came, and they became closer as they dined. After dinner, Teddy took her back to Shutters and ravished her.

18

Peter, Ben, and Leo Goldman sat in Leo's screening room off his office and watched Tessa Tweed be put through her paces by a director who specialized in screen tests. First, she was beautifully lit and photographed from every angle in a dress, sports clothes, evening dress, and a bikini; then she performed two scenes, one dramatic, one comedic, with a young actor who was under contract to the studio. The film ended, and the lights went up. Nobody spoke at first.

Finally, Leo said, "Ben? What did you think?"

"I'm seeing the girl, so I'm not going to have an opinion on this occasion, and I want to note for the record that this test was not done at my behest."

"Duly noted," Leo said. "Ben loves it. Peter, in case you're shy, I'll give you my take on this young woman: she is absolutely sensational. The camera loves her. She reads well. I don't think I've ever seen a better test."

"Well," Peter said, "it's the best test I've ever seen, too, but it's the *only* test I've ever seen. I think she's wonderful, though, and I think she'd be great as Ashley in our current production."

"So do I," Leo said. "Ben, do you have any objections?"

"Are you kidding?" Ben replied. "Of course not."

"Then I'll offer her a seven-year studio contract," Leo said.

"Leo," Peter replied, "I don't think that's going to work. Her mother, Emma Tweed, the fashion designer, is in town. She's Tessa's business adviser, and she's appalled at the idea of her daughter going straight from RADA into the movies. I think it would be better if I offered her a two-picture deal with our production company, with the second picture to be done at a mutually agreeable later date, so there's no pressure for her to move permanently to L.A. I think her mother is less likely to faint at that prospect."

"Smart idea," Leo said. "Don't let her get away."

■ ■ ■ ■

Peter and Ben left Leo's office and got into Peter's cart for the short drive back to their bungalow. "You okay with this, Ben, really?"

"I'm not going to have anything to do with it," Ben said. "You make her the offer. I don't even want to be in the room."

"I got it — you're hands off."

"Right," Ben said, "but if you don't get her signed, I'm going to murder you."

Teddy and Charmaine had breakfast on their terrace overlooking Santa Monica Beach. He marveled at how good she looked without makeup.

"How'd you like to fly up to Carmel for lunch today?" Teddy asked her.

"Just like that? Hop in your airplane and fly to Carmel?"

"Fly to Monterey, actually, then drive to Carmel — it's right next door."

"I'd love that," she said. "It's such a beautiful day for flying, isn't it?"

"Severe clear," Teddy replied. "After all, it's Southern California, where it never rains."

"Except when it pours buckets, and the mountains slide down to the beaches,"

Charmaine said.

"Let's get a shower and get out of here," Teddy said, throwing down his napkin.

Charmaine followed him inside, shedding her robe and running past him toward the bathroom. "Me first," she called over her shoulder.

Teddy followed and stepped into the shower with her. "You have to learn to share," he said.

Igor was working at his desk when the young man at the conference table came alive.

"I've got him!" he called. "He's taking off from Santa Monica!"

Igor rushed over to the table and watched the airplane move away from the airport, north. Then, suddenly, it disappeared from the screen.

"What happened?" the young man asked.

"He turned off his transponder as soon as he left Class B airspace, where it's required," Igor replied, "and I'll give you two-to-one odds that he hasn't filed a flight plan." He checked, and he was right.

"Well, at least we know he's headed north," the young man said. "No, we don't. Anybody leaving Santa Monica is going to get vectored around by air traffic control.

He could be headed back to Las Vegas or north to San Francisco or even east to Phoenix. You'll just have to keep watching that screen. And you'd better watch closely, because Majorov gets into Vegas tomorrow, and he's going to want to see that guy."

"Why does he have the hots for this Billy Burnett?"

"It goes back to a deal to acquire The Arrington that Majorov tried to pull off last year, and failed."

"Burnett's connected to that?"

"Not exactly," Igor replied. "Burnett's connected to Peter Barrington, and his father, Stone Barrington, is connected to The Arrington."

Peter, Hattie, Ben, Tessa, and Emma dined that evening at the newly redesigned Spago Beverly Hills. After they had ordered drinks and then their dinner, Ben excused himself and went off in search of the men's room.

"Tessa," Peter said, "Ben has left the table because he doesn't want to take part in the discussion we're about to have."

"Why not?" Tessa asked.

"Because he doesn't want his friendship with you to play any part in your decision."

"What decision?"

"Leo Goldman ran your screen test this

133

afternoon, and we were there. You did an absolutely wonderful job, and I'd like to offer you —"

"Hold it right there," her mother said, throwing up a hand like a traffic cop. "Don't you dare try to sign her to a studio contract."

"Mother, please . . ."

"I'm not having it. I'll have you bound and gagged and thrown on the first flight back to London if you even consider such a thing."

"Please, Mrs. Tweed," Peter said. "Let me finish. I'd like to offer Tessa a featured role in our production that begins principal photography next week. It's not a seven-year studio contract, not even close. What I'm offering Tessa is a two-picture deal with our production company, and the second film will be shot at some future, mutually agreeable date."

"How long would she have to stay in L.A.?" Emma asked.

"Mother, kindly be quiet for a moment, will you?" Tessa pleaded. "I can't make an informed decision until I've asked some questions. If Peter and I agree, then you can do the deal, all right?"

Emma sighed deeply but said nothing.

"How long would I have to stay in L.A.?"

Tessa asked Peter.

"Only a month or so," Peter said. "Then you'll be free to return to London or to stay here as long as you like. The second picture won't be shot until next year at the earliest."

"She'll be returning to London," Emma said.

"Mother! If you don't be quiet, I'll fire you and get an agent."

Emma threw up her hands. "All right, all right."

"Is this the part of Ashley?" Tessa asked. "I've read the script."

"It is," Peter replied.

"Then I accept, dependent on you and Mother agreeing on a deal."

"Mrs. Tweed," Peter said, "I certainly want you to be happy with Tessa's deal, but I really do think Tessa should hire an agent to represent her. This is a complicated business, and actors who are not well represented don't get the best deals."

"Well, as long as I —"

"Mother," Tessa said, "I want you to be happy with the deal, too, but Peter is right: I'll hire an agent, and you can express your views to him, but you cannot tell him what to do. This is leaving-the-nest time. Look at me — my wings are spread." She flapped her long arms.

Emma fumed a little, but agreed.

Ben, who had been watching from behind a potted plant, returned to the table. "Everything all right?" he asked.

"Everything is all right," Tessa said. "Peter has made me an offer, and I've accepted, in principle. My agent will work out the details with him. You and Mother will stay out of it."

Ben beamed. "I wouldn't touch it with a fork," he said.

Teddy and Charmaine lunched on the deck of a restaurant that was practically falling into the Pacific, watching the waves roll in and crash against the rocks. They took a long walk along the beach, then did some shopping in the village. Late in the afternoon, with the sun threatening to fall into the Pacific, they drove back to the Monterey airport.

When they were approaching Los Angeles airspace, Teddy called air traffic control and requested a VFR approach to Santa Monica Airport, then he was given a vector and a transponder code. He switched on the transponder and entered the four-digit code.

"Igor!" the young man cried. It was nearly

seven PM, and he was still watching the screen. "The airplane is back! It looks like it's landing in Santa Monica!"

"Okay," Igor said. "I'm going home to pack. I'll head to L.A. tomorrow morning."

19

Yuri Majorov's Gulfstream landed at McCarran International in Las Vegas, and a waiting Rolls swept him to his hotel. Once in his enormous suite, he called Igor's cell number.

"Welcome to the United States," Igor said upon answering. "Are you in Las Vegas?"

"Yes. Have you found this Billy Burnett?"

"I've learned where he parks his airplane," Igor said. "At Santa Monica Airport. I'm there now. He must have hangar space, though, because his airplane is not on any ramp — I've checked every one. Don't worry, though, I'll find him."

"I want him in Las Vegas within forty-eight hours," Majorov said.

"Voluntarily or not?"

"I'll leave that to your judgment. Just get him here." Majorov hung up and began to undress for the shower. As he was about to turn on the water, the phone rang and he picked up the bathroom extension. "Yes?"

"Good evening, Mr. Majorov, this is Pete Genaro. Welcome to our inn. Is everything all right with your suite?"

"Yes, it's fine, thank you, Mr. Genaro."

"May I arrange some company for you this evening?"

"Late this evening. I'm going to play some poker after dinner."

"Of course. I'll see to it."

Majorov hung up and got into the shower.

Pete Genaro hung up in a sweat. He was accustomed to dealing with VIPs, but Majorov scared him. The man was a big stockholder in the hotel and casino and demanding in a cold, steely way. He was accustomed to having exactly what he wanted, and to deny him anything was to incur his icy wrath. He called his wrangler and arranged for the most beautiful girl in his stable to be at the poker table when Majorov tired of playing.

Igor had spent the entire afternoon at Santa Monica Airport. It was a small field, but still there were a lot of airplanes parked there and a lot of places for them to park. He had worked his way through the lot of them, until finally he came to the last: Cloverfield Aviation. It was small and a little seedy. He opened the door and walked in to find a lad of no more than eighteen behind the desk, reading a girlie magazine.

"Hi, there," Igor said.

The boy dropped his magazine and set an airport directory on top of it. "Yessir?"

"I'm looking for a friend of mine, and I think he hangars his airplane with you. His name is Billy Burnett."

"What kind of airplane is it?"

"A JetPROP, like a Malibu, with a turbine engine. His tail number is N123TF."

"Oh, yessir, he parks here. He got in less than an hour ago."

"Have you got an address for him? I want to look him up while I'm in town."

The boy flipped through a loose-leaf notebook. "Looks like all we've got is a phone number," he said. He wrote it down on a slip of paper and handed it to Igor.

Igor looked at the number: it was the one he'd called from Mesa Grande, now disconnected. "Is this the only information you have on him?"

"Yessir, that's it."

"Do you know where he's staying?"

"No, sir, I don't."

"Thanks very much," Igor said, and left. He wadded up the slip of paper and threw it into a waste bin on the way out the door. The hangar door was open a couple of feet, and he walked in and looked around. The JetPROP was there, dripping water from having been washed. Igor walked around the airplane, inspecting it carefully. He stopped at an inspection panel on the right side rear of the airplane and read the placard. The emergency locator transmitter was housed there. He opened his briefcase, took out a Leatherman tool and selected the proper screwdriver blade, then un-screwed the inspection hatch and took a GPS locator from his briefcase, along with a Velcro patch, and affixed it inside the panel, but out of sight. He switched on the unit, then walked a few steps away, got out his laptop, and checked the reception. It was working fine.

He got into his rental car and drove to his hotel on Santa Monica Beach, the one called Shutters. As he entered the front door he nearly bumped into a couple walking across the lobby toward the restaurant, a middle-aged man and a younger, blonde woman. "I'm very sorry," he said.

The man looked him up and down for a moment, then said, "Don't mention it."

"Can't you stay another night?" Teddy

asked as he held the restaurant door open for her. But his mind was on the man he had nearly collided with. He fit the physical description that Tom Fields had given him, and there was that trace of an accent.

"I wish I could," Charmaine said, "but I've got to get back. We've got a heavy load of VIPs in the hotel over the next few days, and there's a lot of work to do. Maybe I can come back next week?"

The headwaiter found them a table, took their drink orders, and brought them menus.

"I'm going to look for an apartment tomorrow," Teddy said. "By the time you get back, I'll have a home."

"You're tired of Shutters?"

"I'm tired of paying per day what I'd pay per month for an apartment."

"You're going to find Santa Monica real estate expensive," she said.

"I'll manage."

"I loved our day today," Charmaine said, placing her hand on his.

He squeezed her thigh. "So did I," he said.

After dinner, Teddy stopped by the front desk for a moment and passed the desk clerk two hundred dollars. "Can you tell me the name of the tall blond gentleman who checked in an hour or so ago?"

The clerk consulted his computer. "That would be Mr. Igor Smolensky," he said.

"If anyone should inquire about me, I'm not registered in the hotel, nor have I been."

"As you wish, sir."

Igor checked into his room and immediately plugged in his laptop and turned it on, checking the GPS tracker. The little red dot on the screen was at Santa Monica Airport, exactly where it should be. He ordered dinner from room service.

20

Charmaine was up at five and was soon dressed and packed, while Teddy lounged in bed. She came over and gave him a kiss. "I'll call you next week, then."

"I'll look forward to it and to giving you a new address," he replied.

She left, and Teddy got out of bed, showered, dressed, and packed. He carried his bags down the fire stairs to the garage, then drove to Santa Monica Airport, to Cloverfield Aviation. The boy who sat at the desk all night was just surrendering his seat to the day man, and Teddy took the kid aside. "Did somebody ask about me last evening?" he asked.

"Yessir, he said he was a friend of yours, and I gave him your phone number. Was that all right?"

"Sure, no problem. If he comes back, tell him I've left for New Jersey."

"You're leaving us today?"

"Right. I'll pay my bill and turn in my rental car a little later this morning."

"Yessir."

The boy left, and Teddy carried his luggage into the hangar and stowed it in the airplane, then he took a slow walk around and checked every inspection port. Finally, he came to the ELT port, opened it, and ran a hand around inside. He came out with a GPS locator, identical to the one he had found in Peter Barrington's Cayenne. He found the switch and turned it off, then put it into his briefcase and went back to his car. He drove back to Shutters and parked in the garage, then he took up a position near the fire stairs and switched on the locator. He then telephoned the hotel and asked for Mr. Smolensky.

A sleepy voice answered. "Yes?"

Teddy breathed into the phone for a moment, then broke the connection.

Igor sat up in bed and phoned the front desk.

"Yes, Mr. Smolensky?"

"Did you phone my room just now?"

"No, sir, that was an outside call."

"Thank you." Igor hung up and thought for a moment, then he opened his laptop and looked at the screen. The red dot had moved; it was no longer at the airport; it was now at Shutters. He got into his clothes, put his gun into his trousers pocket, and let himself out of his room, looking both ways up and down the hallway first. The garage, he thought. He went to the fire stairs and ran down two flights.

Teddy could hear the footsteps ringing on the steel stairway. He flattened himself against the wall outside the door to the stairs and waited. A moment later, the door eased open and a hand appeared, holding a semiautomatic pistol. He waited until the man stepped slowly into the garage, then moved behind him and pressed the silencer against the back of his neck.

"Good morning, Mr. Smolensky," he said. The man froze.

"Now open your hand and let the weapon fall to the floor." Smolensky did so. "Now kick it behind you." He followed instructions.

"Mr. Burnett, I presume."

"Quite right. Now tell me, why are you so eager to make my acquaintance?"

"It is the man I work for who wishes to meet you."

"And who might he be?"

"His name is Yuri Majorov. He is intrigued

that you managed to deal with two others in his employ back at Mesa Grande. He is in Las Vegas as we speak, and he would like you to accompany me there for a meeting."

"Who, exactly, is Mr. Majorov?"

"He is a businessman with worldwide interests."

"And why is he interested in Peter Barrington?"

"Not the boy — his father. He and Mr. Majorov have a mutual business interest."

"And he thought that if he murdered the son, the father would become more cooperative? Why would Mr. Barrington wish to cooperate with the Russian Mob?"

"Mr. Majorov would find that an unkind characterization, and I would urge that, when you meet him you not speak in that manner."

"Where is your car?" Teddy asked.

"Over there, to the right — a silver Toyota Camry."

"Give me the keys, very carefully."

Smolensky reached into a pocket and came up with a car key. Teddy pushed him ahead, then picked up the man's gun and slipped it into his own pocket. As they approached the car, Teddy pressed the trunk button and the lid opened. "Climb inside," he said. "I'll drive us to Las Vegas. Which hotel?"

"The New Desert Inn," Smolensky said. "But this is hardly necessary — I've no wish to harm you."

"Climb inside, or I will find it necessary to harm *you.*"

Smolensky climbed inside.

"Make yourself comfortable, now," Teddy said, then he removed the man's gun from his pocket, held it against his temple, and fired once. He wiped the gun down, then dropped it into the trunk with the body, put the car key next to it, dropped the GPS locator inside, and closed the trunk with an elbow.

Teddy got into his car and drove back to Santa Monica Airport, thinking all the way. It seemed likely that Smolensky had put the locator into his airplane only the evening before, so there was only one other way he could have found the aircraft earlier: through flight tracking. He went into the Cloverfield office, paid his bill, and asked that his airplane be moved to the ramp; then he went into the flight planning room and sat down at the computer. He went to the FlightAware website and filled out a form requesting that his tail number be blocked to viewers, then he went out to the airplane and from one of his bags, took out a single airplane number, a 3. He glued it over the 2 in his tail number and did the same on the other side of the airplane, so that now his number was N133TF.

Teddy then got out the airplane's avionics manual and looked up the instructions for changing the tail number in the transponder. He turned on the avionics power switch, and ten minutes later he had changed the number that the transponder would broadcast whenever it was on. He had already listed the new tail number on the FAA registry, along with a number of others, listing a corporation as the owner.

He started the airplane, then called Santa Monica ground control and, using the new tail number, requested a VFR takeoff and vectors to Hawthorne Airport, only a few miles away. After a short flight he landed there and inquired about hangar space, made a deal for it, and rented a car.

He drove back to Santa Monica and looked around for a real estate agency. Having found one, he parked, went inside, and had a conversation with the woman in charge about rental apartments.

He selected two from photographs for viewing, and after he had seen both, chose one on the top floor of a six-floor condominium. The owner of the penthouse was out of the country, and Teddy rented the place for three months, using another identity from his store of documents. He paid in advance, in cash, and accepted a receipt.

Half an hour later, he was unpacked and ensconced in his new home. It was spacious and sunlit and beautifully furnished. He even liked the art on the walls. He got out his cell phone and called Charmaine at the New Desert Inn.

"Hi, there, I didn't expect to hear from you so soon," she said.

"I've found a very nice place to live," he told her, "but now I have to ask you if I can trust you not to tell Pete Genaro where I live or my new phone number."

She was silent for a moment. "Yes, you can," she said.

"Tell him this: that the phone number I gave you has been disconnected and that I said I was checking out of Shutters and headed back East."

"All right."

"Something else: there is a man registered at the New Desert Inn called Majorov."

"I've met him. I didn't like him."

"I'll tell you why later, but it is important that he never hear the name Billy Burnett.

When you next come to L.A., I'll give you another name to use."

"This is very intriguing," she said.

"We'll see how good an intelligence agent you can be," Teddy said. "I'll look forward to hearing from you next week." He broke the connection.

21

When Charmaine finished her shift she went to Pete Genaro's office and knocked on the door. He waved her to a seat.

"Tell me what you've learned about Billy Burnett," he said.

She repeated the biographical information Billy had given her, then she took a deep breath. "I'm afraid he may have left L.A."

Genaro's eyebrows went up. "Oh?"

"He told me he was checking out of the hotel, and when I asked where he was going, he said, 'Back East.' He said he'd be in touch. I tried to call him a few minutes ago, and the number had been disconnected, like the earlier one."

"Do you believe he actually left L.A.?"

"I don't have any reason not to think so."

"How did the two of you get along?"

"Okay, I guess. We had dinner, then went back to his hotel, which was Shutters. I stayed the night."

"Did you have sex?"

"Yes."

"Did he enjoy it?"

"I believe so."

"Then why would he abandon you after such a short acquaintance?"

"I don't know. I'm baffled."

"Our Billy is a slippery character," Genaro said. He threw up his hands. "Well, if he doesn't want to know us, he doesn't want to know us. Thanks, honey, you did your best."

Charmaine left Genaro's office wondering if her story had worked.

Teddy got settled in his new apartment, did some grocery shopping, and picked up a copy of a local magazine. On a rear page was an ad for a tour of Centurion Studios.

In Phoenix the young man keeping watch on the FlightAware screen saw the red light from the GPS locator go off, then, a few minutes later it went on again, this time at a street corner in downtown Santa Monica. He called Igor's cell phone and got voice mail, left a message, then called his hotel and was told there was no reply from the room. He left a message there, then hung up. The GPS marker was still at the same location. He checked a map of Los Angeles and found that the dot was at Shutters.

Later that morning a maid knocked on the door of Smolensky's room, then went inside and cleaned it. She thought it odd that he had gone out but left what appeared to be the contents of his pockets on the dresser — money, wallet, what appeared to be keys. She called the front desk and reported what she had found.

The desk clerk sent a bellman to the room, and he confirmed the maid's story. Then an assistant manager visited the room and noted that a parking ticket for the hotel garage was among Smolensky's belongings, and that he would have needed it to leave the garage. The car keys were missing, but a check of the garage showed the car was still there. Three hours later, when Smolensky had not returned to his room, the assistant manager reported the information to the manager, who called the police.

Two hours passed before a pair of detectives visited the hotel, talked to the manager and the maid, looked at Smolensky's room, then at his car.

"Can we open the trunk without a warrant?" one of the men asked the other.

"If we have reason to fear for Smolensky's life."

"Okay, I fear for his life, how about you?"

"I fear for his life, too." They got a crowbar from their car and pried open the trunk.

In Phoenix, Igor's secretary came into his office and spoke to the young man watching the computer screen. She looked shaken. "The Los Angeles Police just called," she said. "Igor is dead. They found him in the trunk of his rental car in the garage at Shutters. You should talk to them on line two."

The young man went to Igor's desk and picked up his phone. A long conversation ensued, during which he was asked a lot of questions he couldn't or didn't want to answer. As soon as they had hung up, he went to the secretary's desk.

"Have you got a phone number for Mr. Majorov?" he asked.

"He's at the New Desert Inn, in Las Vegas." She wrote down the number for him.

"Have you ever met Mr. Majorov?"

"No," she replied. "I've talked with him on the phone several times, though. He was very businesslike, no charm."

"Would you like to call him and tell him what's happened?"

"I think you should do that," she said. "You're management, I'm just a secretary."

The young man went back to Igor's desk, called the number, and asked for Majorov.

"Yes?"

"Mr. Majorov?"

"Yes?"

"This is Todd German, in Phoenix. I work for Igor Smolensky."

"Yes, Mr. German, what is it?"

"We just got a call from the Los Angeles Police. Igor has been found dead, in the trunk of his car."

After a brief silence, Majorov asked for an account of his conversation with the police. Todd told him everything he had said.

"Did they ask about someone called Billy Burnett?"

"No, sir."

"Did you mention that name to them?"

"No, sir."

"Then they don't know that Igor was looking for him?"

"No, sir."

"Do you have any information on the whereabouts of Burnett?"

"No, sir. I was watching the FlightAware website, looking for Burnett's airplane, which seemed to be based at Santa Monica Airport. Igor planted a GPS tracker in the airplane, and I could see that represented on our tracking screen. Then the marker was turned off and turned on again, and it had moved to Igor's hotel. I think the police must have turned it off, because it isn't alive anymore. I called the place at the airport where the airplane was kept, and they said he left this morning, headed east."

"Call the police back and tell them you'd like to claim the body, then go to Los Angeles and arrange to have it cremated and the ashes disposed of. Igor wasn't married, was he?"

"No, sir, I don't think so."

"Did he have a regular girlfriend?"

"Not that I know of. He worked all the time."

"Yes, he was a very hard worker. Go through Igor's desk and office and remove everything that belonged to him and shred any documents that mention Billy Burnett. Find his desk diary, if he kept one, and his address book. Scrub his office computer clean of any files pertaining to Burnett. If anyone calls the office asking for Igor, they are to be told that he has left the company and you have no forwarding address. When all that is complete, bring the diary and address book and come to Las Vegas. There will be a room reserved for you at the New

Desert Inn. We will talk then." Majorov hung up.

Todd hung up the phone and buzzed the secretary. "Book me a room for tonight at Shutters, and get me a seat on an airplane to Los Angeles, and tomorrow, to Las Vegas." He thought for a moment. "First class. Then come in here and help me. Also, get two thousand dollars in cash from the safe."

"You're going to L.A.?"

"Yes, to claim the body and have it cremated. Then I have to go to Las Vegas and see Mr. Majorov. Do you know of anyone who Igor was attached to that should be notified?"

"No, I don't think there was anyone like that," she said.

"Anyone who calls should be told that Igor has left the company and we don't have a forwarding address."

Todd hung up the phone. He had the feeling that he had just been promoted in the organization.

22

Teddy drove to Centurion Studios after lunch and, at the gate, was directed to the parking lot for tour customers. He arrived to find two dozen people boarding a tram pulled by an electric cart, paid for his ticket, and climbed aboard the last car, sitting next to an attractive woman of about forty. The tram departed.

"Good afternoon, ladies and gentlemen," the driver said over the speaker system, "and welcome to Centurion Studios, one of Hollywood's last intact movie factories. Some of the buildings you'll see date to the beginnings of the movie industry, but most were built after the founder of the studio bought this land and created Centurion."

The driver continued his spiel as they drove past a row of what appeared to be old-fashioned Los Angeles houses. The driver explained that they were called bungalows and housed dressing rooms for

159

stars and the offices of producers and directors. As they passed one particularly nice example, Teddy saw Peter Barrington's Porsche Cayenne parked in front of it, and he made a mental note of the address.

The tram continued down the studio's famous New York street, which had been the standing set for dozens of movies over the decades, then passed the fire department and continued to the back lot, where there was an old Western town set and stables for horses. The tram stopped.

"Now, ladies and gentlemen, we're going to dismount and visit one of the most interesting departments of the studio: the armory. This is where the weapons are kept that are used in Westerns, cop movies, and war movies, and we're going to have a demonstration of shooting by one of the studio's stuntmen."

The group filed into the building and was shown several rooms filled with weapons of every sort, then led into a large room where they were handed headsets that would protect their ears from the noise while amplifying their leader's voice.

He introduced the stuntman, who was dressed in Western regalia, and the group watched as he demonstrated his quick draw and rapid-fire technique with a lever-action rifle. The demonstration came to a halt when his weapon jammed.

Teddy, who was standing a few feet behind the man, watched as he tried to clear the weapon. "Don't force it," Teddy said. "It's going to have to be field-stripped to fix the problem." The cowboy put down the rifle and chose another. The same thing happened.

A man appeared at Teddy's elbow. "Are you familiar with the workings of the Winchester model 1873?" he asked.

"Intimately," Teddy said.

"Come with me," the man said.

Teddy followed him into a workshop where a rifle had been locked in a vise.

"You want to have a go at that?"

Teddy chose a tool from above the workbench, opened the weapon, and pointed to a broken part. "That will need to be replaced," he said. "Do you have spares?"

The man went to a shelf and brought back a box of parts. "There you go."

Teddy quickly replaced the part and reassembled the weapon. He levered it a dozen times without problems.

"Where'd you learn that weapon?" the man asked.

"I used to maintain the guns at a Western shooting club," Teddy lied.

"I'm Jim Garver," the man said, offering his hand. "We've got ninety-odd of those rifles. They're replicas made for the studio by an Italian company in the late 1930s, and they've been used a lot and break regularly. Right now, I've got eighteen that need attention, and I'm short a man. Are you looking for work, by any chance?"

"Not especially," Teddy said, "but I'll be happy to help you out with your problem. I expect that all of the rifles are ready for overhaul, if you have the parts. Otherwise, they'll have to be handmade, unless the Italian company is still in business."

"It's not," Garver said. "What's your name?"

"Billy Barnett," Teddy said, changing a vowel in the surname.

"Billy, I'll pay you twenty-five bucks a rifle to go through the lot and overhaul them. Fifty, if you have to make parts."

"I'm glad to help you," he said.

"Be here tomorrow morning at nine. There'll be a studio pass and a parking permit for you at the main gate."

"I'll see you then," Teddy said, then rejoined the group. They were now watching the cowboy fire a Thompson submachine gun.

Their tour guide spoke up again. "Now

we'll go over to the studio commissary — that's what our restaurant is called — for some refreshments," he said, and everybody got back aboard the tram. They were driven to the commissary, and they filed into one end of the large room, where a table was set up with soft drinks and snacks. Teddy grabbed a Coke and a cookie and stepped away from the table to make room for the others. He cast an eye around the room, now half-empty after the lunch hour, and saw Peter Barrington and his friend sitting at a table talking.

There was a barrier between them, and Teddy walked to it. "Peter!" he called, and the young man turned and recognized him. He got up and came over.

"It's Billy Burnett, isn't it?"

"Barnett," Teddy said, shaking hands.

"What brings you to Centurion?"

"I took the studio tour," Teddy said, "and ended up with a job here."

"Oh? Doing what?"

"Overhauling old rifles over at your armory. It's just temporary — they're short-handed at the moment."

Peter handed him one of his new cards. "When you catch up with the work, stop by and see me," he said. "Call first, to be sure I'm there."

The driver was calling his customers to reboard the tram, and Teddy turned to joined them. "Gotta go," he said. "I'll see you later." He walked outside with the others and got aboard the tram. The woman he had been sitting next to had preceded him.

"I hear you got a job at the armory," she said.

"I'm just going to help them out while they're shorthanded," Teddy replied. "I'm Billy Barnett."

"I'm Margaret Talbot," she said. "Call me Marge."

The tram dropped them off at the parking lot. "Can I give you a lift?" Billy said.

"If you're going anywhere near Santa Monica," she replied. "I took a cab here."

Billy put her into his rental car and aimed it toward Santa Monica. "You're on my way," he said. "That's where I live."

"I've only been in L.A. for a couple of weeks," Marge said. "I'm an actress, and things were a little slow in New York, so I thought I'd try my luck out here."

"Find anything so far?"

"I've had three auditions and one callback," she said. "My agency in New York put me in touch with their L.A. office, so I didn't have to worry about finding an agent."

They drove on toward Santa Monica, chatting easily. Billy looked ahead down the street and saw a Porsche dealer. "Have you got time for a few minutes' stop?" he asked. "I'm in the market for a car."

"Sure, I'm not in a hurry."

Teddy pulled into the dealership, and they walked past a line of sparkling new Porsches to the used-car lot. Something had caught his eye.

A salesman materialized next to them. "Can I show you something?" he asked.

"Let's take a look at that old Speedster," Teddy said, pointing at what was one of the first sports cars Porsche had made.

"Oh, she's a beauty, isn't she? She's the 1958 D model. We picked her up at an auction — an estate was selling the car. The owner maintained it himself since new, and he knew what he was doing."

Teddy got into the car, started it, and listened. He switched off the engine, walked around the car slowly, then popped the hood. The engine bay was clean and, in some places, polished. The haggling began.

23

The whole group, including the Tweeds, gathered for dinner on the terrace outside Stone's house. It was a pleasant California evening, and everyone was relaxed and chatting, until Peter came to Stone.

"Guess who turned up at Centurion this afternoon."

Stone stared at his son. "Billy Burnett?"

"Apparently I got his name wrong — it's Barnett."

"Tell me about this."

"Ben and I had a late lunch at the studio commissary, and there was a tour group there, having Cokes and cookies. They're there most days. Billy was among them. He called to me, and I went over and talked with him for a minute."

"What did you talk about?" Stone asked.

"He told me he'd gotten a job at the studio armory. He described it as temporary."

"Doing what?"

"Overhauling old rifles. I told him to call me when his work schedule allowed."

"Why did you do that?"

"I figured you might like to get a look at him, to see if he's this Teddy Fay guy."

"You're right, I would like to get a look at him."

"If you'd like to see him sooner rather than later, I'll take you to the armory."

"I've seen it before," Stone said, "on my first visit to the studio some years ago."

"You travel with a gun, don't you?"

"Yes."

"Have something break, and we'll take it to the armory to have it fixed."

"Tomorrow?" Stone asked.

"I'm at the bungalow all day. Drop by, and I'll take you to the armory, then we'll have lunch."

"You're on," Stone said.

Teddy drove up to Sunset in his new Speedster with Marge Talbot beside him. The top was down and rush hour was over on Sunset Boulevard, so Teddy drove all the way down to the Pacific Coast Highway and turned north. "Feel like some dinner?" he asked Marge. "I saw an ad for a Greek restaurant that sounded interesting."

"Sure, I'd like that," she said. "This is a delightful car."

"I've always wanted one," Teddy said, "but the time never seemed right until now." He shifted up, and the little car flew along the highway, with the ocean yards to their left. Marge's hair was wild in the wind, but she didn't seem to mind.

Teddy drove into Malibu and turned right into the shopping area. He found the restaurant, and they dined outside on the porch. Teddy felt really comfortable with this woman. He answered her questions with the same answers he had given Charmaine. It made life simpler.

They finished dinner, and Teddy drove Marge home, only a few blocks from his new apartment.

"Where do you live?" Marge asked.

"Over that way a few blocks. Next time I'll cook you some dinner."

"That would be a refreshing change," she said. "No man has ever cooked dinner for me before."

He drove her home to half of an old California duplex, gave her a light kiss on the lips, and went home to his new penthouse.

The following morning, Teddy arrived at

the studio armory at the stroke of nine, and Jim Garver was ready for him; he had cleared the workbench and lined all the Winchester 73s up on a rack beside it. There were four boxes of spare parts on the other end of the bench.

"This is all the parts we've got," Jim said. "Let me know if you have to make any, and I'll find you the right material. There's an apron right over there, unless you'd like some coveralls."

"I'm fine with the apron," Teddy replied. "Why don't I get to work?"

"Have at it, and call me if you need anything," Jim said, then left him alone with the guns and tools.

It was nearly noon when Teddy heard someone at the door behind him.

"Billy?"

He turned to find Peter Barrington at the door, and his father, Stone, standing beside him. "Good morning, Peter," he said. He wiped his hands clean, walked to the door, and shook hands.

"This is my father, Stone Barrington," Peter said.

"How you doing?" Teddy asked, offering his best smile with his new dental veneers.

"Very well," Stone replied, shaking hands.

"I've got a little problem with my Colt Government .380, and Peter said I might get it looked at here." He removed the small handgun from its holster, popped out the magazine, and locked the slide open, then handed it to Teddy, butt first.

"I'll have a look," Teddy said. "Have you ever handled a Winchester 73?"

"No, I haven't," Stone replied.

Teddy handed him the weapon he had just finished. "The rifle that won the West," he said.

Stone hefted the rifle and sighted down the barrel. "Feels nice."

"I think it's my favorite rifle," Teddy said. "They've got nearly a hundred of them — replicas, made in Italy, and they're showing their age. They hired me to overhaul them, and when I'm done, they'll get another fifty years out of them." He stripped the little Colt. "I've always liked this gun, too — feels good in the hand, and a .380 is all you need, if you can hit what you aim at." He stripped the weapon and did something to it, then returned it to Stone. "There you go — just a little adjustment."

Stone returned the magazine to the pistol and holstered it. "Peter said you told him we knew each other from somewhere."

"We met once, at Elaine's — I don't know,

a dozen years ago. She introduced us. I didn't remember it until I saw your name mentioned in a *Vanity Fair* piece."

"Ah, yes, that. Where'd you learn your gunsmithing?"

"I used to belong to a Western shooting club, back home in New York State, and I took it up then."

"Thanks very much for your help. Good to meet you, Teddy."

"It's Billy," Teddy said. "Billy Barnett." He smiled and turned back to the workbench.

Stone and Peter left the armory and got into Peter's golf cart. "Well?" Peter asked.

Stone shook his head. "It's a different man," he said. "Younger, fitter, and Teddy wore a toupee, I think. This guy has a firmer jaw and his own hair. And he didn't bat an eye when I called him Teddy."

"You're right, he didn't," Peter said, steering the cart toward the commissary.

They had just finished lunch when they saw Billy Barnett walk into the commissary with another man.

"That's Jim Garver, who runs the armory," Peter said.

"You know," Stone said, "I'm both relieved

that Billy is not Teddy and disappointed."

"Why disappointed?"

"I don't know," Stone replied. "Maybe I'm just looking for some excitement."

24

Pete Genaro was giving Yuri Majorov a personal tour of the new poker room at the casino.

"Very nice," Majorov said, as if he couldn't care less. "But what matters is the quality of the players."

"Well, this week, we've got Memphis Slim coming in for a few days, and there's Buck Thompson, from Montana. Next week it's all Texans."

"Any of them ever win any money?"

"We had a fellow in here a week or ten days ago who took sixty thousand from what I thought of as a hot group. Name of Billy Burnett."

Majorov stopped walking. "Say that name again."

"Billy Burnett."

"From where?"

"L.A., he says, but he's kind of a mystery man. I ran his identity, and he's real, but his background is pretty skimpy. Looks like he's spent his life flying under the radar."

"I would like to meet this gentleman," Majorov said, and his tone did not sound like a request.

"I tracked him down to a hotel in Los Angeles, Shutters, in Santa Monica, but then we lost him. I even sent one of our best VIP ladies down to see him, but then he just went *poof.*"

"I'd like you to find him," Majorov said. "And I'd like to talk to this lady you mentioned. Right now."

Charmaine tapped on Pete Genaro's office door and stifled a yawn. Pete had woken her from a sound sleep.

"Come in."

She opened the door and walked in. That Russian, Majorov, was sitting on the sofa, and the sight of him gave her the willies. She was afraid of the man; she didn't know exactly why, but she was.

"Have a seat, Charmaine. You met Mr. Majorov, didn't you?"

"Oh, yes, of course," she chirped, and took a chair, primly crossing her legs.

"Charmaine, have you heard from Billy Burnett again?"

"Not yet," she said, "but I wouldn't be

surprised if he called."

"Call him," Majorov said.

"I tried, but his phone had been disconnected. I think he uses throwaway cell phones."

"Is there any other way you can contact him?" Majorov asked.

"No, sir; he checked out of Shutters, his hotel in Santa Monica. He flies his own airplane, so he could be anywhere."

"His tail number is N123TF?"

"Yessir, that sounds right. Maybe you can trace him that way."

"We're working on that," Majorov said. "That will be all, young lady, but if you hear from Mr. Burnett, I want to know about it immediately, do you understand?"

"Yes, sir," she said.

"Thank you, Charmaine," Genaro said.

Charmaine left Genaro's office, walking fast. She turned into the nearest ladies' room, stepped into a booth, and threw up into the toilet. She checked her makeup and hair in the mirror, then went back to the little room in the hotel where she rested between shifts. She took a deep breath, then called Billy.

"Hello?"

"It's Charmaine."

"Hi, there."

"That man, Majorov. I . . . I . . ."

"Hey, take it easy," Teddy said. "Take a few deep breaths and relax."

She did as instructed. "Pete Genaro called me into his office, and Majorov was there. He started grilling me about you."

"That's all right. You couldn't have told him anything that would hurt me."

"What does he want with you, Billy?"

"I had a little run-in with some people who work for him. They tried to kill me, in fact."

"And how did you handle that?"

"By staying alive," he said. "That's why I came to L.A., to get rid of them."

"Majorov said they're tracking your airplane."

"Don't worry, that won't work."

"Billy, I got the impression that Majorov is deadly serious about finding you, and they're putting a lot of pressure on me to help."

"Then do anything they ask you to do — just let me know about it."

"At this number?"

"Got a pencil?"

"Yes."

"Write down a new number." He gave it to her. "Then wait a little while, and tell Genaro that you heard from me. Give him

176

the number we're talking on now. They may check your iPhone for recent calls from this number, so delete them all but this one. Find a Radio Shack and buy a throwaway cell phone, then call me at the new number from that phone, next time you want to talk."

"All right."

"I think we'd better cool it for a while, until the heat from Majorov is off."

"I think so, too."

"Call me whenever you like, but do it from the throwaway. I'd certainly like to know if you have any further contact with Majorov."

"I'll let you know."

"Just relax and live your life as usual."

"I miss you," she said.

"I miss you, too," Teddy replied. "We'll get together again, don't worry. I'll call you in a few days on the throwaway number."

They both hung up, and Charmaine stretched out on the bed and tried to nap, but she couldn't stop trembling.

25

Todd German arrived at Los Angeles International, rented a car, and, using the onboard GPS system, drove to Shutters and checked in. He hung up his clothes, then went online and found a Santa Monica funeral parlor advertising basic services and had a short conversation with them about services and rates. He told them he'd call back later in the day.

That done, he went down to the garage and drove to the West Los Angeles police station. He gave the name of the detective he had spoken to, and after a fifteen-minute wait, a skinny, sandy-haired man in his mid-thirties appeared.

"My name is Detective Sanders," he said. "Please come with me."

He was escorted to a small room containing only a table and four chairs. He was told to have a seat, and Sanders left. He came back ten minutes later with another man, short, dark, and muscular. Gym rat, Todd figured. The man's name was Gonzales.

"Mr. German," Sanders said, tossing a thin file folder on the table, "what is your connection to Igor Smolensky?"

"I believe we went over that on the phone," Todd replied.

"Go over it again for me," Gonzales said. "Please."

"We both work for Amalgamated Enterprises, in Phoenix. Mr. Smolensky was my immediate superior."

"What kind of company is that?"

"It's an international conglomerate made up of about three dozen businesses in various countries."

"Any of these businesses connected to any kind of criminal organization?"

Todd made a show of looking surprised. "Of course not. Neither Mr. Smolensky nor I would be employed there, if that were the case."

"Reason we ask," Sanders said, "is the circumstances of Mr. Smolensky's death fit a pattern associated with criminality. He was lured from his room down into the garage. He left so quickly that he didn't even bother to put his ID or money in his pockets. He was disarmed — he was found with a semiautomatic pistol — placed in the trunk of his car, and shot in the head with a small-caliber weapon. His death had all the hallmarks of a mob killing."

"If that's so, then there must have been a case of mistaken identity," Todd said. "Igor was a straight arrow. He belonged to the Phoenix Kiwanis Club, for God's sake."

"How about you, Mr. German? Do you have any criminal associations?"

"Certainly not."

"Now that Mr. Smolensky is dead, are you going to get his job?"

"I don't know — it's possible, I guess, or they could send someone in from the outside. I've been there less than a year."

"Where were you before that?"

"I was a student at the University of Phoenix."

"That's some sort of Internet school, isn't it?"

"No, but it's a for-profit university."

"What did you study there?"

"I got a bachelor's in economics and an MBA."

"How old are you, Mr. German?"

"Twenty-six."

"Where are you from?"

"I was born in Phoenix. I've lived there all my life."

"Where are your parents from?"

"My father was born in East Germany, my mother in Russia."

"Are you acquainted with something called the Russian Mafia?"

"Only from bad television shows. I'd like to claim Mr. Smolensky's body."

"Does he have any living relatives?" Gonzales asked.

"No — at least, not according to his employment records."

"Wife?"

"No, he was single."

"Was he gay?"

"Not to my knowledge."

"Was he screwing anybody in the office?"

"Not to my knowledge. It's a small office. There's only one woman working for us, and she's married. How do I go about claiming the body?"

Sanders removed a list of names from his folder and slid it across the table. "This is a list of people who checked out of Shutters on the morning that Mr. Smolensky was murdered. Do any of them ring a bell?"

Todd looked at the list: at the top was Billy Burnett. "No, none of them rings a bell. Now, how do I claim Mr. Smolensky's body?"

"We'll give you a document," Sanders said. "You give that to a funeral home, and they'll pick up the body from the city morgue. After that, what's done with him is up to you."

"Was there an autopsy conducted?"

"Yes. The cause of death was a single gunshot wound to the head. There were no other signs of violence on the body."

"Will this murder be solved?"

Gonzales sighed. "I'd say the chances are about fifty-fifty, under the circumstances."

"What are the circumstances?"

"Out-of-town visitor, no local connections, no witnesses, no DNA, no forensic evidence, except for the bullet that killed him."

"So you have nothing at all to go on?" Todd didn't really care, but he thought he should make a show of it.

"That's about the size of it," Sanders said. "We were hoping you might give us something to go on. Why was Smolensky in L.A.?"

"I don't know — he left without telling me, said he'd be back in a couple of days. I don't know of a business reason for his trip. It could have been personal, I guess."

"Did Smolensky know a woman here, or a man?"

"I have no idea."

Sanders took a document from the file

folder on the table, signed it, and handed it to Todd. "This is what you need to claim the body." He gave Todd a card. "Please call us if any further information comes to light."

"I'll do that," Todd said, then he got out of there.

He entered the address of the funeral home into the GPS unit and drove there. He was seen immediately by a gray man in a black suit.

"How may we help you?" the man asked.

"An associate of mine was murdered. His body is at the city morgue." Todd handed him the document. "I'd like you to collect the body, have it cremated, and deliver the ashes to me at Shutters, a hotel on Santa Monica Beach. What is your customary fee for such services?"

The man took a form from his desk drawer and began checking off items. "Hearse, pickup, body preparation, cremation container . . . Would you like to see a selection of urns?"

"No, thank you, just use whatever container is customary."

"An urn is customary."

"Do you have such a thing as a cardboard box of an appropriate size?"

"Yes."

"That will do."

The man added up some figures with a small calculator and wrote a number at the bottom of the page. "Twelve hundred and seventy dollars," he said, sliding the paper across the desk.

Todd counted out the money in cash and was given a receipt. "When will I have the ashes?" he asked.

The man looked at his watch. "By noon tomorrow."

Thank you," Todd said, and left as quickly as possible. Back at the hotel, he booked himself on an early afternoon flight to Las Vegas.

26

Stone, Dino, and Mike Freeman had dinner together in the dining room of the house at The Arrington. It was raining outside.

"I met Billy Burnett," Stone said. "Or rather, Billy Barnett — it seems that Peter got the name wrong."

"You know," Mike said, "changing your name by one letter can be a very effective means of not being found. Most of the legwork in tracing people these days is done by computer. If you enter 'Billy Burnett,' maybe he turns up with a telephone listing or even an address, but computers are literalists: enter 'Billy Barnett,' and it will look for that and only that."

"That's interesting, Mike," Stone said, "but Billy whatever-his-name-is is not Teddy Fay."

"Why do you sound so certain?"

"Because Billy is younger, slimmer, fitter,

and has more hair and a firmer jaw than Teddy."

"Well, slimmer and fitter can make you look younger, and so can a face-lift. Hair can be transplanted and a firmer jaw can be gained with implants, usually slivers of cadaver bone. How about height?"

"I think Billy is taller than Teddy."

"Losing weight can make you look taller, so can lifts in your shoes."

"You're not going to let go of this, are you?" Stone asked.

"I'm just pointing out the obvious," Mike said. "I'm willing to accept that the two men are not the same person."

"There's something you're both forgetting," Dino said.

"Okay, what's that?" Stone asked.

"You're forgetting who Teddy Fay is."

"Who is he?" Mike asked.

"He's a guy who spent twenty years or so outfitting intelligence agents so that they would be unrecognizable as who they are. That means passports, driver's licenses, credit cards — all the paper that a person usually carries. One of our computer kids at the NYPD told me that it's possible, even easy, if you're a good enough hacker with good enough equipment, to go into other computers and manufacture credit reports with long histories of charge accounts, addresses, loans, et cetera. He posits that if a hacker were really, really smart, he could hack into State Department computers and create passport records that would be indistinguishable from the real thing, so that a fake passport wouldn't set off alarms at an airport.

"Now, if he could do all that for CIA agents in the field, he could do it for himself, couldn't he? And if you start looking for him, how are you going to get past all that custom-created background?"

"Fingerprints or DNA," Mike replied.

"When Teddy left the Agency," Dino continued, "he erased his fingerprint records from the CIA and FBI computers and erased every photograph of him on record."

"That makes it tougher."

"And who are you going to compare his DNA to? One of his old identities? Somebody who doesn't exist anymore?"

"I'll tell you one thing," Mike said, "I'd really like to hire this guy."

Stone and Dino burst out laughing. "I don't think he's job hunting," Stone said.

Todd German woke late, had breakfast in bed, and watched an old movie on TV. At eleven-thirty, a package was delivered to his room. He took it into the bathroom, opened it, and looked at the contents: a gray, pulpy substance. He emptied the box into the toilet and flushed it. "Sorry, Igor," he said aloud. "Think of it as a burial at sea."

He got dressed and packed and drove to LAX to catch his flight to Las Vegas.

Todd had just checked into his room at the New Desert Inn when the phone rang. "Yes?"

"This is Majorov. Come up to my suite now." He gave him the room number and hung up.

Todd changed into fresh clothes and went in search of the suite. He rapped on the door, and it was opened by a large man in a suit.

"You German?" the man asked.

"Yes."

The man jerked a thumb in the direction of the next room. Todd walked into a book-lined study and found a man sitting behind the desk, reading a document.

"Sit," Majorov said, then he looked up and gave Todd a long, appraising once-over. "Tell me about Los Angeles."

Todd gave him a concise account of the events of his visit there.

"So the police have no leads?"

"No," Todd said. "And I don't think they're going to find any."

"Why not?" Majorov said. "I thought American policemen never let go of murder cases."

"There isn't anything to find. Billy Burnett doesn't exist, at least, not anymore. He's somebody else, now."

"We have an airplane tail number," Majorov pointed out.

"He's already figured out that we're trying to trace it, and he has, no doubt, already changed it."

"Is it so easy?"

"With stick-on numbers, available at any graphics shop."

"I see. I want you to find this man."

"I don't think I want that job," Todd said.

"Your mother would be shocked."

"I beg your pardon?"

"Your mother and I are first cousins," Majorov said. "How do you think you got this job? With a degree from that . . . *university*?"

Todd was shaken. "She told me that all her relatives are dead."

"She lied," Majorov said. "Now tell me why you don't want Igor's job."

"I would be very pleased to have Igor's job, but not the job of finding this Billy Burnett."

"Tell me why."

"Just look at what's happened so far: he's killed two of what Igor said are your best men and made them vanish from sight."

"Igor found them."

"Only because he knew where to look. And now Igor is dead, too. Burnett is smarter than Igor, or he would be dead and Igor still alive. I have to ask myself why you have become obsessed with finding this man. Is it just revenge over this hotel thing?"

"In my business you don't allow people to take advantage of you, and that's what Burnett has done."

"And he will go on taking advantage of you until you stop looking for him. In fact, what he will do, if you continue to annoy him, is to cut the process short by simply killing you."

"You think he could do that?"

"I walked in here without being searched," Todd said. "I could be armed with a gun or a knife. Why do you think you are invulnerable? Igor thought that."

"You have a very smart mouth," Majorov said. He was becoming irritated, not least because he knew the younger man was right. "Igor was paid four times as much as you," he said, controlling his temper. "If you want Igor's job, go do his job."

Todd stared at him but did not reply.

"Now, I will give you a gift," Majorov said. "There is a woman who works in this establishment who knows Billy Burnett, who spent a night in his bed at this Shutters place. She says she doesn't know how to contact him, but she is lying. Her name is Charmaine." He scribbled something on a sheet of paper. "Here is her address, her phone number, and the number of her room in this hotel, where she rests between shifts." He stapled a photograph to the sheet. "And here is what she looks like." He shoved the paper across the desk.

Todd picked it up, looked at it, and stood up. "All right," he said. "I'll need some cash."

"How much?"

"Ten thousand dollars."

Majorov took a small pad from his desk drawer, wrote the amount on it, and signed it. "The casino cashier will give you the money."

Todd took the chit and left the suite.

27

Teddy worked until three, then went home and spent an hour going through his Barnett identity, cleaning up details, until he was satisfied that everything stood up. Something was nagging at him, but he couldn't figure out what it was.

Then he sat down with the latest issue of *Flying* magazine and on the last pages it came to him. He was reading an article that praised the work of Hawthorne Aircraft Painting, based at Hawthorne Airport. He picked up the phone and called them.

"My name is Barnett," he said. "I have an airplane parked at Hawthorne that I'd like partially repainted."

"Where is the airplane?" the man asked.

"At Million Air. It's a JetPROP."

"I'll run over there and have a look at it," the man said. "What did you want painted?"

"The airplane is red over white, with black

striping. It's fairly new, but I've never liked red."

"So you want just the top color changed?"

"That's right."

"What color would you like?"

"I think a dark green, and I'd like the tail number in white and the stripes in a metallic gold."

"All right, Mr. Barnett. I'll call you back in an hour."

Fifty minutes later, Teddy and Hawthorne Aircraft Painting had a deal, and since the shop had had a cancellation, it would be done quickly. That little bit of anxiety had vanished, and he felt much better.

He called Charmaine on her throwaway number.

"Hey," she said. "How are you?"

"Just fine," he replied. "I've got a part-time job that I'm enjoying."

"Doing what?"

"I'll tell you when I see you."

"When will that be?"

"As soon as you like."

"I've got a long weekend off, starting Friday."

"What time will you leave Vegas?"

"About four."

"Then we'll meet at seven, like before?"

"That's fine. Where?"

"I'll call you when you're on the way. Any noise from Genaro?"

"He invited me to a meeting with Majorov. You were the subject. I didn't give them anything."

"Good girl. Do you own a red scarf?"

"Yes, a silk one."

"If you think you're being followed, wear it around your neck, then go to the restaurant as planned and have a drink at the bar. I'll catch up with you, or call you with a new location."

"Got it," she said. "I'll call you around five on Friday. Do you have a new number?"

He gave it to her. "See you Friday." He hung up.

Todd found the hotel room where Charmaine spent her rest periods and tapped lightly on the door.

"Who is it?" a woman's voice called out.

"Hotel services. I have to change the lock on your door." He smiled into the peephole.

"Just a minute," she answered. "Let me get decent."

He waited patiently until the door began to open, then he pushed it hard, knocking her back a few paces. She was wearing a hotel robe, and her hair was wet. She seemed too shocked to scream.

Todd swung hard and struck her cheek and ear with the flat of his right hand, knocking her nearly unconscious. He grabbed her hair and jerked her to her feet, then he stripped off the robe, pushed her onto the bed, and sat on her. Holding his left hand over her mouth, he reached into a back pocket, retrieved a switchblade, and held it to her face. "Scream, and I'll cut you, understand?"

She nodded.

He moved his hand from her mouth to her throat. "This is how it is," he said quietly, but with threat in his voice. "I want to find Billy Burnett, and I know you know how to do that. If you don't tell me right now, I'm going to fuck you a few times, then cut your throat. There won't be a second chance, so you'd better get it right the first time. Go."

"All right," she said. "All I have is a new phone number. He called only a few minutes ago." She gave him the number.

"Where does he live?"

"He told me that when he left Shutters he was going to find a place in Santa Monica. The last time I talked to him, he said he had found a place, but he wouldn't tell me where. He's very cautious."

"I told you there wouldn't be a second

chance," he said, pressing the sharp blade to her face.

"I swear to you, that's all he would tell me. He wants me to come to L.A. on Friday, but we'll meet at a restaurant, the way we did last time, then go to his place. He'll call me en route with the name of the restaurant."

He squeezed her throat. "There's something else. Tell me."

"That's all I know, I swear it."

"When do you leave on Friday?"

"At four."

"Pick me up in front of the hotel. I'll ride down to L.A. with you."

"Whatever you say."

"Don't bother going to Genaro," he said. "Genaro sent me. You're being watched. Fuck with us, and you're a dead girl. Do you understand?"

She nodded.

He got up, walked to the door, and left the room, without another word.

Charmaine opened the bedside drawer and removed a .25 caliber pistol that she was licensed to carry in Nevada. She ran to the door, opened it, and looked up and down the hall. He was gone. She closed the door and found her throwaway cell phone but stopped before making the call. If the man hadn't been lying, her room might be bugged; her car, too. There might even be a camera.

She took a few deep breaths, dried her hair, got dressed, and went to work, as usual. All evening she gave a performance, one that said everything was normal. She smiled at Genaro when she saw him on the floor, and he smiled back.

She had to hang on until Friday, she thought; she had to keep it together. If they were watching, she would betray nothing. But on Friday, she would be wearing that red scarf.

28

Teddy was working on a Winchester 73 when his boss, Jim Garver, came into the workroom, pulled up two chairs, sat down in one and offered Teddy the other.

"I'm impressed with your work," Jim said. "How'd you like to come to work full-time here?"

"I don't know, Jim, I've just retired from thirty years in my own business, and I'm having a good time. I'm happy to help you out from time to time, but I don't want to commit to a full-time job."

"Here's my problem," Jim said. "I've got more than two thousand weapons here, and a lot of them are old and in the same shape as the Winchesters. What I'd like to do is to overhaul every single one of them, and I think you're the man to do that."

"Tell you what, Jim, when I finish the Winchesters I'll draw up a plan in writing for overhauling your stock, and I'll make a start on it, but part-time. You start looking for a good gunsmith, and I'll help you evaluate applicants by working side by side with them until you find the right guy. But — and I know this is a big but — I'll set my own hours and work at my own pace, and you can pay me by the hour — fifty dollars per — instead of by the weapon."

"You've got yourself a deal," Jim said, offering his hand. "I'll get you some new credentials that will make it easier for you to move around the lot. I'll throw in free meals at the commissary, too."

Teddy shook his hand.

Mike Freeman was having lunch in the commissary with Peter Barrington, having completed a private tour of Centurion Studios, which he had greatly enjoyed. They were finishing their lunch when a man came into the commissary and was waved over by Peter.

"Billy," Peter said, "we're leaving shortly, but if you'd like to sit down, you can keep our table."

"Thank you, Peter," Teddy said, and sat down. A waitress brought a menu and he ordered the daily special.

"I'm sorry," Peter said, "I didn't introduce Mike Freeman. Mike, this is Billy Barnett."

The two men shook hands.

"Mike is a friend of my father's," Peter explained. He put his napkin down. "Mike, will you excuse me? I've got to be back at the bungalow for a meeting. You finish your lunch."

"Thank you, Peter," Mike said. He stood and shook the younger man's hand, then sat down again. "A fine young man," he said to Barnett.

"That is certainly my impression of him," Teddy replied.

"I'm very pleased to meet you, Mr. Barnett," Mike said.

"Please call me Billy — everybody does."

"Thank you, Billy. I've been hearing about you from Peter and Stone."

"Oh?" Teddy asked, frowning.

"Only favorable things," Mike said. "Billy, may I tell you a story you might find interesting?"

"Please do," Teddy said. "I like a good story."

"Many years ago," Mike said, "my name was not Michael Freeman, it was Stanley Whitehouse." Mike thought he saw a flicker of recognition on Barnett's face at the mention of the name. "I was an intelligence officer with MI-6, which you probably know is the British foreign intelligence service."

"I've heard of it," Teddy said. His lunch arrived, and he began eating. "Please go on."

"I was having a good career," Mike said, "and had been earmarked for promotion, perhaps to a high office, by my superiors. Then one day, my direct superior, a man named Palmer, invited me to his country house for the weekend, so that we could discuss an intelligence operation without being interrupted by office business."

Mike waved over the waitress and ordered another glass of iced tea. "Not a very British beverage, really," he said. "They prefer it hot."

"I've heard," Teddy said.

"So I went down for the weekend, and I was introduced to Palmer's daughter, Penelope, who was a doctoral candidate at Cambridge. She was considerably younger than I, but we really hit it off. By the end of the weekend I was in love with her, and she, with me. It can happen very quickly."

"I'm acquainted with the syndrome," Teddy said.

"We agreed to meet in London for dinner, and by the time a few more dinners had passed, we were living together at my flat. It was early summer, and she would not return to Cambridge until the fall. Before much time had passed, she became pregnant — an oversight on both our parts. I was married and in the throes of a divorce, which in Britain at the time, with the best will in the world on the part of both participants, could take a couple of years, so this was very inconvenient for both of us. She told me that she wished to have the child. I asked her to marry me, and she accepted, understanding that she would be a single mother for a while.

"The following day, I was dispatched to the Middle East on an assignment, and not until I returned some three weeks later did I discover that much had happened in my absence. She had told her father of her pregnancy and the name of the child's father. He did not react well and pressed her to abort the pregnancy. She refused, there was a fight, and she left her father's house and went to my flat. Over a weekend, she reconsidered the desirability of carrying the fetus to term, and she asked a close friend who was a medical student to help her. He was the son of a man named Prior, who was the parliamentary private secretary to the foreign minister.

"The boy had seen an abortion performed but had not conducted one himself. Nevertheless, he thought he could handle it, and he brought the necessary implements for the procedure to a friend's country cottage, where he met Penelope. The procedure seemed to go well, and he spent the night with her to be sure she was all right, then he returned to London to see his boyfriend — he was gay. Later that day she became ill, and he had not left her with an antibiotic. By the time he returned the following day, she was in extremis, and he called an ambulance. It turned out that he had perforated her uterus during the abortion, and infection had ensued. In spite of heroic efforts to save her life, she died in the hospital."

"I'm very sorry," Teddy said.

"I, of course, had gained the enmity of her father, who blamed me entirely, so my position at MI-6 was untenable. I had to leave the service and make my way in the world by other means. Fortunately, I had made the acquaintance of an important businessman who found the skills and languages I had gained in MI-6 useful to him. I was sent to Egypt to work there. In the meantime, the Prior boy, who had performed the abortion, was arrested and sent to prison for two years. While there, he was raped and murdered."

"Good God!" Teddy said. "Your story gets worse and worse."

"There's more," Mike said. "Palmer left MI-6 and went into politics, and both he and Prior were elected to seats in parliament. When the Conservatives came to power some years later, they both became cabinet members — Prior, foreign secretary, Palmer, home secretary. As such, Prior held sway over MI-6, and Palmer over the police. Not long after that, an attempt was made on my life, unsuccessfully, and it became clear that other attempts would follow.

"My employer introduced me to an Englishman, now an American citizen, who ran a large security company in New York called Strategic Services."

"I've certainly heard of that," Teddy said.

"I used the skills I had learned in MI-6 to create a new identity for myself and came to this country to work for Jim. I learned through friends in England that Prior and Palmer were still pursuing me, and Jim Hackett came under suspicion of being me — Stanley Whitehouse. As a result of that, he was murdered. Shortly afterward, the current head of MI-6, a friend of Stone Barrington, managed to expose Prior and Palmer as being behind Jim's murder. As a result, they were expelled from the government and tried for his murder. They are both now in prison."

"I've read bits and pieces of your story," Teddy said, "but I didn't know the whole thing." He looked a little uncomfortable. "Why are you telling me all this?"

"Because I want you to know that, having been on the run and in constant danger for years myself, I understand what you must have gone through the past few years."

Teddy stared at him. "I don't know what you mean," he said.

"I know that you are Teddy Fay, and I have every sympathy for your position. Stone Barrington, by the way, suspected you of being who you are, but after meeting you, decided that he was entirely wrong. I helped convince him."

"So you are the only person who thinks I'm this Teddy person?"

"Quite so. And I am no threat to you. In fact, I want to offer you employment at Strategic Services. I think someone with your skills could be very valuable to us. For your part, you could establish a permanent new identity and live in the open as a free man. Since you have obviously changed your appearance to the extent that no one who knew you in your earlier existence would ever recognize you, you would finally be safe. I will offer you a handsome salary and a full package of benefits, and your future would be assured."

Teddy took a deep breath and let it out. "And why do you think I have all the skills you mention?"

"Because I read your CIA file, when such a file still existed. Don't worry, I don't have a copy, and, I suppose, neither does anyone else."

"Well, Mike," Teddy said, "this has been a very interesting lunch."

"We will not meet or speak again, unless that's what you want," Mike said. He gave Teddy his business card. "This is how you can get in touch with me, should you ever wish to. My offer will remain open indefinitely." He stood up. "Now, if you will excuse me, I will exit your life until such time as you may wish to rekindle our acquaintance." He offered his hand, and Teddy shook it.

Mike left the commissary, and Teddy was left staring into his lunch plate. He felt exposed and, unusually for him, panicky. Gradually, as he thought it over, he became calm. What Freeman had said to him had obviously been sincerely offered. By the time he had left the table to return to work in the armory, he felt some comfort, knowing that he had a way out of his life as a fugitive, if he wanted a way out. Right now, though, he had things to do.

29

Charmaine was leaving the New Desert Inn to retrieve her car from the parking lot when her assailant fell into step with her.

"My car is in the employee lot," she said, pointing.

"We'll take my rental car," Todd said. "It'll be a nice surprise for Mr. Burnett."

"As you wish," Charmaine said.

"Here we are," Todd said, as they approached a black Camaro. He handed her the keys. "You drive."

He put her bag in the trunk, and they started their journey to Los Angeles.

Teddy worked until three at the Centurion armory, then went home to his new apartment, showered, then, at five o'clock, he called Charmaine on her cell phone.

A ringing came from her handbag. "It's my phone," Charmaine said to Todd.

"I'll get it for you," he said. He found the phone in her purse, opened it, and pressed the speaker button.

"Hello," she said.

"Hi, there. Why are you on the speakerphone?"

"It's against the law to use a cell phone in the car. It's not so obvious when the speakerphone is on."

"Are you on schedule?" Teddy asked.

"Right on the button. Where are we meeting?"

"Would you mind going to Michael's again?"

"Not at all. I liked it there."

"Michael's, then, at seven-thirty."

"You're on."

"Are you wearing my favorite scarf?"

"The red one? You bet!"

"Great, I'll see you at the bar." Teddy hung up.

"What does the red scarf mean?" Todd asked, stuffing her phone back into her purse.

"Mean? Nothing — he just liked it the last time I wore it, so I wore it again."

He squeezed her thigh. "You sure about that?"

"Oh, don't be so nervous," she said. "Billy has no way of knowing you're coming."

Todd checked his watch. "Step on it," he said. "I want to be a little early."

At Todd's instruction, Charmaine pulled over to the curb down the block from the restaurant, instead of giving it to the parking valet. It was seven o'clock. Todd pressed the button to lower the windows, then switched off the ignition.

"I like the night air in L.A.," he said, making himself comfortable in the passenger seat. "All you have to do now is to alert me when you see your Billy drive up to the restaurant."

Teddy reached through the car window and placed the silencer to the back of the man's head. "Why wait to be introduced?" he asked.

"Shit," Todd muttered.

"Charmaine," Teddy said, "please get out of the car. Is your bag in the trunk?"

"Yes," she said, getting out and pressing the trunk release.

"Move over into the driver's seat," Teddy said, prodding Todd with the silencer.

Todd scrambled over the console as instructed.

"Charmaine, go into the restaurant and have a drink at the bar. The gentleman and

I will have a little chat, then I'll be back. I won't be long."

"I'm here to deliver a message to you," Todd said.

"Start the car, and let's drive over to Shutters," Teddy said. "You haven't checked in yet, have you?"

"No, but they're expecting me."

"While you drive, you can give me the message."

"Mr. Majorov would like to meet you in Las Vegas," Todd said.

Teddy chuckled. "I've already received that message, from the last gentleman Mr. Majorov sent, and you may recall, I declined."

Todd drove the short distance to Shutters and, on Teddy's instructions, pulled into the garage.

"I should warn you," Todd said as he parked, "Mr. Majorov doesn't like having his invitations declined, and he doesn't like his messengers shot."

"You needn't worry about that," Teddy said. "We're going to call Mr. Majorov after you've checked into your room, and I'll speak to him. Get your luggage from the trunk."

Todd pressed the trunk release, and the two men got out of the car. They walked to the rear, and when Todd leaned over to retrieve his bag, Teddy shot him in the head. He quickly folded the body into the trunk and closed it with his elbow, then he put away the pistol and walked the short distance back to Michael's.

Charmaine was sipping a margarita at the bar, and he sat down beside her and ordered her another and one for himself.

"I think he meant to kill us both," Charmaine said.

"So do I," Teddy replied.

"He's not going to get a chance to do that, is he?"

"No, he's not."

"How am I going to explain this to Pete Genaro and Majorov?"

"I'm going to make a proposal," Teddy said, "and if you accept, you'll never have to worry about either of them again."

"I'm all ears," she said.

"First, let me ask you some questions: Do you have any family?"

"My mother died last year, and she was my closest remaining relative. I have a couple of cousins, but I haven't been in touch with them for years."

"Is there anything in your Las Vegas apartment that you can't do without?"

She thought about that for a moment.

"Nothing that can't be replaced on a shopping spree."

"Do you want to go on working at the casino and hotel?"

"No, it's getting too scary there. I mean, they sent that guy to kill me, as well as you."

"Then come and live with me, and let me take care of you. I'll give you a new, foolproof identity, and Genaro and Majorov will never be able to find you. I'll give you a wonderful life."

She took his face in her hands and kissed him. "Yes," she said. "Yes, yes, yes."

"Oh, where is your car?"

"In the employees' parking lot at the hotel. It's leased. I can have the leasing company pick it up."

"Tomorrow I want you to write to the leasing company, then write a letter to Pete Genaro, resigning your job and asking him to wire any money owed to you to your bank account in Vegas. We'll transfer any funds you have there to an offshore account I have, then I'll give you the cash. We'll find a moving company on the Internet, and you can have them pack your belongings and deliver them to a charity. You'll write to the phone, electric, and gas companies and to the credit card companies, closing your accounts. When all that is done, you will, effectively, have disappeared."

"As long as I'm with you," she said.

30

Ten days passed. Stone and Dino flew back to New York with Mike Freeman. Stone managed to convince Emma Tweed to come with them for a visit.

Peter began shooting his new feature, starting with Tessa's scenes, so that she could finish shooting in under a month. Ben was grateful for Emma's absence; Tessa moved into the house at The Arrington.

Five days after it had been left there, the body of Todd German was found in the trunk of his rented Camaro in the parking garage at Shutters, and the two detectives at the West Los Angeles police station had a new murder to solve. They were now getting crazy.

Pete Genaro looked up from his desk to find Yuri Majorov filling his doorway.

"I have had a call from my Phoenix office telling me that the body of Todd German has been found in exactly the same circumstances as the body of Igor Smolensky and in the same place," he said. "Where is your Charmaine? Did Burnett contact her?"

Genaro handed him a sheet of stationery. "I received this from Charmaine today," he said. "I sent someone to her apartment. It was empty, and the lease had been paid up."

"I expect you have a skip tracer employed here," Majorov said.

"Do you want to find Charmaine that badly?"

"Where Charmaine is will be Billy Burnett."

"Mr. Majorov, if that's what you want, then I'll do it. But you should consider that the bodies are stacking up. Do you want that to continue?"

"What I want is for you to assign a skip tracer to find these people. When he has done that, you will report their location to me, and I will take care of the rest."

"As you wish," Genaro said.

Teddy continued working part-time at the Centurion armory, overhauling weapons and interviewing applicants for his job.

Charmaine followed Teddy's instructions, shutting down her old life, and she visited an upscale hairdresser in Beverly Hills, who cut her hair shorter and colored it to its natural shade of chestnut brown. She bought new clothes and jewelry, replacing the things she had left behind, paying with cash that Billy had given her.

One late afternoon, when all that had been accomplished, Billy sat her down with a drink. "You're going to have a new name," he said. "What would you like it to be?"

She thought about that. "When I was a child," she said, "I hated my name. I always wanted to be Elizabeth and to be called Betsy."

"Then that is who you will be," he said. "Would you like to be Mrs. Barnett?"

"Very much."

"Then that will be done, too. It will all be accomplished by tomorrow evening, then we will go out and celebrate."

Teddy didn't go in to work the following day. He spent the time creating a new identity for Elizabeth Barnett — passport, driver's license, credit report, work history, and Social Security number, and he had a credit card issued from his Cayman Islands bank and mailed to him in Los Angeles. He also created a birth certificate and a marriage certificate and filed them both in the relevant city and state computers.

Betsy came home to find her new identity

arrayed on the dining room table. "You did all this?" she asked.

"I did, and it's all indistinguishable from the genuine article. You exist under your new name on more than a dozen computer systems around the country. You can travel anywhere in the world with these documents. I also removed your application for a casino worker's card from the Nevada state computers, and your employment record from the computer at the hotel. Were you ever fingerprinted for any reason other than the casino application?"

"Yes, for my carry license."

"I'll delete that record tomorrow and make up a California license for you."

"You, sir, are a marvel," she said to him.

"Get changed into your new clothes," he said. "I've booked a table at Spago Beverly Hills."

While Betsy Barnett was applying her makeup, something occurred to her. If her ex-husband, Jimmy Sayer, tried to get in touch with her and failed, he would start looking for her, and she knew him to be tenacious. After a moment's consideration, she called him.

"Hello?"

"Jimmy, it's Charmaine."

218

"Hey, babe, I was just thinking about you. How about dinner and a roll in the hay?"

"I'm afraid not, Jimmy. I got married."

"Really? Anybody I know?"

"No, you don't know him."

"One of your customers?"

"Yes."

"And where are you living?"

She hesitated. "That's not important, Jimmy. You won't be hearing from me again, and I don't want you to try to find me."

"You sound serious," he said.

"I'm absolutely serious. For all practical purposes, I no longer exist. Understand?"

"I can't say that I do, but if this is what you want . . ."

"It's exactly what I want, Jimmy. This is goodbye." She hung up, relieved that she was done with him forever.

Harry Katz knocked on Pete Genaro's door and was invited in and told to sit.

"How many cases you working on, Harry?" Genaro asked.

"Three, at the moment."

"Hand 'em off to somebody else. I've got a special case for you, and I want you to devote a hundred percent of your time to it."

Harry produced a notebook and a pen.

He was an ex–LAPD detective, and he had been trained to take copious notes. "Go."

"Remember Charmaine? One of my hostesses?"

"The little blonde?"

"That's the one."

"What's her last name?"

"Evans."

Harry sighed. "Why do they all have such common names? Does she have any family?"

"I'm working from memory, here," Genaro said, "because her personnel file has been deleted from the hotel computer."

"No kidding? How'd she do that? Did she have anything to do with computers in her work here?"

"Just her schedule."

"How about the state record of her casino worker's application?"

"Good idea, check that."

"Any close friends?"

"Not that I know of. Her apartment's been cleaned out, and her car was picked up by the leasing company from the employees' lot."

"How about that husband of hers, the one we busted for that card-counting scam?"

"Now, there's a thought — I forgot about him. Last I heard he was working as a parking valet at the Sands. He won't ever work indoors at a casino again."

"You have an address on him?"

Genaro turned to his computer and searched the out-of-date employment files. "Got one, but who knows if he's still there?"

Harry made a note of it. "Well," he said, "it's a start."

"There's something else, Harry."

"Shoot."

"Charmaine has a boyfriend named Billy Burnett. He checked in here a few weeks ago, wired us a quarter-million, and played poker for three or four days. Walked away up sixty grand. I ran every sort of check on the guy and came up with the standard stuff, but nothing that would help track him down."

"Billy Burnett," Harry said, writing down the name.

"William J. Burnett. Harry, the man is dangerous."

"How so?"

"He doesn't like being tracked. One of our major stockholders has lost four — count 'em, four — men who tried to track him. Two of them are buried *in their car* in the New Mexico desert. The other two have been found in the trunks of their cars in the parking garage at Shutters, in Santa Monica."

"Holy shit!" Harry said. "I guess that is what you'd call dangerous." He noted the names of the four men, then took down the colors and tail number of Burnett's airplane.

Genaro was still typing away at his computer. "Well, shit," he said, "her casino card application is gone from the state's records, too."

"This Burnett sounds like a major computer geek," Harry said.

Genaro told him everything he could remember about both Charmaine and Billy Burnett. "Go get 'em," he said. "When you find 'em, do nothing — just call me. And, Harry, don't turn up dead."

"Gotcha," Harry said, then left.

31

Stone and Emma, Dino and his wife, Viv, and Mike Freeman were having dinner at Patroon, a new favorite restaurant of Stone's. When the ladies went to the restroom, Mike spoke up.

"I sort of had lunch with Billy Barnett before we left L.A.," he said.

Stone was surprised. "Why?"

"It was accidental, really. Peter and I bumped into him at the Centurion commissary, then Peter left and Billy and I had a chat."

"About what?"

"I offered him a job."

"Doing what?"

"I haven't figured that out yet, but I'm sure he'd be a useful employee."

"Did he have any idea that we suspected him of being Teddy Fay?"

"He does now," Mike said. "I told him so."

"Mike, that's crazy," Stone said. "That makes him dangerous."

"I told him my story as a way of warming him to me."

"Did it work?"

"He admitted nothing — the man is icy cool. I'll bet he could beat a good polygraph."

"Did he take the job offer?"

"No, but he has my card. Stone, I don't think you have anything to worry about, as far as Peter is concerned. He seems very protective of the boy."

"Well, I'm relieved to hear that," Stone said.

The women returned, and the subject changed.

Harry Katz ran the usual background check on Billy Burnett, just to see what turned up. Pete Genaro had been right: it was unrevealing, as far as the man's whereabouts were concerned. He was going to have to go to L.A., he guessed. He told his secretary he was going away for a few days, and as an afterthought, he asked her to book him into Shutters, where the two dead men had been found.

But Harry had another stop to make before he left town. He found James Sayer

224

in the valet parkers' break room at the Sands and introduced himself.

"Yeah, I remember you from the Desert Inn," Sayer said. "What can I do for you?"

It wasn't a warm greeting, Harry thought. "The Desert Inn people are concerned about your ex-wife," he said. "She quit her job and apparently left with somebody who could be dangerous."

"I didn't know Pete Genaro was concerned about anything but his bottom line," Sayer said.

"It's true he's not concerned about people who steal from his casino," Harry said, "but Charmaine was a valued employee, and he doesn't want her to get into trouble."

"Well, she called me yesterday," Sayer said. "She said she had gotten married and left town, and she wouldn't be seeing me again."

"Did she say who she married?"

"No name. She said he was a former client at the Desert Inn."

"Did she say that she got married, then left town?"

Sayer thought about that. "No, she just said she got married. I didn't get the impression she got married in Vegas. In fact, she had a low opinion of the marriage chapel business here. I don't think she would have

225

gotten married at one of those."

"Did she say anything else that might have indicated where she was?"

"Nope, not a thing."

Harry thanked him, got into his car, and headed for L.A.

His first stop was at the West Los Angeles police station, and it took him only a minute or two to find out which detectives were assigned to the homicides in the Shutters garage. Turned out, he had been a mentor to one of them, Sanders, when they had both been assigned to the Ramparts division. Sanders seemed glad to see him.

"I hear you guys are working the homicides at Shutters," Harry said.

" 'Working' isn't the right word," Sanders said. "We're mostly sitting on our asses, trying to figure out what to do next. These are the cleanest killings I've ever seen."

"Tell me about the ballistics," Harry said.

"Same gun, a .380 semiautomatic. There was a shell casing in each trunk, too."

"No prints on the shell casings?"

"Clean as a whistle. This guy is a pro, no doubt about it. Both victims worked for the same company in Phoenix, an international conglomerate. The second victim came in here and talked to us, told us nothing, then claimed the first victim's body and had it cremated. We think he must have been hunting for the killer on his own and found him."

"You think there was a crime other than homicide connected to these two killings?"

"Maybe, but we can't prove it."

"Do you have a list of the other guests in the hotel at the time?"

Sanders fished a document out of the case file. "Here's a list of people who checked out the morning Smolensky was shot. That's all we got from the hotel."

Harry glanced at the list and immediately saw a W. J. Burnett, but he said nothing. This was his case for the moment, and he didn't want the two cops in his way.

"What's your interest in these homicides, Harry?" Sanders asked.

"I may be looking for the same guy your two victims were looking for."

"What's his name?"

"Doesn't matter — it changes often," Harry said.

"What does your casino want with the guy? He steal from them?"

"Nope. It's a confidential matter."

"If it's connected to our two homicides, it's not confidential."

"If I find out anything along those lines, I'll let you know," Harry said. He thanked them and left.

■ ■ ■ ■

Teddy checked his computer for messages and found flags he had placed on various websites, indicating to him that somebody was doing a background check on William J. Burnett. It had to be the casino again, since he had never given that name to anybody else.

So, there was somebody else on his tail again.

32

Teddy had begun to think that the only way to put a stop to this relentless hunt for him would be to take Majorov out of the picture entirely. Apparently, nothing less would discourage him.

He logged on to the CIA mainframe, routing his path through half a dozen other computers around the country. Anyone who stumbled onto his presence there would find that the computer being used was in a real estate office in Boise, Idaho.

He did a search for Majorov, and the man not only had a file, but a large one. He was the son of a colonel in the KGB who had been in charge of a Spetsnaz, or special forces, unit that had been tied to a misbegotten plan to invade Sweden back in the 1980s. The father had begun his rise in the KGB when he was chosen as the English instructor to the former Soviet premier, Andropov.

Yuri Majorov, the son, had been trained as a KBG officer right out of Moscow University, but his career had been rocked by the Glasnost movement, which changed nearly everything in the former Soviet Union, even to some extent the KGB. After that, he had made large sums of money by putting together syndicates of investors to buy former state enterprises that were being privatized. His investors were largely criminal organizations.

Majorov was believed to have combined and reorganized these Russian Mafia groups into a kind of criminal conglomerate, which had many investments in legitimate businesses. They were very big in hotels.

Then came the interesting part: Majorov had been involved in an attempt to take over The Arrington, a new hotel built in Bel-Air, Los Angeles, by a group formed by Stone Barrington, who had inherited a large piece of land in that community from his murdered wife, Arrington, who had been the widow of the movie star Vance Calder, who had assembled the land over decades.

Majorov was believed to have been in New York when a friend of Barrington's had been kidnapped by a Russian Mafia group, and to have been in a helicopter shot down in the ensuing battle between the Russians and a combination of NYPD and CIA units. He was thought to have perished in the crash.

Teddy thought of adding an addendum to the file, pointing out that Majorov was alive and well in Las Vegas and still trying to get The Arrington, but he thought better of it. Such a note would simply start a search for whoever had put it there, and he didn't need the attention. Instead, he closed the file and did a search for Michael Freeman. In reading the file he confirmed the story that Freeman had told him at their meeting. He logged off the mainframe and considered his options.

It was clear that Teddy would be doing a favor to just about everybody — Barrington, the CIA, the NYPD, and the group that owned The Arrington — by simply eliminating Majorov. This, though, was not as easy as he would have liked it to be. First of all, his face was now known at the New Desert Inn, as was the Burnett alias, and Majorov would surely have heavy personal security.

Teddy had come to a point where he had been offered a way out of his fugitive existence and into an interesting and safe environment, and to risk that over a revenge killing, however satisfying, would be foolish.

There was a better way. He dug out Michael Freeman's card and called the cell phone number written on the back.

"Mike Freeman."

"Mike, this is Billy Barnett."

"Hello. Good to hear from you so quickly. I hope you are calling to accept my offer."

"I'm giving that very serious thought, and I think it might be a favorable alternative for me, but there's something in the way, something I thought that you, and perhaps some of your acquaintances, would like to know about."

"Please tell me about it. I have about fifteen minutes before a meeting is convening in my office."

"If this conversation is being recorded, please turn it off."

"This is an ordinary cell phone, and no recording is being made at this end."

"Good. Have you ever heard of a Russian named Yuri Majorov?"

"I have. I am under the impression that the gentleman is now deceased."

"Mr. Majorov is not only alive, but he appears to be the person who sent two men to track a certain Porsche Cayenne and kill Peter Barrington and his two friends. Fortunately I overheard a conversation the two men were having in Russian when they stopped for gas at the garage in New Mexico where I was working."

"Perhaps you could enlighten me on the subject of what happened to those two men? I was told you, quote, 'had a word with them, and they turned around and went home.' I found that story implausible."

"Quite right," Teddy said. "I think they suspected me of overhearing their conversation, and they came after me. They are now buried inside their large SUV in the New Mexico desert and are extremely unlikely ever to be found."

"Now," Mike said, "I find *that* story to be extremely plausible."

"As a result of that incident, Mr. Majorov sent two other men, separately, to find and kill me."

"And what happened to those two?"

"The bodies of both were discovered, on separate occasions, in the trunks of their rental cars in the garage of a Santa Monica hotel."

"So is your trail now free of Majorov's employees?"

"I fear not. There are indications that another is now sniffing around. It occurs to me that now would be a good time to accept your offer, adopt a new identity, and join Strategic Services, in whatever capacity you deem best."

"I'm extremely glad to hear that, Billy,"

Mike said. "What's holding you back?"

"I don't think I should do that while Majorov is still dispatching his minions to find me and do me harm. Eventually, somebody would turn up at Strategic Services, looking for Billy Burnett."

"A good point," Mike said. "Why do I think you have a plan to prevent that happening?"

"As it happens, I do. I considered cutting off the head of the snake, but there would, no doubt, be other snakes involved who might be as tenacious as their colleague."

"A reasonable assumption. Do you have an alternative plan?"

"It seems to me that you have connections with people who would be pleased to see Mr. Majorov not only out of business, but out of breath, as it were."

"That is entirely possible," Mike replied.

"I thought that, rather than my taking on the Majorov task personally, it might be better for everyone involved to have him brought to heel in a more legally satisfying manner. Do you think that it might be in the best interests of your acquaintances if you initiated that process with a phone call to someone I don't need to know about?"

"I think that is a very sensible suggestion," Mike said. "Is there a number where I can reach you?"

Teddy gave him the number of a new throwaway phone. "That should be operative within the hour, whereas the number I'm now calling from will terminate shortly."

"Got it," Mike said. "I'll get back to you when I can. Oh, can you tell me the present whereabouts of Mr. Majorov?"

"I believe him currently to be an honored guest of the New Desert Inn hotel and casino, in Las Vegas."

"Thanks, and goodbye for the moment."

Teddy hung up, hoping that he had done the right thing. Still, he had one more call to make. He called the New Desert Inn and asked for Pete Genaro. "Tell him it's Billy Burnett," he said to the operator.

Genaro was on the line in a flash. "Well, hello, Billy. How are you?"

"I'm very well, Pete, although I realize that may not be good news to you."

"I don't know what you mean," Genaro said, sounding wounded.

"Pete, you and I have had a cordial relationship up until now, but I suspect that you may be in cahoots with Mr. Majorov in seeking my demise."

"Nothing like that, I assure you," Genaro said. "Mr. Majorov only wishes to meet you."

"You may tell Mr. Majorov that I have no wish to meet him, but that if I should do so, he would not enjoy the meeting."

"Now, now, Billy, don't misjudge the man."

"I know just about all I need to know about Mr. Majorov, and my advice to you would be to put as much distance between you and him as possible, and as quickly as you can. The relationship will not profit you or your business. Now, I will hang up before you can complete your trace, but I did want to mention that whoever is tracking me now will meet with the same end as the previous trackers, if he is not called off immediately. Good day, Pete." He broke the connection.

"Did you get it?" he asked his chief of security, who was standing next to his desk.

The man hung up the other phone. "Not enough time," he said. "All I can tell you is that the call came from somewhere in the southwestern United States."

Genaro was alarmed. "Could that mean Vegas?"

"Could be."

33

Mike Freeman called the new director of central intelligence, Lance Cabot, on his private office line. It was the first time that Mike had used that number.

"Cabot."

"Good day, Lance, it's Mike Freeman. Have you a moment?"

"Yes, but not much more than that, Mike."

"This won't take long. It's my understanding that some of your people came up against a Russian named Yuri Majorov not so very long ago."

"That is correct, and Mr. Majorov did not survive the encounter."

"I have come across some very reliable information to the effect that not only did Majorov survive the encounter but that he is presently in the United States."

Lance was quiet for a moment. "May I ask the source of your information?"

"I'm sorry, I can't divulge that, but I

believe it to be solid, or I wouldn't have troubled you."

"Do you have a location?"

"He is staying at the New Desert Inn hotel and casino in Las Vegas."

"And how long will he be there?"

"I don't know that, but I believe he may have been there for a couple of weeks."

"And what do you expect me to do about it?"

"I have no expectations in that regard. I simply thought that you would like to know, and that if you want something done about it, you have the appropriate tools at your disposal. I won't take any more of your time, Lance. Goodbye."

"Goodbye, and thank you," Lance said.

Harry Katz sat at the bar at Shutters and went over his notes carefully. He had thought that he might have missed something, and he found it: Jimmy Sayer had said that Charmaine had gotten married. If that were so, and if she got married in Los Angeles County, there would be a record of it. He opened his laptop on the bar, went to the L.A. County website, and clicked on public records, then marriage licenses and marriages.

He looked at licenses and found them arranged alphabetically. There were two dozen Burnetts, in the current year, but none of them a William J. or W. J. Disappointing.

Harry ordered another drink and thought it over, then he went to the list of marriages. About the same number of Burnetts, but still not the right ones. Then Harry had a little accident: he pressed the up arrow, and it stuck and began scrolling. He poked at it a few times before it released, and he found himself looking at a list of Barnetts, one letter different. And there, at the bottom of the list, was a W. J. Barnett, of 1147 Third Street, Santa Monica. It occurred to him that simply changing one letter in a name would throw off computer searches. He wrote down the address and checked the map app on his iPhone. It was only a few blocks from where he sat. He signed for his drink and left the bar, returned his laptop to his room, and left the hotel.

Five minutes later he stood in front of the address he sought. It was Michael's restaurant. He went inside and approached the headwaiter.

"May I help you, sir?"

"I hope so. Do you have an employee here by the name of William J. Barnett? Or Burnett?"

"I believe I know all the employees," the

man said, "and there isn't one by that name. I'm sorry I can't be of more help."

"Perhaps you still can help. Do you have a table for one?"

The man checked his reservations list. "I'm sorry, sir, but I don't. However, if you like, you can order dinner at the bar."

"Thanks, I'll do that." Harry took a seat at the bar, ordered a drink, and asked for a menu.

A couple of blocks away, Teddy sat at his computer and saw a flag from the public records page of the Los Angeles County website. "Uh-oh," he said aloud. "Not good." Intriguing, though. How, he wondered, would anyone know to search that particular record in looking for him?

"Betsy," he called.

She came out of the bathroom.

"Did you tell anyone that we got married?"

"No," she said, then went back into the bathroom. A moment later she came out again. "Wait," she said, "I called my ex-husband, because I knew he'd start looking for me if I left town without telling him. He's never been able to accept the divorce and keeps trying to win me back."

"So, you thought if you told him you were

240

married, he'd let go?"

"Exactly. Was it the wrong thing to do?"

"Maybe. I'm not sure."

"Could someone find us because I told him that?"

"Probably not, but it could help someone who was looking. Now that I think of it, I don't believe we should go to Michael's anymore."

"Why not?"

"Because when recording our marriage, I used Michael's as a home address."

Harry Katz had an excellent dinner at Michael's bar, but questioning the bartender about the existence of a Barnett or Burnett employee got him no further. He asked for a check.

His cell phone went off, and he answered it. "Harry Katz."

"Harry, it's Pete Genaro."

"Hi, Pete."

"Where are you?"

"At a restaurant in Santa Monica. Charmaine's ex-husband said he got a call from her and that she said she had gotten married. I believe that Billy Burnett changed his name to Barnett and married Charmaine under that name. There's a marriage recorded, and it gives his address as the address of this restaurant."

"Harry, I had a call from Burnett, and he knows somebody is on his trail again. This is not good for you, and I think you should break off your investigation."

"But, Pete, I feel I'm getting close, here."

"Harry, the closer you get the more danger you're in. Have you forgotten what I told you about the last two guys who did what you're doing?"

"No, and I had a conversation with the LAPD about that. One of the investigating detectives was somebody I knew."

"And how are they doing in their investigation?"

"They're completely stymied."

"That should tell you even more about Billy Burnett."

"I see your point. Do you want me to come home?"

"Do this, Harry: trace Burnett if you can but don't approach him. Just let me know where he is, and I'll pass it on to Majorov, then it's his problem."

"All right, Pete, if that's what you want."

"That's what I want, Harry."

"Then you got it." Harry paid his check and left the restaurant. It was a pleasant night, and he decided to walk a bit. He wondered if Billy Burnett had used a nearby address for his marriage certificate and might, perhaps, live a few doors away, but he had no further information that might tell him where.

34

Kerry Smith, deputy director for investigations at the FBI, took the call from Lance Cabot.

"Kerry, I have some new information on one Yuri Majorov," Lance said.

"What, where he's buried, maybe?"

"According to my information, from a source I respect, Majorov is not only alive, but is, at this moment, at the New Desert Inn, in Las Vegas."

"What's your source?"

"Giving you that wouldn't help you, and my source wouldn't reveal his source."

"So this is a third-hand rumor? If you believe it, why don't you do something about it?"

"I suppose you could characterize it as a rumor, but pursuing Mr. Majorov is not within the purview of my charter. I have now done my duty as a citizen, having reported the information to a responsible law enforcement official, and that splashing sound you hear is me washing my hands of this matter. Good day to you, Kerry." He hung up.

Kerry sighed, went to the contacts menu on his computer, and clicked on the number of the agent in charge for the FBI office in Las Vegas.

"This is AIC Carney."

"Good morning, Arch. This is Kerry Smith."

"Hello, Director."

"Arch, have you ever heard of a man called Yuri Majorov?"

"Ummm, that may sound familiar."

"Arch, it's okay if you've never heard of him."

"In that case, I've never heard of him."

"Some time back, maybe a couple of months ago, there was a big brouhaha in New York — a woman was kidnapped by some members of the Russian Mafia, and some of our people, along with some CIA people, tracked her to Brooklyn, in the area known as Little Russia. She was freed after a big shoot-out that included a couple of helicopters, one of them, apparently, operated by the Russian Mob. This fellow Majorov was said to have been aboard that one, and it was shot down, but his body was never recovered."

"How can I help you, Director?"

"I have some information that says that Yuri Majorov is a guest in a hotel in Vegas called the New Desert Inn. I assume you know it."

"Yes."

"Word is, Majorov has been there for a couple of weeks."

"What would you like me to do about it, Director? Do we have enough for an arrest warrant?"

"No, I don't think we do, so don't go over there with a SWAT team. I'd like you to visit the hotel and ask, politely, to speak with Mr. Majorov. If you find him there, question him on what he's doing in the country. You might check, first, to see if he entered the country legally. If he didn't, then you can turn him over to Immigration and Naturalization. If he's in the country legally, then just make him uncomfortable about being here and get as much information from him as you can."

"Yes, sir, I'll get right on that."

"Thank you, Arch. Let me know what you find out." Kerry hung up and forgot about Yuri Majorov.

Archibald Carney buzzed his assistant.

"Check the last thirty days with Immigration and see if somebody named Yuri Majorov entered the country legally, then send me two agents — whoever's looking idle."

"Yes, sir."

Three minutes later his assistant buzzed back. "A Yuri Majorov entered the country legally at JFK in New York twelve days ago." Carney thanked him. Two special agents appeared in his office. He explained what he knew, and the source of his information. "Go over to the New Desert Inn. If Majorov is there, brace him politely and find out why. He's apparently Russian Mob, so try and make him feel that he might be happier in Moscow."

The two special agents, Morris and Thomas, presented themselves at the front desk at the New Desert Inn, flashed their badges, and asked for the manager.

"How can I help you, agents?" the man asked.

"Do you have a Russian citizen named Yuri Majorov registered here?"

"I'll check," the manager said. He turned to a computer terminal and sent an e-mail to Pete Genaro: *Two FBI at front desk, asking for Majorov. What do?* A moment later, a message came back: *Send them up, then inform the guest that they are coming.*

The manager turned back to the agents. "Yes, Mr. Majorov is registered here. He's in suite 1530, top floor. The elevator is to your left." He watched them walk away, then called 1530.

"Yes? What you want?"

"Please tell Mr. Majorov that the FBI are on the way to his suite."

"Shit."

"Just tell Mr. Majorov."

"Okay." The man hung up, and the manager went back to his office.

The man who answered the phone, a muscular, not very bright man named Rackov, was terrified. "Tell the boss FBI are on the way up," he said to his colleague, "then help me." The man went to the bedroom to tell Majorov, who was in bed with a hooker and awoke only slowly, then he came back.

"He's getting up, I think."

Rackov tossed him a light machine gun just as the doorbell rang. Rackov ran to the door and looked through the peephole to find two men in business suits standing there. "Yes?" he shouted. "What you want?"

"FBI," one of them said, and they both held badges up to the peephole. "Open up."

Rackov motioned over his colleague.

"Open door," he said. The man opened the door, and Rackov opened fire, driving the two agents backward across the hallway until they fell in a bloody heap against the opposite wall.

Majorov burst out of the bedroom, tying a robe around his naked body, and rushed over to the door. "What happened?" he demanded.

"FBI are here," Rackov said, pointing to the hallway.

Majorov took one look at the two dead men, then started yelling orders. He ran back to the bedroom, ignoring the hooker, who was sitting up in bed, and started getting dressed.

"What's happening?" she asked.

"I am checking out of the hotel," Majorov replied, and started throwing the contents of his closet into two suitcases.

The desk clerk looked up from his work to see Mr. Majorov striding through the lobby, followed closely by two large men pushing a luggage cart laden with bags. He picked up the phone and called the bell captain. "I think Mr. Majorov is going to want his car," he said. "Right now."

As he hung up the phone, it rang while it was still in his hand. "Front desk."

"It's Margie, the housekeeper. One of my maids on the fifteenth floor says there are two dead men in the hall outside 1530."

"She must be crazy," the desk clerk said. "Check it out yourself, then call me back." He hung up, then thought perhaps he should tell the manager about this.

"Airport," Majorov said to the driver. The car moved away, and he turned toward Rackov. "Why did you shoot them?" he asked.

"They were FBI," Rackov said. "They showed badges."

"But what did they want?"

"They wanted to come in the suite."

"They said nothing else?"

"Nothing else."

Fifteen minutes later they arrived at the airport and were admitted to the ramp, where Majorov's Gulfstream 450 awaited. The two pilots were walking around the aircraft, inspecting it.

Majorov and the two bodyguards got out of the car, and the first thing they heard was approaching sirens. Majorov looked around him and found no one watching. He reached into his jacket and came out with the small Beretta Nano that he habitually carried. He pointed it at the two bodyguards and said, "Take out your weapons." As they did, he shot both of them, then he ran around the car and shouted to one of the pilots, "Call the police!" Then he rapped on the window of the car. "Call Mr. Genaro at the hotel and tell him to send a lawyer to the police station."

He didn't have long to wait for the police, because they were now driving onto the ramp, lights and sirens on. He set the Beretta on the tarmac and raised his hands.

"Thank God you're here!" he shouted, as two uniformed officers approached him.

35

Genaro answered the phone and listened for a moment. "Why does he need a lawyer?" he asked the driver.

"I think because he shot the two bodyguards."

Genaro began blinking rapidly. "Where are you?"

"At the airport."

Genaro hung up and found the hotel manager standing in his doorway. "What?"

"I sent the two FBI agents up to 1530, and the housekeeper just called to say that they're both dead, lying in the hallway."

"Two FBI agents are dead in my hotel? What the fuck?"

"I have no idea. Mr. Majorov and his two bodyguards left the hotel right before I got the call. I don't know where he was going."

"He was apparently going to the airport," Genaro said. "Elsie!" he shouted at his secretary. "Get me the hotel's lawyer —

whatshisname, Greenbaum!"

Kerry Smith's private line rang. "Deputy Director Smith."

"Sir, it's Arch, in Las Vegas."

"Yes, Arch. How did the meet with Majorov go?"

"Very badly, I'm afraid. Both my agents are dead, apparently shot by Majorov's bodyguards."

"*What?* Say that again."

Arch repeated the information. "LVPD picked up Majorov at the airport. He had shot the two bodyguards, and he claims they shot the agents, then kidnapped him. They're holding him at the main police station."

"That is the most insane thing I've ever heard!" Kerry said.

"And ten minutes after they got him to the police station a lawyer for the New Desert Inn showed up, met privately with him, and is now demanding his release."

"Did Majorov mention why his own bodyguards would kidnap him?"

"The lawyer told the police that some criminal element in Moscow had ordered him kidnapped and forcibly brought home."

"Jesus Christ!"

"What do you want me to do, sir?"

253

"There's nothing you can do, since he's in the hands of the local police."

"Killing two federal agents is a federal crime."

"Don't you think I know that? Unless we have evidence that Majorov killed them himself or ordered them killed, then all he's done is shoot the bodyguards. Are they dead?"

"Yes, sir, they were both shot in the head."

"Get the ballistics report and find out if Majorov's weapon — I assume he had a weapon — killed our two men. If it only killed the bodyguards, we don't have a federal case against him, unless there were witnesses."

"The only other person in the suite at the time of the shootings was a hooker, who apparently was in bed with Majorov. She says she heard gunfire, and one of the bodyguards came into the bedroom where they were sleeping and got them up."

"So Majorov has a witness who exonerates him."

"It would appear so, sir."

"Get over to the police station yourself and interview everybody concerned, including the hooker, then get back to me."

"Yes, sir." The AIC hung up.

Kerry thought for a few seconds, then

called Lance Cabot.

"Cabot."

"It's Kerry Smith."

"Yes, Kerry?"

"We sent two special agents to the New Desert Inn to interview Majorov, and his bodyguards killed both of them."

"I'm sorry, Kerry, you're not making any sense."

"You're not listening, Lance. Majorov's bodyguards killed both our agents when they went to his suite, then they apparently hustled Majorov out of the hotel and to the airport, where he shot them both. He now claims they were kidnapping him." He gave him all the information he had.

"My condolences on the loss of your agents," Lance said. "Is there anything else I can do for you? I'm in a meeting."

"Nothing!" Kerry shouted, then banged down the phone.

Lance called Mike Freeman.

"Yes, Lance?"

"Your information about Majorov was correct," Lance said.

"Will anything come of his being there?"

"A great deal has already come of it," Lance said. He relayed what Kerry Smith had said to him.

255

"That's bizarre," Mike said. "What are the charges against Majorov?"

"None, so far. He lawyered up immediately, and he may very well be released shortly, if he hasn't been already."

"Is there anything I can do?"

"No, Mike, this is merely a courtesy call. Goodbye." Lance hung up.

Mike called Billy Barnett on the cell number he had been given.

"Yes?"

"It's Mike Freeman."

"Hello, Mike. What's up?"

"I made a call about Majorov to someone who made a call to the FBI, who sent two agents to see him. As far as I can tell, Majorov's bodyguards killed the agents, then Majorov killed the bodyguards at the airport and is claiming they kidnapped him."

"If I read that in the newspapers I wouldn't believe it," Teddy said.

"Neither would I."

"I don't know what to say."

"Neither do I. I'll let you know when I hear more." Mike hung up.

Pete Genaro sat in his office, staring at the blotter on his desk. Majorov sat across from him, sipping a brandy and soda.

"Thank you for sending Mr. Greenbaum,"

Majorov said. "He was very good."

"You're welcome," Genaro said. "Mr. Majorov, I would be grateful if you would not kill anyone else in my hotel."

Majorov shrugged. "I have not killed anyone in your hotel, only the two bodyguards who were kidnapping me. I believe Mr. Greenbaum has convinced the police that that is so. However, the police have asked me to remain in Las Vegas until their investigation is complete — a few days, Greenbaum says. I suppose my suite is still available?"

"Yes," Genaro said tonelessly.

"What have you heard from your skip tracer fellow?"

"Oh, that."

"Yes, that."

"Billy Burnett has disappeared without a trace. My man is the best in the business, and he has been unable to find him or the girl."

Majorov set down his drink and spread his hands. "I must ask you to provide security for me while I am in the hotel," he said.

"All right," Genaro said. "I can spare one man, but not outside the hotel."

"I will remain in the hotel and the casino,"

Majorov said, rising. "Now I will go to my suite."

"Of course," Genaro said.

36

Stone walked into the Four Seasons at lunchtime; Mike Freeman was waiting for him at the bar. The headwaiter seated them immediately at Mike's usual table, and half a bottle of a good Chardonnay was waiting for them in an ice bucket.

As soon as they had ordered, Mike took a deep breath and began. "I have news of Yuri Majorov," he said.

"Did they find his body?"

"In a manner of speaking. It's occupying a suite at the New Desert Inn, in Las Vegas."

"Is it breathing?"

"I'm afraid so."

"Then we should probably call someone in law enforcement, shouldn't we?"

"I have already done so, if rather indirectly. As a result, two FBI agents were sent to the hotel to question him, and his bodyguards killed them both."

"Holy shit."

"Exactly, but that's not all: Majorov was taken to the airport by his bodyguards, and there he shot both of them, then called the police. When they arrived, he claimed that they were kidnapping him."

"Hold on, I'm getting dizzy," Stone said, taking a gulp of his wine.

"You're going to get dizzier. Majorov was released by the LVPD and is back at the hotel. Turns out, he entered the country legally, and there are no charges of any kind against him."

"How did you learn about this?"

"From Billy Barnett."

"Is he in New York?"

"Not yet." Mike thought about that for a moment. "Well, he could be in New York — he could be anywhere, for that matter — but my assumption is that he's still in L.A."

"Does this mean that Peter is in danger from Majorov?"

"I don't believe so. In the circumstances, I don't think Majorov is likely to do anything more boisterous than playing blackjack at his hotel. Too many law enforcement and intelligence agencies are now aware of his presence in the country."

"I'm going to go back to L.A.," Stone said.

"I'll go with you," Mike said.

"Do you have business there?"

"My business is such that I have business everywhere, or at least, wherever I want to go. We'll take the company airplane."

"Thank you, Mike."

"When would you like to go?"

"I've got a few things to clear up at the office. I'll pick you up at, say, four o'clock? We can beat most of the rush hour to Teterboro and we'll be at The Arrington in time for dinner."

"Sounds good," Mike said.

"I'll let Peter and the staff know we're coming in."

Their lunch arrived, and they devoted their attention to that.

Back in his office, Stone called Emma Tweed, who was at her New York office.

"Hi, there."

"Hi. Mike Freeman and I both have some business in L.A., so we're going back out there. Would you like to come?"

"I'd really like that, but my being in the New York office has caused a kerfuffle, and it's going to take me a few days to sort it out. How long are you staying?"

"Just a few days."

"Then I'll be here when you get back," she said. "Give my love to Tessa and the kids."

"Will do."

They landed at Santa Monica at seven PM, Pacific time, and were shortly at The Arrington. Peter, Ben, and the girls greeted them in the living room.

"Dinner in half an hour," Peter said. "What brings you two back so soon?"

"It's complicated," Stone said. "We both have business to conduct out here. Let's leave it at that."

"If you say so," Peter said.

"How's your shooting going, fellas?"

"We're a week into it and two days ahead of schedule," Ben replied. "There are advantages to shooting on soundstages instead of on improvised locations."

"How are you getting along with Leo Goldman?"

"Very well. He's been helpful in moving things along."

"Have you seen Billy Barnett?" Stone asked Peter.

"I've seen him in the commissary at lunch a couple of times. I believe he's still working at the armory."

"He seems like a very useful fellow," Stone said. "What's he going to be doing when he finishes renovating all those weapons?"

"I don't know," Peter said. "I'll ask him."

"I would have thought that such a competent and versatile fellow might be of use to you in your work," Stone said.

"You know, the same thought occurred to me," Peter said, "but I haven't done anything about it. Maybe I'll have a chat with him this week."

Suddenly Stone liked the idea of having Teddy Fay around Peter. The man had been protective of him before, and perhaps he would continue to be.

37

Teddy Fay sat at his usual table at the Centurion commissary and picked at his lunch while reading the *Los Angeles Times* story about the adventures of Majorov the previous day. Why wasn't the guy in jail?

He began to wonder if the events of the day before had made Majorov more vulnerable. Had he replaced his bodyguards? If he turned up dead now, would the police blame the Russian Mafia? Still, Teddy's face was known at the New Desert Inn, and that face was connected to a name. Those odds were too long for Teddy.

He finished his lunch and went back to the armory. The new gunsmith had started, and he would have the man well broken in before another day had passed.

Teddy was calling it a day at three when he had a phone call.

"Billy Barnett."

"Billy, it's Peter Barrington. How are you?"

"Very well, thanks, Peter."

"I wonder if you could stop by my bungalow and see me when you finish work today?"

"I've just finished," Teddy said. "Is right now good for you?"

"That's fine. You know where we are?"

"I think so, I saw the Cayenne parked there."

"See you shortly, then."

They both hung up, and Teddy wondered what Peter could want.

It didn't take him long to find out. He gave his name to Ruth Pearl at the bungalow and was shown into the editing suite.

"Hi, Billy," Peter said, stepping away from the console. "I'm just adding this morning's footage to the rough cut. I do this every day, so that when we wrap, we'll already have a cut in the can. Come into my office and let's talk."

Teddy followed Peter into the adjoining room, and they took seats around the coffee table.

"Billy, will you tell me something about your background?"

Teddy gave Peter the same story he had

given Betsy.

"You've led an interesting life," Peter said.

"And it seems to be getting more interesting since I retired."

"We're a little shorthanded around here," Peter said. "Ben and I are new at this kind of studio work, and we could use some help of a general nature."

"What could I do for you?"

"Tell me what your skills are, in general."

"Well, I can make machine parts, repair weapons, service computer and audio equipment, cook, repair airplanes, and give flying instruction."

"Flying instruction? That's interesting. Ben, Hattie, and I all got our private licenses while we were at Yale. Do you have an airplane?"

"I have something called a JetPROP. Do you know what that is?"

"Yes, my father used to have one, until he got the jet. I need to get my instrument rating."

"I can train you for that," Teddy said. "I'm a certified instrument flying instructor."

"How long would it take?"

"Well, if you worked on it full-time, we could do it in under two weeks."

"I can't do that at the moment, but I can fly on weekends and occasionally I can take a couple of hours off in the late afternoon."

"Then we could probably get it done in six or eight weeks."

"Where do you keep your airplane?"

"At Hawthorne, but I can move it to Santa Monica, if that's more convenient for you."

"That sounds good. It's my ambition to eventually own and fly my own jet, as Dad does. What sort of training will that involve?"

"You'll need your instrument rating and a multi-engine rating — that one can be done over a long weekend. Then you'll need some turbine time before Flight Safety will accept you as a student for a type rating in a jet, then you'll need a couple of weeks of type-specific jet training in the simulator. You could get all this done in a year, if you take it very seriously and work hard."

Peter nodded. "I'm certainly willing to do that. I've also been thinking of trying to buy a hangar at Santa Monica for when I buy an airplane."

"I can ask around about that. In the meantime, you should sign up for one of the online instrument courses — that way, you can learn the classroom stuff at your leisure. I'd recommend working on it at least an hour a day."

"All right, I'll do that."

"We can start the practical instruction this weekend, if you have the time."

They discussed money and agreed on a salary for Teddy. "I'll charge you by the hour for the airplane, and you can pay the FBO for the fuel."

"Sounds good. Can you start here tomorrow?"

"I can start the day after tomorrow. I need another day to make sure my replacement at the armory has a grip on the work."

"Great. You'll be working for us, not the studio, but Ruth will set you up with the credentials you need to be on the lot, and she'll give you a parking pass. What are you driving?"

"A 1958 D model."

"Wow, that's a neat car. Won't take up much room in the lot, either."

The two shook hands, Teddy filled out some forms for Ruth, then he went home to Betsy.

"Hey, hon," she said, as he walked in the door.

"What have you been up to?" he asked.

"More shopping. I've pretty much replaced my wardrobe. Did you see the papers this morning? About Majorov?"

"Sure did. Maybe all that activity will take his attention away from you and me."

"I hope so."

"I got a new job today, as an assistant to two young filmmakers on the Centurion lot."

"Assistant what?"

"Whatever they've got. I'm going to give one of them some flight instruction, too, for his instrument rating."

"I didn't know you were an instructor."

"You still have a few things to learn about me," he said, kissing her.

"I know the things that are important to me," Betsy said. "When do you start the new job?"

"Day after tomorrow," Teddy said. "I've got an offer from a security company, too. We'll use that for a backup, in case we need to move on." He had already explained to her that there might be times when they would have to move on short notice, and she had accepted that.

"Want to take a walk down the beach?" she asked.

"Sure."

Harry Katz sat in his car outside the apartment building. He didn't know what Billy Burnett looked like, but he knew Charmaine Evans, and he had come across her shopping on Rodeo Drive and followed her home.

Now he watched as Charmaine left the apartment building in the company of a somewhat older man.

"Good day, Mr. Burnett," he said aloud, and with a chuckle.

38

Pete Genaro was working at his desk when the fateful call came. "Genaro."

"Pete, it's Harry Katz. I've found your guy."

"Really?"

"I got lucky and ran across Charmaine shopping in Beverly Hills, hitting the expensive shops. I followed her to an apartment building in Santa Monica and staked it out. A couple of hours later, she left the building with an older man, and I figure it's Billy Burnett. I've just e-mailed a couple of photos of them together. I'll hold while you check them out."

"Okay." Genaro checked his e-mail and found the photos. "Harry? That's Billy Burnett."

"Great! What do you want me to do?"

"Absolutely nothing. Come back to Vegas, and don't mention a single word of this to anybody."

"As you wish, Pete. I'll be home tonight and at work tomorrow." Both men hung up.

Genaro sighed. He realized that, with all that had happened, this situation was not what he wanted. He liked Billy Burnett, and he especially liked Charmaine, and he did not like Yuri Majorov, especially since he had started shooting people in his hotel and at the airport. He had a board meeting in an hour, and he wanted to be ready for it. He called his banker.

"Good afternoon, Pete."

"Afternoon, Abner. Are we all set?"

"I've been to my people with your proposal, and we'll back you, Pete. Go ahead and put it to your board. A cashier's check for the funds will be on your desk momentarily."

"Thank you, Ab. I'll get back to you after the meeting."

"Goodbye, Pete, and good luck with your board."

Genaro hung up. He left his office and decided to take the long way to the boardroom. He walked through the public rooms of the hotel and then through the casino, stopping to chat now and then with a customer or an employee or to suggest some small change in the decor or other arrangements. He loved this place; it was what he had always wanted.

Shortly before the board meeting he entered the boardroom to find the CEO and chairman, William Stein, chatting with his vice chairman, Albert Hegelman. The corporate counsel, Abby Greenbaum, sat at the conference table, going over some documents.

"Hello, Pete," Stein said.

"Hello, Bill, Al," Genaro replied.

"I see you've got something on the agenda today. Want to tell us about it?"

"I'm sorry, Bill, but there isn't time. This came up on short notice, and I'd rather put it to the full board. I will tell you that I very much want your support for what I propose. I think it's important to the future of this business."

"We'll hear you out, Pete," Stein said, "and I'll support you if I can."

The others were entering now and taking their seats as per their place cards. Only Majorov was late, and when he came in, he didn't bother to apologize or respond to any of the greetings he heard. He took his chair at the end of the table and glared malevolently at his fellow directors, as if to intimidate them.

"Gentlemen," Stein said, "the board will come to order. The first order of business on the agenda is a proposal from our chief financial officer, Pete Genaro. Pete?"

Genaro stood up and smiled at the group. "Gentlemen, I know that you have all become aware of the events of the past few days, during which two FBI agents were murdered on our property by bodyguards of Mr. Majorov, and a few minutes later, when those two bodyguards were murdered by Mr. Majorov himself."

"They were not murdered," Majorov shouted, slamming his hand on the conference table. "It was self-defense!"

"The police may have bought that," Genaro said. "I don't."

Majorov sprang to his feet. "Have you forgotten the importance of my investment in this property?"

The chairman gaveled him into silence and told him to sit down and be quiet. "Please continue, Pete."

"I am also aware that Mr. Majorov has twice attempted to murder a valued customer of our casino. Gentlemen," Pete said, "these actions hark back to a day when a different element held sway in this town, when a casino was not looked upon as a legitimate business. That day is past, and we must act to preserve our reputation as honest businessmen."

There was a murmur of assent around the table.

"As you know, gentlemen, our bylaws provide for the buyout and removal of any investor whose conduct brings our corporation into disrepute. Today, I wish to make a personal offer, backed by the Las Vegas Investment and Trust Company, to purchase the shares owned by Mr. Majorov, valuing them by the formula stated in the bylaws, and simultaneously, I wish to move for Mr. Majorov's removal from further ownership participation and immediate expulsion from these premises." Genaro sat down.

"Second the motion," Albert Hegelman said.

"Move the question," Abby Greenbaum echoed.

"With no further discussion," Stein said, "the board will vote." Greenbaum called the roll, and the vote was unanimous in favor, except for the vote of Majorov. "The motion having carried, Mr. Genaro will be treated henceforth as owner of the shares formerly owned by Mr. Majorov, and the paperwork is ready for signature in the adjoining room. Mr. Majorov, you are excused from this meeting."

Majorov stood and glowered at the gathering. "There will be blood," he said.

"If so, sir," Stein said, "it will be yours."

"Hear! Hear!" everyone shouted.

Genaro walked around the table, took Majorov by the elbow, and escorted him from the conference room. The two security men assigned to him awaited.

On a table in the room were two documents and a cashier's check. Genaro handed Majorov his pen. "Sign both documents," he said.

Majorov hesitated for a moment, then sagged. He signed both documents and received the check.

"Gentlemen," Genaro said, "please escort this gentleman from the premises. Housekeeping has already packed his bags and they are waiting for him, as is a car to drive him to the airport. Put him aboard his airplane, and watch it take off before you leave the airport."

Majorov leaned close. "I will kill you for this," he hissed.

Genaro leaned in, too. "If you want to get to the airport alive, you'd better shut your mouth and get out of here, you miserable son of a bitch."

He returned to the boardroom and got a round of applause from his fellow directors.

"Pete," Stein said, "in your brief absence the board has accepted my resignation as

CEO and appointed you as my replacement. I will remain as chairman, of course."

"Thank you all, gentlemen," Genaro said.

At the airport, Majorov got out of the car and boarded his airplane, while the pilots loaded his luggage.

The pilots got back aboard. "We're ready to start engines, Mr. Majorov," the captain said, "and we've filed for Moscow with a fuel stop in Iceland."

"Scrub that," Majorov said. "Refile for Teterboro, New Jersey."

39

Teddy was done with his work in the armory by noon the following day. After lunch in the commissary, he dropped his car at his apartment building and took a taxi to Hawthorne Airport. He inspected the new paint on his airplane and, finding it excellent, paid the shop, then flew to Santa Monica.

He taxied to Atlantic Aviation and spoke with the chief lineman about any hangar that might be available for purchase.

"I heard a rumor that Craig Livingston, the rock star, might be selling his hangar," the chief said. "I know for a fact he's already sold two of his three airplanes. His chief pilot has an office in the hangar. You might speak to him." He pointed out the hangar, which was not far from Atlantic.

Teddy walked over there and found the pilot at his desk, updating a maintenance manual.

"I'm Billy Barnett," Teddy said, offering

his hand.

"I'm Tim Peters," the man said. "What can I do for you?"

"I heard a rumor that Mr. Livingston might want to sell his hangar."

"Well," Peters said, "he's already sold the Pitt Special and the Caravan. Only the Citationjet Four is left, and he wants to move it to Burbank and rent hangar space there."

"What do you think he would take for the hangar?" Teddy asked.

The man named a very high figure.

"Are you his only pilot?"

"Yes, it's a single-pilot airplane. I'm an airframe and powerplant mechanic, and I'm type-rated in all the smaller Citations, and I'm a certified instrument flight instructor."

"Will you go to Burbank with the airplane?"

Peters looked uncomfortable. "I haven't had any assurances about that. Livingston is type-rated as single-pilot in the airplane, so he doesn't necessarily need me."

"And what do you think Livingston would take for the hangar, if the deal included keeping you on here?"

"Come to think of it," the man said, "I think he might take a percentage less, probably a lot less."

"That sounds interesting," Teddy said.

"There's an apartment upstairs, too, but I don't use it — I've got a place nearby. Let me show it to you."

Teddy liked what he saw. "I'll get back to you in a day or two," he said.

The man handed him two cards. "That's my card, and the other is for Livingston's lawyer. Make your offer to him, and a word of advice: bargain hard. Livingston has had some cash flow problems, and he wants out bad."

Teddy shook his hand and left.

Pete Genaro moved into the CEO's office immediately, and after he was completely settled in he went to FlightAware.com and entered the tail number of Majorov's Gulf-stream. The airplane was over New York State and headed southeast, originally filed for Reykjavik, but diverted to Teterboro.

There was a knock on his door, and he waved in Harry Katz.

"Nice new digs, Pete," Harry said, taking the offered chair.

"Thanks, Harry, and thanks for your good work the past few days. I'm sorry it was for naught."

"Don't worry, you'll get my bill." Harry handed him a slip of paper. "That's their address in Santa Monica, should you need it."

Pete slipped the address into a desk drawer. "Majorov is out of my hair," he said. "I've bought him out, and the board has elected me CEO."

"Congratulations, Pete. Anything else I can do for you?"

Pete leaned back in his chair. "Harry, we've never talked about this, but are you available for wet work?"

"How wet are we talking, Pete?"

"Soaking wet."

"What did you have in mind?"

"I would like for Majorov not to return to Vegas — in fact, I'd like him not to return to anywhere."

"I'm not opposed to that degree of wetness in general," Harry said, "but you're talking about a Russian Mafia guy with personal security."

"I understand that such an undertaking would be expensive. I was thinking twenty-five grand."

"Do you know the whereabouts of said fellow?"

"His jet is about to land at Teterboro."

"Do you know where he stays when he's in New York?"

"At one of his company's properties, the

Excelsior — in the penthouse."

"If I recall, there's a taller building directly across the street."

"I believe that is so."

"If a person could gain access to the roof, then the deed could be done, but I'd need fifty grand."

"Forty grand, and you pay your own expenses."

"I'll need to make a couple of phone calls," Harry said. "Can I get back to you?"

"Use my old office," Pete said, "but not my telephone. Use your own."

"Give me an hour," Harry said.

"I don't know how long he'll be in New York," Pete said.

"I understand. Do you have a photograph of the gentleman?"

Pete turned to his computer. "I believe we took one when he joined the board several months ago." He scanned for the shot. "Here we go." He printed out the photo and handed it to Harry.

"That will do nicely," Harry said. He got up and went down the hall to Pete's old office. He photographed the photograph of Majorov with his cell phone, then he used a throwaway cell phone to call a number in New York's Little Italy.

"Who are you calling?" a man's voice answered.

"I'm calling the person I'm speaking to. You know who this is?"

"Right."

"I'm in need of some extermination work," Harry said.

"What kind of pest are we talking about?"

"A large rat — you don't need a name."

"Tell me what I need."

"The infestation is in the penthouse of the Excelsior Hotel. You know it?"

"How about access?"

"From the roof of the taller building across the street. It's well within spraying distance of standard equipment."

"What sort of markings does the rat have?"

"Give me an e-mail address, and I'll send you a photo."

The man gave him an address, and Harry e-mailed the picture.

"Nice one," the man said.

"You'll know him when you see him."

"When is that?"

"He should be there in a couple of hours."

"Write down this number and wire twenty large."

"No success, I'll need a full refund."

"You got it."

"Give me an hour, then check and call me

back." He gave the man the number. He hung up and went back to Genaro's office.

"It can be done tonight," he said. "I'll need twenty grand wired to this offshore account number right away and the other twenty in cash."

Genaro took the account number. "You'll be responsible?"

"I'll return the money if it doesn't happen."

Genaro nodded. "Go."

40

Jolly Tonio got the call and agreed to ten thousand for the job.

"It's gotta be tonight," his client said. "There'll be a photo in your mailbox in five minutes." He recited the address and details of the building. "The custodian will spend the evening in a bar down the street. A key to the building will be taped to the photo."

Jolly noted everything, then opened the case that held the custom-made sniper's rifle that he relied on for such work. He checked the weapon's action and the number of rounds in the magazine, then closed the case and went to a closet, where he selected his wardrobe: a gray business suit, white shirt, dark tie, and a black fedora, then a reversible raincoat — tan on the outside, black on the inside. He tucked a folding stool into an inside pocket of the raincoat, then folded the soft fedora and stuck it in the inside pocket. Finally, he went into his bathroom and selected a dark, bushy mustache from an assortment, tucked it into a little box with some adhesive, and selected a pair of black eyeglasses with nonprescription lenses.

He put on the raincoat, black side out, locked his apartment, then opened the mailbox and removed a blank envelope. On the cab ride to a corner a block short of his destination, he checked the photo and slipped the building key into a pocket, then, using his reflection in a window, he glued the mustache in place and put on the fedora and the black glasses.

As he walked to the building he presented a dark figure — dark everything — and older. He stopped in front of the building. The lobby was lit only by a single fixture, and his key worked. He checked a back exit and found that it opened into a walkway to the street behind the building. Ideal. He unfolded his stool, stood on it, and un-screwed the bulb in the fixture; he wore driving gloves so there would be no prints.

Jolly took the elevator to the top floor, then blocked the door open with a trash can from the hallway; he walked up a flight and, using his key, let himself onto the roof. He walked to the parapet and looked down one floor and across the street at the Excelsior

Hotel. The penthouse was, literally, a house set down on top of the building, surrounded by a planted deck. The living room lights were on, and a bedroom was lit by a single bedside lamp. Two people were standing at a bar in the living room having a drink. The man was the man in the photograph; the woman was wearing a tight black dress, low-cut.

Jolly unfolded his stool and sat down on it, the case in his lap. He opened it and assembled the weapon, bolted on the scope, then laid it carefully on the parapet. He used a pocket range-finder to get the correct distance, then sighted in the weapon and adjusted the sight for the range. Finally, he shoved in a magazine of six rounds and laid the rifle on the parapet again.

Jolly took an iPhone from his pocket, switched it on, and plugged an earpiece into his ear, then selected an album of Chopin waltzes and settled in for the duration. He was a calm person who could sit for hours, unmoving, as long as he had music to listen to.

Most of an hour passed while the two people chatted and drank, then they moved into the bedroom and began to undress. The process was businesslike; the woman was a hooker. That meant she wouldn't stay long after her work was done; the man would then be alone, and there would be no one to call the police until the following morning, when the maid found him.

The two people had sex by the light from the living room and the single lamp by the bed. They were done in twenty minutes.

Jolly rechecked everything as the woman got dressed, collected her money from the dresser top, and left. The man went, naked, into the bathroom, and the light came on. Jolly decided to take him as he came out of the bathroom. He would be a better target standing than in the bed. The rifle was semiautomatic; he would fire three times rapidly: the first to shatter the glass of the sliding door, the second at the man's chest, the third to the head. Jolly liked head shots; they were final. He took careful aim through the scope at the empty space outside the bathroom.

The man stepped out of the bathroom, and Jolly fired the first round through the thick glass. It shattered. A second later, as he was squeezing off the second round, the man dived back into the bathroom. *Shit!*

The bathroom light went off. Jolly waited for a moment, but it was clear the man wasn't coming out, not until he had summoned the police or hotel security from the bathroom phone.

Jolly quickly picked up the ejected shells, dismantled the rifle, and packed it into the case. As he stood to leave he heard a police car in the distance, then saw it come around the corner and head for the hotel. He walked quickly to the door, let himself into the building with his key, and removed the trash can blocking the elevator door. As the car moved down he used a corner of the rifle case to break the light fixture over his head, so that when the door opened, light would not pour into the dark hallway downstairs.

Once down, he let himself out of the building through the rear exit, set down his case, folded the fedora and put it into a pocket, then took off the raincoat and reversed it, so that it was tan on the outside. He removed the mustache and the glasses and put them into his pocket, then he walked to the street behind the building, then another two blocks before hailing a cab.

Once headed downtown, he made a quick phone call.

"Yeah?"

"It's me. Negative result — couldn't be helped."

The man at the other end hung up, and

so did Jolly. He wouldn't get paid for tonight, but there would be other nights.

Harry Katz got a cell phone call a few minutes later.

"Hello?"

"The operation failed — the patient survived. A wire is on its way back to you."

"What happened?"

"It couldn't be helped." The man hung up.

"Damn it," Harry muttered to himself. Tomorrow morning, he'd have to refund Genaro's money.

41

Yuri Majorov sat down on the toilet lid, breathing hard. He took some deep breaths to try to slow his heartbeat, but he was seriously frightened. He reckoned that if he had been a fraction of a second slower, he would be dead. When he got his breathing under control he called the hotel manager, who said he would call the police.

"Don't do that," Majorov said. "Nothing will come of it, and I don't wish to speak to the police. Move me to another suite, immediately, then tomorrow morning, replace the glass, patch the bullet holes, and clean up."

"Yes, sir."

Majorov sat on the toilet lid a little while longer, thinking. Who would have the temerity to order this hit? Surely not Pete Genaro, whom Majorov judged to be a timid man, accustomed to doing what he was told. The name Barrington occurred to him. Since he had ordered the hit on Peter Barrington he had lost four employees to assassination. This experience had to be the fifth attempt. Then he heard the approach of a wailing police car, then another.

His assailant would be gone by now, and Majorov got into his clothes. Fortunately, he had not unpacked, and he didn't wait for a bellman. He tidied the bed, then carried his case to the door and opened it to find an assistant manager about to ring his bell.

"I have another suite for you, sir," the young man said. "One floor down, at the rear of the hotel."

"Let's take the stairs," Majorov said. The young man escorted him to the suite and left. Majorov called the manager.

"I'm sorry about the police, sir," the man said. "We didn't call them — a neighbor must have heard the shots."

"Tell the police the suite is empty, that this must be an act of vandalism." He hung up and poured himself a stiff brandy. He was still not calm.

Half a brandy later, he took out his cell phone and called his pilot.

"Yes, sir?"

"Have the airplane ready at eleven tomorrow morning," Majorov said. "File for Santa Monica."

"Yes, sir. Any other passengers?"

Majorov thought for a moment. "One," he said, then he hung up and found another number in his contacts list, a fellow Russian who lived in Brooklyn.

"Good evening, Yuri," the man said in Russian.

"Good evening, Boris. I am in New York for the night, departing for Los Angeles at eleven tomorrow morning from Atlantic Aviation, at Teterboro. I would like to take with me the most accomplished and reliable assassin you know."

"That will be Vladimir Chernensky," Boris said without hesitation.

"Is he available?"

"I will see that he is. How long will he be gone?"

"A few days, perhaps a week — less, if he is very efficient. He should bring his own tools."

"He will be at Atlantic Aviation at ten-thirty."

"How much should I pay him?"

"I will deal directly with him, and you may reimburse me later."

"Thank you, Boris. Is all well?"

"Things have calmed down in Brooklyn since your last visit," Boris replied, wryly.

"Good. Thank you for your assistance."

Majorov hung up.

Harry Katz knocked on Pete Genaro's office door and was bade to enter and sit.

"Good morning, Harry," Genaro said. "I just got a call from my bank. The money I wired abroad has been returned. What happened?"

"I was told that the operation was a failure, the patient survived, and that it couldn't be helped. That's all I know, but I take it literally. My contact is not a stupid person, and he doesn't employ stupid people." Harry took a thick envelope from his pocket and pushed it across the table. "Here's the rest of your money."

"I see," Genaro said. "No, I don't, not really."

"These things happen. Do you want me to pursue it further?"

A little chime from his computer caused Genaro to turn and look at the screen. "Well, well," he said. "Majorov's airplane has just taken off from Teterboro, filed for Santa Monica. ETA is three-ten PM, Pacific time. It's a Gulfstream 450, and the likely FBO will be Atlantic Aviation." Genaro read out the tail number. "Plenty of time for you to get to Santa Monica, Harry. I'd like you to handle this personally."

"Pete, I'm sorry, but I do not possess the requisite skills to accomplish that mission the way you would want it done."

Genaro looked at him hard for a moment, then relaxed. "All right, who do we know who could take care of this?"

"I don't have a man you can trust," Harry replied, "but there is someone you know in L.A. — in Santa Monica, in fact — who has proven adept at dealing with such problems."

Genaro's eyebrows went up. "Ah, Billy Burnett."

"Exactly."

Genaro opened a desk drawer and fished out the slip of paper Harry had given him. "I have an address, but not a phone number."

"I can get the number through a contact at the phone company in L.A. I'll call you with it."

"Mr. Burnett seems to communicate exclusively through throwaway cell phones," Genaro said.

"He's almost certainly renting his apartment," Harry said, "and there is very likely a phone there."

Genaro pushed the thick envelope back across the desk. "This should cover all you've done so far, plus another trip to

L.A., if necessary," he said. "I want you to ensure, by whatever means necessary, that Mr. Burnett gets the message in plenty of time to meet that airplane."

Harry tucked the envelope back into his pocket. "I'll get it done, Pete." He got up and left.

It took Harry less than half an hour to track down the number of the penthouse apartment in Santa Monica. He thought about making the trip, but first he would try the phone number. It rang five times before it was picked up by a woman.

"Hello?" She sounded uncertain — worried, even.

"Charmaine, don't be alarmed, this is a friendly call. It's important that you give Billy Burnett a message."

"I don't know what you're talking about. You have the wrong number."

"Don't hang up until you have the message, and you should write it down." There was no reply, so Harry continued. "Yuri Majorov is landing at three-ten PM at Santa Monica Airport. He is aboard a Gulfstream 450." He recited the tail number. "There is reason to believe that he is coming to Los Angeles to harm Billy."

"I know your voice — this is Harry Katz,

isn't it?"

"Pete Genaro asked me to get the message to Burnett."

"Does Majorov know our address?"

"No, he does not. Only Pete and I know it. I saw you shopping in Beverly Hills and followed you home — that's how I got the address. I got the number through a friend at the phone company."

"Why was Pete looking for Billy?"

"At Majorov's behest. He seemed to want badly to find Billy, but Pete has now ousted Majorov from his ownership position at the casino and taken over as CEO. He despises Majorov and wants no harm to come to you and Billy."

"Are you in Los Angeles?"

"No, I'm in my office at the casino. No one is looking for Billy, except Majorov. I don't know what resources he has in L.A., but if I learn anything else, I'll call this number."

"Let me give you a cell number," she said. "I may not be here when you call again."

Harry wrote it down.

"Give me your cell number."

He gave it to her.

"Thank you, Harry. Goodbye." She hung up.

Harry called Pete.

"Yes?"

"Mission accomplished," Harry said.

"Keep me posted," Pete replied, then hung up.

42

Teddy was on time at Peter Barrington's bungalow for his first day. Peter greeted him and waved him to the sofa.

"I'm looking forward to my first lesson in your airplane tomorrow," Peter said.

"I think you'll enjoy the airplane," Teddy said. "By the way, I've found you a hangar at Santa Monica Airport."

"It's a little early, isn't it?" Peter asked. "I don't even have an airplane, yet."

"I'm told that hangars for sale at Santa Monica are rare, and this is a very good opportunity. The hangar belongs to a rock singer named Craig Livingston."

"Sure, I know who he is."

"It's big enough to hold a jet and two smaller airplanes. Livingston is having financial problems, and he wants out of the hangar badly. He's already sold his two smaller airplanes."

"How much does he want for the hangar?"

Teddy told him. "I think he'll take half that and be glad to get it." He handed Peter Livingston's attorney's card.

"Tell me about the track to learning to fly a jet," Peter said.

"What kind of jet?"

"A Citation Mustang."

"You'll need your instrument rating and a multi-engine rating, and probably some turbine time, before they'll accept you for training at Flight Safety. Livingston's pilot is also a mechanic and a flight instructor. He could give you a lot of dual time in a Mustang."

"I got a multi-engine rating when I was at Yale," Peter said. "Relax for a minute while I make a phone call." Peter went to his desk, picked up the phone, and dialed a number.

Teddy flipped through a flying magazine that was on the coffee table.

"Dad?"

"Good morning, Peter."

"I'm sitting here with Billy Barnett, talking about my flight training, and Billy has found a hangar at Santa Monica Airport that I can buy."

"Why do you need a hangar?" Stone asked. "You don't have an airplane."

"I thought I might remedy that. You've

300

got the new Citation M2 on order. What are you going to do with your Mustang?"

"Well, I was going to sell it."

"Then sell it to me."

"Do you know what's involved with learning to fly a jet?"

"Yes, Billy has briefed me on all that."

"And you're willing to take the time to train?"

"I can start now, and then do it more intensively when we've finished this film."

"Then I'll make you a gift of the airplane," Stone said.

"Dad, I can afford to buy it from you."

"And I can afford to give it to you."

Peter grinned. "All right, I accept."

"And you want to buy this hangar?"

"Yes, and I think it's a really good deal." Peter explained the circumstances and Livingston's need to sell quickly. He gave his father Livingston's attorney's number. "Will you negotiate the deal?"

"I'll call him now and get back to you," Stone said.

They hung up.

"Did you hear that?" Peter said.

"Are you buying his Mustang?"

"He's giving it to me."

Billy laughed. "That's a much better deal."

They talked about flight training in the

Mustang for a few minutes, then Peter's phone rang.

"Hello?"

"Congratulations, kiddo, you've just bought yourself a hangar. His attorney accepted our offer, after calling his client. He faxed me his ground lease with the airport, which runs another eighty-six years, which looks good, and we can wrap it up today."

"That's great, Dad."

"And one of Mike Freeman's pilots is available to fly your new Mustang out here. He's waiting for my call after we've closed."

"Perfect."

"Livingston's pilot is making a hundred grand a year, and with all the work he's doing — servicing his airplanes, taking care of paperwork, training — he's worth it. I think you should hire him.

"I've pulled a boilerplate contract from our database, and after I've typed in the parties' names and made a few small changes, I'll fax it to you. Fax it back to both me and the lawyer and ask the bank to wire the funds to the lawyer, then we've closed. The bank will want you to fax them a letter."

"I'll do it the moment I get the contract." He saw Billy answer his cell phone, then leave the room. "Thanks, Dad." He hung up and waited for Billy to return.

■ ■ ■ ■

Teddy closed the door behind him. "Betsy?"

"Yes. I've just had a phone call on the line at the apartment."

"Who has that number? I don't even have it."

"A man named Harry Katz, who works for Pete Genaro."

"All right, start packing. I'll be there in half an hour, and we'll get out."

"No, no, Billy, we don't have to move." She began explaining what Katz had said. "For some reason, Pete wanted you to know that Majorov is coming to town." She gave him Majorov's ETA and the description of his airplane. "What are you going to do?"

"I'm not convinced that Majorov is looking for me in L.A.," Teddy said. "I'm going to look into it, though."

Peter's fax machine spat out the contracts. He looked them over, then signed them and faxed them back to the two numbers, then he wrote and printed a letter to his bank with the wiring instructions, asking for a confirmation when the funds hit the seller's account. He called his father back.

"We're closed, Dad. Thanks so much for

your help."

"Your Mustang will arrive at Santa Monica on Sunday afternoon, late. I've got the hangar number, and I'll direct the pilot. Give him two thousand in cash and tell him to enjoy an evening in L.A. before flying back to New York."

Peter turned to see Billy returning to the room. "Thanks, Dad. I'll talk to you later." He hung up.

"We've closed on the hangar," he said. "Dad says I should hire the pilot. What's his name?"

"Tim Peters."

"He makes a hundred grand a year now, and he does a lot for it. We can add flight instruction to his duties."

"I've just had a call about my airplane," Teddy said. "I have to go out to Santa Monica and move it right now. I can hire the pilot for you, if you like."

"Great, do that. Tell him Ruth will send him an employment package next week, outlining the benefits and the health insurance. And you can put your airplane in the hangar. The Mustang arrives from New York late Sunday afternoon."

"Great. I'll be back later. Is that all right?"

"Sure, take the rest of the day off. Billy, I'm really excited about this."

"You're going to enjoy the experience," Teddy said. "I'll see you tomorrow morning at eleven, in your hangar." He told Peter how to find it, then he left and headed for Santa Monica Airport.

43

Teddy drove quickly to Santa Monica, got buzzed through the gate, and drove to the hangar. He walked inside to find Livingston's jet gone and Tim Peters packing things into boxes.

"Going somewhere?" Teddy asked.

"Home, I guess. Livingston sold the hangar, and less than half an hour ago fired me and flew his airplane to Burbank."

"Did he give you any severance pay?"

"A month. I've been with him five years."

"Put that in your pocket, then, and come to work for Peter Barrington."

Tim blinked. "Who's he?"

"My boss — a young film director and producer at Centurion Studios. He's offering you a hundred grand a year and a package of benefits, including health insurance."

"Then I accept," Tim said.

"He's an enthusiastic pilot. I'm starting his instrument training tomorrow in my airplane, a JetPROP, and as soon as we're done with that, you can start giving him all the time he can handle in the Mustang. Flight Safety will want him to have some turbine time before he trains."

"Not only can I do that, but there's a training outfit on the field that's bought a Mustang simulator from Flight Safety, so he can do his training here. They've got a night class to teach the ground school, and simulator training starts the first of the month. The biggest part of it is learning the avionics."

Teddy gave him Peter's card. "You can start by getting the utilities and phone switched to his company name, B&B Productions, and you can call Atlantic and ask them to tow my airplane over here. It's going to live in the hangar, along with the Mustang."

Tim sat down at his desk and picked up the phone. "What a relief! The wife is going to love it!"

"Oh, and get a cleaning service over here to clean the hangar and the apartment upstairs. I may be using it, myself."

"I forgot to show you the pilot's lounge," Tim said. "It's in the back left corner, and it has a computer station that connects to weather planning and Flight Services. There are a couple of reclining chairs for visiting pilots and a big-screen TV to keep them entertained while they're waiting."

"Good, I can use that for giving Peter ground school."

"Are you type-rated for the Mustang?"

"No, just the 535 series of Citation jets, but I have the same Garmin 1000 software in my airplane, so getting typed wouldn't be much of a jump, and that will be a help to Peter, since the Mustang has the same avionics."

"I'll get you type-rated. If you can learn the operator's manual description of the systems, we can do it with some simulator time, a few hours of dual, and a checkride, and there's an FAA examiner on the field."

"Great, Tim."

Teddy's airplane arrived, and was backed into the hangar, leaving room for the Mustang. Teddy pulled his Porsche Speedster inside, too.

Teddy sat down in the pilot's lounge and thought. If Majorov didn't know where to find him, as Harry Katz had said, why would he be coming to L.A.? And if Teddy wasn't his target, that left Peter. He looked at his watch; Majorov's G-450 was due in shortly. He went to his airplane and got some things, including a pair of binoculars that had a built-in camera, from his equipment case and left the hangar. He found an out-of-the-way perch at one side of the Atlantic Aviation ramp and waited.

Majorov pulled a file from his briefcase and handed it to the man who sat across the folding desk from him. They were half an hour out of Santa Monica and descending. "Mr. Chernensky," he began.

"Call me Vlad, please," the man said, in Russian.

"This is the material I have on the people who are your targets. There is a young man named Peter Barrington and his father, Stone Barrington. Young Peter does something in the movies, I'm not sure what, but I expect he lives in his father's house at The Arrington. Security is very tight there. His father is a New York lawyer who is very influential on the board of The Arrington and is the key to my gaining control. He is based in New York, and when his son is dead, I feel he will be much more likely to wish to sell his interest in the hotel, and at my price.

"The third man is named William J. Burnett and is known as Billy. You should regard him as extremely dangerous."

"I regard all targets as extremely dangerous," Vlad replied. "No one is a lamb if he knows he is hunted. Does Mr. Burnett know he is hunted?"

"Yes, but it's likely he feels that recent events have made him safe."

"Do you mean your leaving Las Vegas?"

"Yes."

"Why should he be concerned with whether or not you are in Las Vegas, if he is in Los Angeles?"

"I sent two men, on separate occasions, to deal with him. They both are dead. One of them was my sister's boy. Neither of them was stupid."

"I see. I will keep those facts in mind. On the other hand, he does not know me, does he?"

"Certainly not."

"He will not expect someone of my age and mien of being an assassin."

"Perhaps not — I cannot say. But you must remember, he is very wily."

Vlad smiled a tight little smile, revealing gray teeth. "I am pretty wily, myself."

Teddy watched as the big Gulfstream set down on runway 21 and engaged its engine reversers. Shortly, it taxied to a halt on the ramp at Atlantic Aviation, guided by the chief lineman. A large Mercedes van pulled up as the airstair door was lowered by a crew member.

Teddy trained his binoculars on the open aircraft door, focused them, and waited. A crew member came down the stairs carrying two large suitcases. He was followed by a large mustached man whom Teddy assumed was Majorov, and he took a rapid series of photographs. Then came someone Teddy had not expected.

A small, gray man in a black suit, white shirt, black tie, and black fedora, who might have been an undertaker, came slowly down the stairs, carrying a large, apparently heavy case that he would not allow anyone to take from him. He looked to be between sixty and sixty-five.

Intrigued, Teddy got as many shots of him as possible before he disappeared into the van with Majorov, and they drove across the ramp to the electrically operated security gate and waited for it to open. Teddy ran back into the hangar, tossed his equipment into the Speedster, and got it started. "Tim," he called to the pilot, "if you want to meet your new boss, be here at eleven tomorrow morning."

Tim ran over and held out a key ring. "Here are a few keys to the place. One key works in all doors."

Teddy pocketed them and drove out onto the ramp. He saw the Mercedes van driving through the now-opened gate and hurried to catch the gate before it closed.

44

Teddy pulled into the parking lot outside the gate and, after noting the license plate number, let the van get a couple hundred yards from him before following. The van made a right turn, then a left, and then turned right onto I-10. At the next exit it turned onto 405 North, and Teddy followed, always keeping two or three cars between him and the van, which was easy to follow, because it was so tall. Teddy had seen photographs of that model given the sort of interior one would expect in a corporate jet.

Traffic was moving moderately well on I-405, and soon the van got off at the Sunset Boulevard exit and made a right. Five minutes later, at UCLA, it turned left onto Stone Canyon Road.

Is he headed for The Arrington? Teddy asked himself, but after another five minutes, the van turned into the entrance of the Bel-Air Hotel. Teddy drove straight on, then when out of sight, made a U-turn and went back to the hotel. He saw Majorov and the older man leave the van and head toward the check-in lobby, while a bellman unloaded their luggage.

Teddy parked on the street; he put on a blue blazer and a porkpie straw hat, then he ran across the road and the bridge into the grounds of the hotel. He saw Majorov's back as he disappeared into the lobby. He walked around the freestanding building and saw a bench and a newspaper someone had left. He parked himself there, put on his sunglasses, and began to leaf through the paper. Ten minutes passed, then the two men left the lobby in the company of an assistant manager, who was chatting to them and getting little response.

Teddy made a point of not lifting his eyes from the paper as they passed him. He watched them take a turn past the outdoor restaurant, then got up and stood at the corner of the building, watching as they continued up a covered walk and past the swimming pool. He kept as much distance as possible between himself and his quarry, but he still managed to see which building they entered. After the door was closed, he got close enough to read the suite number, then he walked up a service road, out of the hotel's grounds, and back to his car.

Teddy didn't like the Bel-Air Hotel as an environment for killing — at least, not alone. There were two many people about, too many ends to tie together. Dealing with Majorov and/or his friend was a job for a team, not one man, and he did not work with a team.

Back at the airport, he drove into the hangar. Tim Peters was sitting at his desk, putting his belongings back into the drawers. Teddy went to the pilots' lounge and went to work on the computer. He took the memory chip from his binocular-camera, inserted it into the computer, and copied the photographs of Majorov and his friend onto the hard drive, then he encrypted the file. He set up a path through half a dozen other computer sites to the CIA mainframe, and logged on to it. After another half a minute's work he was into the Agency's face-recognition program.

The program identified Majorov almost immediately and brought up a file on him. Teddy read it avidly and committed the salient details to memory. Then he switched to the photographs of Majorov's companion; the computer took much longer and it required all the photographs before the man was identified. Teddy read the file:

Vladimir Ivanovich Chernensky, born Kiev, Ukraine, 1951, served in Soviet Army 1969–74, trained as a sniper. Tried for murdering his platoon sergeant, acquitted, but discharged. Seems to have become associated with criminal gangs in Moscow as a young man. Entered U.S. 1997 on a Polish passport, then disappeared, probably now in Brooklyn, NY. Rumors of use by the Russian Mafia as an assassin, acquiring sobriquet "the Viper." Said to be a crack shot with rifle or handgun and good with knife and razor. Said to be inventive in his work.

That was all, but it was more than enough to worry Teddy. He made a phone call on his cell phone.

"Mike Freeman."

"It's Billy Barnett."

"Hi, Billy, you ready to come work for us?"

"Not yet — probably not for several months."

"Is something else occupying your time?"

"Yes. Majorov landed in Santa Monica a couple of hours ago and has checked into the Bel-Air Hotel." He gave Mike the suite number.

"That's interesting to know," Mike said. "Do you think he's an immediate threat to anyone I know?"

"He brought with him a man from New York — write this down: Vladimir Ivanovich Chernensky, early sixties, five-seven, a hundred and thirty, gray hair. Known in Brooklyn as 'the Viper.' "

"I don't like the sound of that," Mike said.

"There isn't anything to like about this man. He's an assassin, pure and simple: rifle, handgun, knife, razor — probably poison and a dozen other ways to kill. He's not the sort of person a sane man would choose to travel with. He was carrying a heavy suitcase that he wouldn't let anyone touch."

"I'm in L.A. I'm going to talk to Stone about this and suggest putting some people on him and Peter."

"If you'll forgive the suggestion, I think you should do it surreptitiously with Mr. Barrington and confine your protection of Peter to transporting him between The Arrington and Centurion Studios. I'm doing some work for him at the studio and at Santa Monica Airport, and we'll be spending a lot of time together, so I can watch his back. I'll e-mail you photographs of Chernensky and Majorov, and you can distribute them to your people."

"Maybe I can get Chernensky arrested before he has time to move."

"He has no criminal record in the United States and by this time probably has an ironclad identity," Teddy said, "so it would be difficult to have him arrested. If he gets anywhere near Peter, I'll deal with him. If he gets near Mr. Barrington, I recommend he be dealt with . . . informally."

"That's out. We don't do that sort of thing — too much to lose."

"Then tell your people not to get in my way," Teddy said, then hung up. He e-mailed the photographs to Freeman, printed out some copies, then got into his car and drove back to Centurion Studios.

Peter was editing when Teddy walked in.

"I thought you were taking the day off," Peter said.

"I finished my work, and I'd like to talk to you."

Peter switched off the machine, and they moved into his office.

Teddy placed the hangar keys on Peter's desk. "The hangar is all yours. One key works every lock. I'd like your permission to make use of the apartment in the hangar, if you don't need it."

"Of course."

"I hired Tim Peters, and he was very happy about it. You'll meet him at the airport tomorrow morning at eleven, before we fly."

"Great! Anything else?"

"Yes. From now until further notice, you must not go anywhere except in a vehicle driven by a Strategic Services employee. Do you own a handgun?"

"No, I'm not much interested in guns."

"Do you know how to shoot?"

"Not in any sort of serious way."

"Then let's go down to the armory right now and get you familiarized."

"But why? I don't have a license."

"I'll have one for you tomorrow morning."

"You can do that?"

"Don't ask too many questions, Peter."

"Why am I in danger?"

Teddy handed him photographs of Majorov and Chernensky. "The larger, younger of the two men is Yuri Majorov, who sent the two men to follow you in New Mexico. You are unlikely to see him, but the other man is very dangerous, and you must be on the lookout for him every time you leave this bungalow."

"And what if I see him?"

"Either tell me, or if I'm not available, shoot him."

"Are you serious?"

"Yes. Let's go over to the armory and spend an hour on the range."

45

Peter turned out to have a good eye and a steady hand, and Teddy was pleased with his performance, standing, kneeling, and prone. Next he had him fire while moving left and right, and he was not so happy with his prowess in that mode. Still, he could shoot — if he could bring himself to shoot. Teddy didn't know how to teach that.

Teddy checked out the handgun and holster for the .380 pistol Peter had been firing, then they rode back to the bungalow in Peter's golf cart, with Teddy on high alert.

"Well," Peter said, when they got back inside, "that was fun, but I'm glad it's over."

"You need more work on shooting while moving," Teddy said.

"You know what's scary about this?" Peter asked. "How seriously you're taking it."

"You'd better take it seriously, too, until I can neutralize the Viper, or you won't finish the film you're working on. And by the way, when you come to the airport tomorrow morning, have the driver pull into the hangar before you get out. There's nothing to hide behind at an airport, if shooting starts."

A voice came from behind him. "Shooting? What shooting?" Ben Bacchetti and Hattie Patrick stood in the doorway.

"Ben, Hattie, you remember Billy Barnett, from New Mexico?"

"Sure," Ben said. "Hi, Billy. We've been in the recording studio. What's going on?"

"Well," Peter said, "you remember the car following us on the road?"

"Yeah, I think so."

"The guy who sent the car is in L.A., and Billy thinks he might send somebody else to look us up." He handed Ben the photographs.

"This guy is a threat?" Hattie said. "He looks like somebody's grandfather."

"That's because he has survived every encounter he has ever had with an opponent," Teddy said. "You would be unwise to underestimate him."

"What do we do if we see him?" Hattie asked.

"Run," Teddy replied.

"Ben shoots," Peter said to Billy.

"Good. You want me to get you something

to shoot with?" Teddy asked.

"I've got the old man's .38 back at The Arrington," Ben said.

"Carry it. I'll get you a license."

"What about me?" Hattie asked.

"Do you want to walk around armed?"

"Well, no."

"Then let me worry about you. Just keep a lookout for that old man in the photograph."

"This is playing like a movie," Hattie said.

"Don't make the mistake of believing that," Teddy replied. "Everybody needs to be wary for the next few days."

"What happens in a few days?" Ben asked.

"Don't ask."

Stone left the Wilshire Boulevard office of Woodman & Weld and drove back to The Arrington. He noticed a brown SUV a couple of cars behind him that turned whenever he did.

He found Mike Freeman sitting by the pool with a Bloody Mary frozen to his fist.

"Did you have a good day?" Mike asked.

"Pretty good. I've been going over Peter's contract with the studio. Our L.A. office did the dogwork, and they did a good job."

"God forbid a partner in a law firm should

get the crease in his pants wrinkled."

"Mike, your people drive brown SUVs, don't they?"

"Brown, black, blue — whatever the dealer has when we're shopping for cars."

"A brown one followed me from the Woodman & Weld offices just now. What's going on?"

"You remember why you came back out here?"

"I do."

"Your fears were warranted. Majorov has turned up in L.A. with an assassin in tow, and I'm taking precautions."

"I see. What precautions have you taken with Peter?"

"Billy Barnett."

"Is he enough?"

"I believe he is."

The door slammed, and the kids came out of the house.

"Welcome home," Stone said. "How was your day?"

"Extremely interesting," Peter said. "I spent part of it learning to shoot a handgun. Billy was my instructor."

"How'd you do?" Stone asked.

"Pretty good, I think. Billy seemed pleased, except I was a little wild when moving."

"Get better at that," Stone said.

"That's what Billy said."

"Listen to Billy."

"I do."

"We all do," Hattie said. "Ben and Peter are packing now, and I have instructions to run if I see this man." She handed Stone the photograph Billy had given her. "He's called the Viper."

Stone sucked his teeth. "I don't like the sound of that."

"Who does?" Mike asked. "I assume you're packing, yourself?"

"I will be, starting tomorrow."

"The Viper is staying at the Bel-Air with Majorov."

"You're so comforting," Stone said. "How do you feel about the security at The Arrington?"

"It's excellent. Strategic Services provides it, if you recall. I had a word with our team leader this afternoon, and I circulated that photograph in your hand."

"Where did the photograph come from?"

"From Billy Barnett."

"And how did he get it?"

"He photographed them when they got off Majorov's airplane at Santa Monica."

"How is Billy so on top of this?"

"I don't know, and I don't much care, but

I'll say this: I'm glad I offered him a job, and I'll be very pleased if and when he accepts it."

"Dad," Peter said, "thank you for suggesting I hire Billy. I'm very glad I did. We're going to start working on my instrument rating tomorrow, in his airplane. He has a JetPROP, like your old airplane, but newer and better equipped."

"And your Mustang will be here by dark," Stone said. "The pilot called from his last refueling stop."

"And the pilot I hired is going to give me dual in the Mustang," Peter said.

"As far as I'm concerned," Stone said, "the more time you spend in the air for the next week or two, the better."

46

Teddy and Betsy showered together, as had become their habit, then had breakfast.

"Betsy," he said.

"You sound serious."

"Don't I always sound serious?"

"Well, you have a sense of humor, you know."

"Right now, I'm serious." He showed her the photo of the Viper. "This man is in town with Majorov, and he's very dangerous. If you see him, avoid him and call me."

"All right."

"I've told you before that we might have to move on short notice."

"You have."

"That time may be near. I want you to come to the airport with me this morning and see where we'll be moving, if we need to."

"All right."

"And I want to make a stop along the way."

"I'm yours for the day."

"Okay, give me a hand with a couple of bags, will you?" Teddy went to a locked closet, opened it, and handed Betsy a duffel and a small suitcase. He grabbed another, heavier duffel and a briefcase, and they took the elevator down to the garage and stowed the things in the Speedster's tiny trunk and behind the two seats. Betsy held one duffel in her lap.

Teddy drove to a large office supply depot and bought a roomy safe with a digital combination, then paid extra to have it delivered to the airport immediately.

He was at the hangar by ten o'clock, where he found Peter's Mustang parked alongside his own airplane, and the keys on Tim's desk. Then, while they waited for the safe to be delivered, Teddy showed Betsy the apartment.

"This is nice," she said, checking out the modern kitchen and the view of Santa Monica from a large window. "I could live here."

A truck's horn blew downstairs, and Teddy went to show the driver where to put the safe, which was in a closet in the pilot's lounge. He tipped the man, then gave Betsy the car keys. "You have two assignments this morning," he said. "While I'm flying with Peter, I'd like you to buy some things for the apartment — whatever it needs — and get it ready for us to move in."

"That's easy — what else?"

"I want you to buy a car."

"What kind of car?"

"Whatever you want."

"New or used?"

"Whatever you want, but it should be large enough for us to make a move in, maybe an SUV." He went to the large duffel he had brought, which was full of cash, and gave her ten bundles of $100 bills. "Here's a hundred thousand dollars," he said. "That's your budget."

"I don't think I'll need that much."

"Then keep the change." He unpacked the rest of the cash, put it into the safe, along with his briefcase and a suitcase, set a new combination, and locked it. "If we need to leave, the money is what we take first," he said. He got her to memorize the combination and open the safe twice.

Tim Peters arrived, and Teddy introduced him to Betsy, then she left. Teddy sat Tim down, gave him a photograph of the Viper and the lecture on how dangerous the man was.

"I keep a nine-millimeter in my bottom

desk drawer," Tim said.

"Don't use it unless you have to, but if you have to, use it fast and aim for the head."

"Gotcha."

Peter arrived in an SUV with a Strategic Services driver, and Teddy introduced him to Tim, then they unlocked the Mustang and had a good look at it.

"Now to work," Teddy said. They towed Teddy's airplane out of the hangar, and Teddy showed Peter how to perform a preflight inspection. That done, they got aboard, with Peter in the left seat, and Teddy ran through the prestart checklist with him.

"Have you used the Garmin 1000 avionics suite before?" Teddy asked.

"Yes, I trained in airplanes equipped with it."

"Then you have a head start on your instrument training *and* your Mustang training," Teddy said. He took the younger man through engine startup, then they got permission from the tower for a VFR departure to the north.

Peter took off and flew the airplane with some assurance, which encouraged Teddy. They flew north and west and found some airspace, and Teddy took Peter through some turns, slow flight, and stalls, then they made some landings at a small airport and returned to Santa Monica.

Teddy chocked the airplane and took Peter into the pilots' lounge. "I'm going to use this room as an office, if that's all right with you."

"Sure it is."

He sat Peter down and started ground school with a long lesson in how to read IFR charts and approach plates, then they walked to a restaurant on the field and got some lunch.

"I have the feeling I'm traveling with the Secret Service," Peter said over burgers. "Mike's people and you are always watching."

"That's why I took the gunfighter's seat," Teddy said. "In the corner, facing the room and the door."

"Yeah, I noticed that."

"Are you armed?"

"The holster is on my belt, under my shirttail," Peter said. "There's a magazine in the weapon, but the chamber is empty."

"When we're back in the hangar, pump a round into the chamber, leave the hammer back, set the safety, and holster the gun. You may need to move fast, and all you'll have to do is thumb the safety down and fire. Also, replace the ejected round in the magazine."

Peter nodded.

When they returned to the hangar there was a shiny Mercedes station wagon inside, and Betsy was unloading shopping bags. Teddy introduced her to Peter, who left them to make some phone calls.

"New?" Teddy asked.

"Two years old, nine thousand miles," she said. "And it's got the V-8 engine. I paid forty-six thousand and I put the change into the safe, less some walking-around money."

"You done good, sweetheart."

"Thank you."

"You want to come flying with us, see some California countryside?"

"Maybe next time. I think I'll get the apartment sorted out."

Teddy kissed her, then went to the airplane with Peter, took off, and headed north again.

As Peter made his first right turn, Teddy looked back at the airport and saw a large black Mercedes van being allowed through the gate at Atlantic Aviation. *Not the only such van in town,* he said to himself. *Probably picking up arriving passengers.*

47

Teddy watched from the right seat as Peter made his third landing at Santa Monica. He was pleased with the way the boy had adapted to the single-engine turboprop. Teddy himself had taken a while to get used to landing the airplane, and he thought of himself as a pretty hotshot pilot.

They taxied to the hangar and went through the shutdown procedure, then Teddy took a few minutes to review what they'd done that day and to question Peter on approach plates. "We'll start flying instrument approaches tomorrow," he said.

They got down from the airplane and attached the little electric tow to the nose-wheel, then Teddy used the remote control on his key to open the bifold hangar door. He stood and stared. Except for the Mustang and his Speedster, the hangar was empty. Tim Peters was absent, and so were Betsy and her new station wagon. Teddy drew his gun. "Stay there," he called over his shoulder to Peter.

Teddy walked into the hangar, the gun in his hand, watching for movement, listening for a footstep, sniffing the air for the smell of cordite. Tim's office was empty, as was the pilots' lounge. Teddy kicked off his loafers and ran lightly up the stairs to the apartment, stepping on the outside of each step to avoid squeaking. He checked the apartment quickly, finding it in excellent order — sheets on the beds, dishes in the cupboards, dusted, vacuumed, perfect. Then from downstairs he heard the closing of a car door — quietly, as if not to attract attention.

He ran down the stairs and found Peter and Betsy leaning on the Mercedes station wagon and chatting. Teddy heaved a huge sigh of relief and put the gun away before they could see it.

"Hi, there," Betsy said.

"Where you been?" Teddy asked lightly, stepping into his loafers.

"I went back to the apartment to pick up a few things — some of your clothes, the liquor."

"Betsy likes a martini at the cocktail hour," Teddy said to Peter. "Where's Tim?"

"Gone for the day. He said you didn't

seem to need him," Betsy said. "Peter has been telling me I ought to learn to fly."

"I think that's a good idea," Teddy replied. "I've got my hands full right now, but there's a flight school on the field." He pointed at the sign across the runway. "Why don't you go over there and inquire about training, while Peter and I run over a few things?"

"Help me with the liquor and the bags, and I will," she said.

The two men carried the things upstairs for her, then went back to Teddy's new office in the pilot's lounge. "Let's do a weight and balance calculation," Teddy said, "and get that behind us." His anxiety had finally melted away.

When they were done for the day, Teddy handed Peter two California carry licenses, one for him and one for Ben.

Peter looked at them closely. "Are these bogus?"

"If you go to the state website, you'll find your names listed there as license holders."

"Then I won't inquire further," Peter said. He shook hands and stepped into the Strategic Services SUV, which had just pulled into the hangar.

Betsy returned and parked her car in the

hangar, then Teddy closed the main door. He checked the lock on the rear door, near his office, then they went upstairs.

"Can I force a drink on you?" he asked.

"I believe you can," she said.

Teddy made her a martini and poured a bourbon for himself, while she spread something on some crackers. They sat down in the living room on the comfortable sofa.

"I start Monday with my flying lessons," Betsy said. "I'll fly three days a week and do ground school the other three. Sundays off."

"To flying through the air on gossamer wings," Teddy said, raising his glass.

She raised hers and they took their first sip.

"I've brought enough things here so that I can live here without returning to the apartment," she said.

"You're a smart woman," Teddy said.

"You can do the same."

Teddy laughed. "And getting smarter and smarter."

"Now tell me what might make us move?"

"At least two people know where we are," Teddy said.

"Harry Katz and Peter Genaro," she replied. "Who else?"

"Whoever they might tell."

"I've known them both pretty well for a few years, and I don't think either of them will tell anybody."

"I hope you're right," Teddy said, "but I'm alive and free because I'm a cautious one."

"Nothing wrong with caution. Are you ready to tell me what you're running from?"

"Quite frankly, I thought I was through running," Teddy said. "I made a . . . an arrangement with the people who wanted most to find me, but then . . ."

"Then, what?"

"Then Peter Barrington and his friends came into my life, pursued by bad men, and I got involved. Now I'm very probably being pursued by the friends of those bad men."

"Majorov and the Viper?"

"Exactly. And those two, in turn, have friends, and I don't know how far that extends."

"What is your plan?"

"I plan to stay in Los Angeles until I feel that Peter and everyone associated with him are perfectly safe, and then I plan to go to work for Strategic Services."

"What's that?"

"It's the second-largest security firm in the world," Teddy said. "Throw a dart at a map of the world, and you'll hit one of their offices."

"And where will we move when you take that job?"

"That is undetermined, but I am of the impression that I may have some choice. I like Los Angeles. How would you feel about living here sort of permanently?"

"I'm just fine with that, as long as you feel safe," she said. "As it is, how long do you think we'll be here?"

"Long enough for you to get your pilot's license and for Peter to learn to fly his new jet."

"So, what, three months?"

"More likely six, but we'll see. I like working at Centurion Studios, too. If we stay on, maybe I can find you a job there."

"I wouldn't object to working in the movie business," Betsy said.

"After you've got your private license," Teddy said. "Maybe your instrument rating, too."

"When I've done all that, will I be your copilot?"

"Sweetie," he said, kissing her, "after you've done all that, I'll be *your* copilot."

She laughed, but Teddy was still worried. He had a history of seeing things go wrong after he had made plans.

48

Majorov returned to his large suite after a good breakfast at the Bel-Air's outdoor restaurant, and as he closed the door, he was immediately struck by the smell of gun oil. He walked to the door of the bedroom adjoining the living room, rapped and opened the door. He was met by the sight of Vlad, sitting on the bed, pointing a pistol at him.

"That was very close," Vlad said in Russian. Various gun parts were spread on a towel on the bed.

"You are not here to shoot me," Majorov said. "What are you doing to find Burnett?"

"I will bring you up to date," Vlad said. "There is no such person listed in any directory of any sort in the Greater Los Angeles area — no telephone, no mail delivery, no utilities, nothing. These are the tools for searching for someone, and Mr. Burnett has avoided them all. We know only two things:

that Mr. Barrington is at The Arrington, up the street, and competently guarded, and that his son goes to the movie studio every day in a different car with an armed guard."

"Why can't you get at him at the movie studio?"

"Because it is fenced and guarded by its own police force, and because, even if I could get inside, I would not be able to find Peter Barrington. The place is like a small city."

"So you have nothing?"

"Let me finish. You gave me details of Burnett's airplane, but no such airplane with that registration number is registered with the Federal Aviation Administration, and no airplane of that color and with that registration number is parked at any airport in the Los Angeles area."

"Then Burnett is gone from Los Angeles."

"Possibly," Vlad said. "But we know some people who might know something."

"And who might they be?"

"The two gentlemen from Las Vegas: Genaro and Katz."

"They have denied knowing."

"Katz has a reputation as the best skip tracer in Vegas," Vlad said. "I cannot believe he spent several days looking for Burnett without finding him. And if he knows where the man is, Genaro knows, too."

"Then why wouldn't he tell me?"

"Why would he tell you anything? The man drove you from a profitable business and ran you out of town. Genaro hates you."

"You're right, he would never tell us anything."

"Katz might," Vlad said.

"Why do you think that?"

"Katz works for money. He sells the location of people to his employers."

"So I should offer him money?"

"It would seem the best thing to do." Vlad spread his hands. "And if that doesn't work, there are other methods. After all, personal safety is as important to a sane man as money."

"So you want to go to Las Vegas?"

"I'm told it is only a few hours by car."

"I can't go to Vegas."

"I'm not suggesting you do. I don't require your assistance to do my work. All I require is your money."

Majorov left the room for a couple of minutes then returned and tossed a bundle of hundred-dollar bills on the bed. "Here is thirty thousand dollars," he said. "You may keep anything you don't have to pay Katz. The concierge will obtain a rental car for you." Majorov walked out of the room and closed the door behind him.

Vlad began repacking his weapons case, while whistling a little tune from his childhood. It brought back a fond memory: his father had been singing it when Vlad cut his throat with the man's own razor. He had liked the razor as a tool ever since.

Harry Katz sat in his office near the casino late in the day; he finished transcribing his notes to his computer, shut the laptop, bent over and reached into his bottom drawer for the bottle of scotch and glass he kept there. When he straightened up, a little man was standing in the doorway to the small reception area, holding a suitcase in one hand. "I'm sorry," he said, "I didn't hear you come in."

"Excuse me, please," the man said. He was harmless-looking, six-tyish, maybe older, dressed in a black suit and wearing a fedora. "May I speak with you for a moment, Mr. Katz? About some business?"

Harry couldn't place the accent: something foreign with some New York in it. "Have a seat," he said, waving him to a chair in front of the desk. "Would you like a drink?" He held up the bottle.

"Thank you, perhaps a little later, after I

342

have stated my proposition."

"Suit yourself," Harry said. He poured himself two fingers and took a sip.

The little man set down his suitcase next to his chair and bent over, out of Harry's sight. Harry heard the snap of the locks opening, and when the man straightened, he was holding a pistol equipped with a silencer in one hand and a roll of duct tape in the other. As if that weren't alarming enough, he was also wearing surgical gloves.

"Forgive me," the man said, "but since I am not a strong person I would prefer it if you were temporarily immobilized while we talk." He rolled the duct tape across the desk, and Harry caught it. "If you would please roll your chair from behind the desk."

"What's this about?" Harry asked, not moving.

"If I must I will shoot you a little."

Harry rolled his chair sideways, following the motions of the pistol from behind the desk.

"Good. Please tape your feet to the bottom of your chair."

Harry did so, but not too tightly.

"Good. Now, please tape your right hand to the arm of the chair."

Harry couldn't think of anything else to

do that would not get him shot, so he did so.

The man got up, walked over to Harry, and placed the silencer to his head. "Now grip the arm of the chair with your left hand."

Harry did so, and the man tore off a piece of the tape with his other hand and his teeth, then taped Harry's left hand to the chair.

"Now," the man said. He took a bundle of money from his case and placed it on the desk. "There is twenty thousand dollars," he said. "I wish some information."

"Why didn't you just ask?" Harry said.

"Because I feared you would not tell me what I want to know. But now I will give you twenty thousand dollars to tell me where to find Mr. William Burnett." The man set his pistol on the desk, reached into an inside pocket, and came up with a straight razor. He unfolded it. "And if you do not tell me everything I want to know, I will cut your throat. But not before I have caused you quite a lot of pain."

Harry's insides turned to water, and he reasoned quickly. He might tell the man everything and earn the money, or he might tell him everything and still get his throat cut. It wasn't much of a choice. "I'll tell you what I know," he said.

The man folded the razor and set it on the desk beside the gun. "Please continue."

"There's a pad and pencil on the desk, if you want to write this down," Harry said.

"That will not be necessary. I have an excellent memory. Now, please, I am becoming bored."

Harry recited the address in Santa Monica. "Mr. Burnett lives in that building in the penthouse — the top floor."

"With Charmaine?"

"Yes, with Charmaine."

"And what security precautions has Mr. Burnett taken?"

"I know of none. I have not visited the apartment. I found Charmaine shopping in Beverly Hills and followed her home. Later I saw the two of them leave the building. I bribed the superintendent to tell me which apartment they occupied."

"What else do you know?"

"They are married. I found a record of their marriage at the Los Angeles County Clerk's Office."

"Ah, I did not think to look there. You are a good skip tracer. Does Peter Barrington visit Mr. Burnett at his apartment?"

"I'm sorry, I don't know that name."

345

The man picked up the razor and opened it.

"Truly I do not know this Barrington. Who is he?"

"A producer of movies."

"I know nothing of him and Burnett."

The man considered that. "Anything else? Last chance."

"Ask me anything you like. That is what I discovered in my investigation. I never spoke to Burnett, I just reported my findings to Pete Genaro at the casino."

"Please give me a complete physical description of Mr. Burnett and Charmaine."

"Charmaine is about thirty-five, five feet, seven inches tall, busty, but with an otherwise trim figure. She had blonde hair when I knew her, but since moving to Santa Monica she has dyed it a dark brown, blue eyes, very pretty."

"And Mr. Burnett?"

"Mr. Burnett is difficult to describe because he is so ordinary-looking. He is between forty-five and fifty-five, about five-eleven, maybe six feet, maybe a hundred and sixty or seventy, fit-looking for his age. He was wearing a hat when I saw him, but I think his hair is dark, but graying. He was wearing sunglasses when I saw him."

"I believe you, Mr. Katz, so I will give you

your life." He walked over, the razor still in his hand.

Harry winced as the man went through his pockets, relieving him of his pistol and cell phone.

The man pocketed the cell phone and tossed the pistol into the next room. He tore off another piece of the tape and wrapped it securely around Harry's head, covering his mouth completely, then he reinforced the bindings of his hands and feet. Finally, he unscrewed the silencer and put it and the pistol into his case and pocketed the razor. "There is your money," he said. "Does a person come to clean your office at night?" he asked.

Harry nodded.

"What time?"

Harry shrugged.

The man found a sheet of paper and a marking pencil in a drawer and wrote DO NOT DISTURB on it. "I will place this on your outer door," he said. "If you tell Mr. Burnett or Mr. Genaro of our conversation, I will come back and kill you slowly and painfully. Do you understand?"

Harry nodded.

The man reached over, lifted Harry's glass of whiskey, sniffed it, then poured it slowly down his throat. Then he picked up his suitcase and, with the note in his other hand, left the office.

Harry started to sweat at the thought of what he had avoided. He tried moving his hands and feet, to no avail. He was securely attached to the chair, and he needed badly to urinate. He would have to wait for the cleaning lady, and he didn't know what time she came, or if she would ignore the sign on the door. After that, he would decide whether to call Charmaine.

Harry held it together for nearly an hour, before he peed in his pants. Then he began to cry, softly.

49

When he was back on I-15, driving toward Los Angeles, Vlad telephoned Majorov.

"Yes, Vlad?"

"I have spoken with Mr. Katz and he has very kindly given me the address of Mr. Burnett."

Majorov was suspicious. "He did?" he asked incredulously.

"He was not forthcoming at first, but after the sight of the money and a brief chat, he told me everything he knows. Believe me, everything."

"And where is Burnett?"

"Living in an apartment building in Santa Monica." Vlad gave him the address. "In the penthouse apartment, no less. I am on my way there now."

"Good. Report to me after your visit, and may it be successful."

"From your lips to God's ear," Vlad replied, then hung up. Using the GPS unit supplied with his rental car, Vlad had no difficulty finding the apartment building. It was now just past eleven PM. He parked his rental car on the street, went to the trunk, opened his case, and removed what he needed, secreting the implements on his person. He noted the building's garage, but did not enter it. He did not know, after all, what kind of car Burnett drove.

He walked into the building's lobby, which was deserted, and examined the elevator buttons; there were eight of them, plus one marked PH. He pressed that button and got on an elevator, which rose quickly, then he stepped out of the car into a hallway. The elevator door closed silently behind him.

He examined the edges of the penthouse apartment's double door: no light escaped from the apartment. He removed the silenced pistol from its holster, then rang the bell. He waited a minute, put an ear to the door, heard nothing, then rang it again. There was no response.

Vlad knelt by the doorknob and examined the lock. Very ordinary; no problem. He took a small leather case from an inside pocket, selected a pair of lock picks, and went to work. In under a minute the lock turned. Vlad stood up, put away his tools, and, holding his pistol in one hand and a small flashlight in the other, slipped inside and closed the door gently behind him.

He stood in the dark for a minute or so, listening for any sign of life: a television set, someone breathing or turning over in bed, a toilet flushing. Dead quiet. There was enough light from outside filtering in so he didn't need the flashlight. First, he found the bedroom, its door wide open; no one there. He checked the living room and the kitchen: no one.

Then he turned on the flashlight and went to work. A few clothes, not many, both male and female, in the closets. Not much in the bathroom, either. He searched for a computer, but did not find one; there was no liquor in the bar. The refrigerator held milk, orange juice, and not much else. Very unsatisfying. Had his quarry moved? He went into the bathroom, lifted the toilet seat and urinated, then flushed. It had been a long drive.

He let himself out of the apartment, rode down to the lobby, left the building, and got into his car. He was not going to wait there all night.

As he turned the corner, two people came out of the restaurant across the street from the building, but Vlad did not see them.

■ ■ ■ ■

Teddy and Betsy crossed the street, entered the building, and rode up to the penthouse. "That was the best dinner Michael's has given us yet," Betsy said. "I'm stuffed."

"Not too much to be stuffed again," Teddy said, leering a little.

"We'll see."

Teddy let them into the apartment and switched on the living room light, while Betsy went into the bedroom.

Teddy opened the sliding door to the terrace to let in the cool night air, then he heard a shriek from the bathroom and ran toward it. Betsy was struggling to her feet, her panties around her ankles.

"What's wrong?" Teddy asked.

"You left the toilet seat up again, and I fell in," she said crossly.

"I didn't do that," he protested. "At least, I don't remember doing it."

"You're the only one who lives here who lifts the seat to pee," she said, lowering the seat and sitting down.

"I'm sorry, sweetheart, I guess it was just automatic."

"You have to break yourself of that habit, Billy, there's a woman living here now."

"I promise, I'll break the habit."

They went to bed, but there was no sex that night.

Majorov was sill up, watching TV, when Vlad returned to the suite at the Bel-Air. "Is the work done?" he asked.

"No. I got into the apartment, but there was no one there, just some clothes and things."

"Why didn't you wait?"

"Because I've been traveling all day, and I'm tired," Vlad said, with the air of a man who didn't want to be questioned. "I'll call on them again tomorrow."

"See that you do."

"Yuri," Vlad said irritably, "don't annoy me again, otherwise you'll have to do this job yourself. Now I am going to bed."

And he did, while Majorov smoldered.

50

Teddy got up early and shaved and showered, while Betsy slept on. He got dressed, and by that time she was showing signs of life. He leaned over and kissed her awake.

She glanced at the clock. "Why so early?"

"It's my first day on a movie set," Teddy said. "They start early. What's your plan for the day?"

"I'm going to take a few more things to the hangar," she said, "and buy some better towels for the apartment there."

"See you later, then." Teddy took the elevator down to the garage, got into the Speedster, and drove to the studio. Something was nagging at him, but he couldn't bring it into his frontal lobe; it just festered, somewhere in his brain.

Vlad woke early, as usual, and planned his day. First, he would visit Mr. and Mrs. Burnett and complete his business with them, then he would drive to Universal City and take the studio tour. He had already looked it up on the Internet and reserved a ticket.

Majorov was breakfasting in the Bel-Air's outdoor restaurant, and Vlad ignored him as he passed. He ordered his rental car from the valet, got into it, and drove toward Sunset. It was only after he had turned onto the boulevard that he realized his error: rush hour. It took twenty minutes just to get on the freeway, which had pretty much become a parking lot.

Teddy was very impressed with what he found on the soundstage: Peter's production designer had constructed a Century City apartment inside the huge space, and as he walked around it, he wished he lived there. It was complete in every way, down to the dishes in the kitchen cabinets.

A loud buzzer went off, and an amplified voice announced, "All quiet on the set. Cell phones off." Teddy switched off his phone. A red light over the entrance to the stage went on, signifying that they were now sealed inside the huge space.

Then Teddy's frontal lobe lit up, and he knew what had bothered him: the toilet seat. He had a clear memory of visiting the bathroom before they left the apartment for dinner, and of closing the seat, reminding himself that he no longer lived alone. Another man had been in their penthouse.

He stepped into a corner and switched his cell phone on again, waiting impatiently for it to boot up. He pressed the favorites button and selected Betsy's number, pressing it to his ear and waiting for her to pick up. Nothing happened. He looked at the screen and found a "call failed" message. He tried again, to no avail. The studio, in spite of the earlier announcement, was jamming cell calls from the soundstage, just in case.

Betsy struggled out of bed and into the shower. She shouldn't have had that extra glass of wine after dinner, she now realized. Coffee would fix her, though. Then, as she got out of the shower and wrapped a towel around herself, she heard the doorbell. At least, she thought it was the doorbell; it had never rung before.

She padded to the front door in her bare feet and peered through the peephole. A man stood outside, his back to the door; he was dressed in a black suit and a black fedora. Then he turned toward the door and rang the bell again. There was a gun in his hand.

Oh, shit, she thought. As silently as she

could, she slipped the security chain into its receptacle, then ran for the bedroom. She struggled into some clothes and looked for her handbag. Where the hell was it? She had her driver's license and passport and car keys in the bag, and she couldn't leave it here.

Vlad knelt and began using his lock picks.

Inside, Betsy heard the lock being tampered with. She looked around, panicked, and saw her handbag on the living room coffee table. She grabbed a pair of shoes, not bothering to put them on, ran into the living room, and snatched her handbag from the coffee table, knocking over a martini glass left there from the cocktail hour the evening before, and smashing it.

Outside, Vlad heard the glass break and put his ear to the door.

Betsy took the longest leap she could, trying to clear the broken glass, and failed. A sharp stab flashed through her foot and up her leg, but she ran anyway, ignoring the pain, past the front door and toward the kitchen and the service elevator. She pressed the button and waited, fidgeting with anxiety. The overhead light was on B. That meant the super could be holding the elevator in the basement. She thought about the stairs, but, remembering her foot, now bleeding copiously, she continued to watch the light. It began to move up. *Please,* she thought, *no stops!* As the elevator neared the penthouse, she heard the front door unlatch and open, then she heard a banging noise and what sounded like the screws of the chain lock tearing out of the doorjamb.

Vlad stepped inside and saw the broken glass on the floor next to the coffee table and, running away from it, a trail of blood leading toward the kitchen. He racked the silenced pistol and moved in that direction.

The elevator door finally opened, and Betsy pushed the G button. Seconds elapsed, and the door began to close. Through the remaining six inches of closure, she saw the little man enter the kitchen and turn toward her, raising his gun.

She flattened herself against the elevator wall, and as it began to move, a small hole appeared in the door.

Vlad swore to himself. He watched the elevator light as it moved downward. Should he wait for it to return, or use the main elevator or the fire stairs? He opted for the main elevator, hoping the car would still be waiting.

Betsy struggled into her shoes as the service elevator descended, then began looking through her handbag for something. As the elevator door opened in the garage, she found a pack of tissues and crammed it into the elevator door, hoping that would prevent its closing, then she ran for her car, keys at the ready.

The main elevator was still at the penthouse level, and Vlad pressed the G button, gambling that there was a car involved in the woman's escape plan. The elevator started down.

Betsy got the car started and backed hurriedly out of her parking space, narrowly missing a concrete column in the process. She got the thing into gear and drove as quickly as she could through the garage and up to the street, turning toward the boulevard.

Vlad ran out of the elevator and began searching the garage for the woman. She couldn't have gotten away this quickly; she must be in her car, somewhere in this space.

Peter Barrington yelled, "Cut," and the red light over the soundstage door went out. Teddy ran outside, got a signal on his phone, and tried Betsy again.

As she turned onto Bundy, toward the airport, Betsy heard her phone ringing in her handbag. She managed to get it out without wrecking the car. "Billy?"

"Get out of the apartment now," Teddy said. "Don't take anything, just get out."

"I am out," Betsy said.

"The toilet seat was left up by someone else."

"That evil little man got into the apartment," she said. "I barely made it to the service elevator."

"Is anyone following you?"

"I don't believe so. I think I made it out of the garage before he could get downstairs."

"Make a few turns, and watch your rearview mirror. If he's following you, he'll be a couple of cars back. If you spot him, find a policeman. If you don't, continue to the airport, and call me the minute you get inside the hangar. I'm on my way."

■ ■ ■ ■

Vlad got to his car and started it, but he didn't know what she was driving. He searched the boulevard for a woman driving erratically, but saw nothing.

Betsy pulled into the hangar, and called Teddy.

"Where are you?"

"In the hangar. Nobody followed me, I'm sure of it. I waited within sight of the gate, and nobody came through for five minutes. You go back to work."

"Is Tim in his office?"

"Yes, he's at his desk."

"He has a gun. Tell him that if anyone follows you into the hangar, to shoot him and quickly."

"All right." She hung up, got out of the car, went to the hangar door, and looked around, then she closed the hangar door. Tim looked up from his computer and waved. She waved back. She wasn't about to tell him to shoot anybody.

51

Teddy spent the day watching the shooting, helping when he could, and when they were done, rode back to the bungalow with Peter in his golf cart.

"Have you got a couple of hours after work for some flying?" Peter asked.

"Sure," Teddy said. "I should be through here by five-thirty, and I can meet you at the hangar by six."

"I have to interview a woman for a job at five, but that shouldn't take long."

"What sort of job?" Teddy asked.

"We're learning that Ruth Pearl can't handle everything alone," Peter said. "We're getting a lot of invitations to industry functions and requests for interviews, and we need somebody to handle those, plus make personal arrangements — travel reservations, et cetera."

"You met my wife, Betsy, at the hangar," Teddy said. "She used to be a VIP concierge at a Las Vegas hotel. Would you interview her for the job?"

"Sure. Her background sounds good for us."

They arrived at the bungalow and found Stone Barrington on the front porch in a rocking chair. "Good morning," he said. "I thought I might buy you lunch, Peter, if you've got the time."

"Sure, Dad. Give me a few minutes to return some calls, and we'll go over to the commissary."

"Will you come with us, Billy?" Stone asked.

"Of course," Teddy replied. He knew why Stone wanted him there — to watch Peter's back.

"Sit with me while Peter makes his calls," Stone said.

Teddy took a rocking chair.

"What's new with Majorov and his assassin?" Stone asked.

"He managed to find out where my wife and I are living and paid a visit this morning. She got out just in time."

"Is there any way you can take a more offensive tack?" Stone asked.

"Only if I catch them outside the Bel-Air. That's a very tightly secured place — not as tight as The Arrington, but tight."

"I see."

"For the moment I think the best use of my time is to cover Peter," Teddy said. "Blocking an attempt on him is the best way for me to go on offense."

"I'll trust your judgment," Stone said.

"Thank you. I want Vlad off the street as much as you do. My wife had a very close call this morning."

Peter finished his calls, and they went to lunch. After that, Stone excused himself, saying that he had to visit the Woodman & Weld offices on Wilshire.

"Is someone driving you?" Peter asked. "I can get a studio car to take you."

"It's all right," Stone said. "One of Mike Freeman's people is driving me."

Later in the day Vlad parked across the street from the main gate at Centurion Studios and watched the employees leave work. One of them was driving an old Porsche Speedster, a car Vlad had admired in his youth.

A few minutes later, a brown SUV drove through the studio gate with Peter Barrington in the front passenger seat. Vlad's heart leaped; finally an opportunity. He waited for a couple more cars to follow the SUV, then he fell in behind it.

■ ■ ■ ■

Half a block down the street, Stone Barrington sat in the front passenger seat of another brown SUV, with a Strategic Services agent at the wheel. "There," Stone said, pointing. "I think that black car is following Peter's."

The agent pulled into traffic. "How do you want to handle this?" he asked.

"You're armed, aren't you?" Stone said.

"Yes."

"So am I. Look for an opportunity to force that car over without attracting too much attention."

"I'm not sure that's going to be possible," the agent said. "We're talking L.A. rush hour here."

"Do the best you can."

Five cars now separated Stone from Peter, and the black car following him was two cars ahead of Stone's.

"See if you can get alongside him," Stone said, unholstering his pistol.

"Wait a minute, now," the driver said. "I can't be involved in a shooting — that's strictly against company policy, unless we're shot at first."

"What kind of glass is in this car?" Stone asked.

"This one has our stage one protection package," the agent said. "The glass will stop a nine-millimeter bullet, and so will your door. It has a Kevlar lining."

"Then let's crowd him — maybe he'll take a shot at us, and I can fire back. I have the advantage of not driving, while he is."

"I don't know about this," the agent said. "Provoking a gunfight in rush hour traffic."

"I'll take the responsibility with Mike Freeman. You have nothing to worry about."

"Except getting shot," the driver said, but he pulled into the left lane and managed to get a car closer to the black vehicle.

Stone racked his pistol and switched it to his left hand, leaving his right free to operate the window control.

"How much noise are you going to make?" the agent asked.

"It's a .380 — not as much as a nine-millimeter or a .45."

"There's a small blanket folded on the seat behind you," the agent said. "Hide your weapon in that. You'll get a better jump on the guy if he can't see your gun, and the blanket will suppress noise and muzzle flash."

"Good idea." Stone turned around, found

the blanket on the rear seat, and pulled it into his lap. He twisted it around his left hand; he would be firing through the soft wool. "Whenever you're ready," he said, rolling his window halfway down.

Vlad caught sight of a movement in his side mirror that brought him to attention: a brown SUV, like the one Peter Barrington rode in, suddenly pulled out into coming traffic and passed the car behind him, pulling up close, riding his bumper. He looked for a way to get away from the car, but he was in the middle of a block, moving slowly, and was surrounded by other cars; there was no way out. Then the SUV swerved and pulled up in the lane beside him.

Vlad yanked the silenced pistol from its holster; he recognized the front passenger as Stone Barrington, from photos he had seen. As the car pulled alongside him he did not hesitate; he fired two shots at Barrington.

Stone saw the two stars appear in the armored glass. He had his left hand, wrapped in the blanket, up to the window's edge and got off two quick shots. The blanket burst into flames.

■ ■ ■ ■

Vlad's hat flew off, exposing his white hair, and he felt the passing of another bullet. He stomped on the accelerator and gained half a length on the SUV, then he yanked the wheel to the left, forcing the other vehicle into oncoming traffic, where it collided with a delivery truck and stopped. Vlad then got around two cars and was only one behind the other SUV.

The agent produced a cell phone and used it as a walkie-talkie: "Sierra Sierra One, this is Sierra Sierra Three! Black car behind you. Take evasive action immediately! Repeat, take evasive action immediately!"

Stone got the blanket off his hand and stomped at the flames, finally extinguishing them. Out of the corner of his eye he saw an LAPD foot patrolman coming toward them from across the street. He threw the smoldering blanket out his window and ran the glass down, to hide the bullet marks.

"I've got this," the agent said. "Just sit there quietly."

Stone stuck the gun back into its holster and sat there, trying to look benign, as the agent began explaining to the officer how the other car had forced him into traffic.

Vlad was ready to make his move when the vehicle beside him turned left. He swung into the left lane and gunned his car past the one car separating him from Peter Barrington. Then, to his astonishment, the brown SUV made a sudden right turn down a side street, leaving him stuck in the left lane. Traffic came to a halt as a light turned red half a block away. He had lost his opportunity, and what was worse, Stone Barrington had made him. How could the man know him? he wondered; they had never met.

Then he felt something running down the side of his face. He looked into the rearview mirror and found a little nick in the bridge of his nose. The son of a bitch had grazed him!

52

Teddy opened the hangar door with his remote control and drove inside and parked next to Betsy's Mercedes. Tim Peters was doing something to an engine of the Mustang jet and gave him a wave.

"Anything wrong?" Teddy asked.

"Just topping off the oil," Tim replied. "This bird had a long flight out here."

"Peter will be here fairly soon," Teddy said. "Will you close the hangar door after he arrives?"

"Sure."

Teddy went upstairs and found Betsy putting away new towels. "Peter's going to be downstairs in a few minutes, and he wants to hire someone to work for him. You've got a job interview as soon as he gets here."

Teddy went down to his new office and made sure Peter's logbook was up to date. He heard the hangar door close and car doors slam, and a moment later Peter came into the room.

"Have a seat, and we'll go over what we're going to do this afternoon," Teddy said.

"We just had a brush with the Viper," Peter said. "At least, I think it was the Viper."

"What happened?"

Peter told him.

"Sounds like your agent is a good driver."

"He sure is, and he told me the Strategic Services cars have bulletproof glass in them. I was happy to hear that!"

Vlad had been lying in wait for Peter outside the Centurion main gate, Teddy thought. *He must have gotten a look at me, too, though he wouldn't know who I am. He might remember the Speedster, though.*

Betsy rapped on the door, and Teddy left them alone. As he walked out of his office, someone rang the bell for the entry door built into the larger, bifold door. Tim opened the big door and another brown SUV drove in, and Stone got out.

"Peter had a run-in with Vlad," Teddy said to Stone.

"I know, I was there. I got off a couple of rounds at his head, and I think I hit him, but he outmaneuvered us and got away. We hit a delivery van and had to spend a few minutes with a cop, but it ended well, except for a dented fender."

"Vlad is getting closer," Teddy said. "He was lying in wait for Peter outside the studio. We can't make it easy for him anymore."

The Strategic Services agent walked up. "You need to get a different car for tomorrow," Teddy told him, pointing at the two SUVs. "No more identical SUVs — Vlad is on to that."

"Right," the man said. He produced a cell phone and called his headquarters.

"It troubles me," Stone said, "that *I'm* the one who got to take the shot. Where were you?"

"I'm Peter's body man at the studio. During transport, he's in the hands of Strategic Services, as are you," Teddy said. "Everybody did his job, except you — you didn't have a job. You took matters into your own hands, and you missed. What was the range?"

Stone looked embarrassed. "Maybe four feet."

"I don't think Mike Freeman would hire you."

The agent returned. "We'll have different vehicles tomorrow — no SUVs."

Teddy looked toward the rear of the hangar and saw Peter and Betsy standing outside the office, chatting. They shook hands, and Teddy joined them.

"I've just hired myself a personal assistant," Peter said. "I'll see you tomorrow, Betsy, and I'll leave a studio pass and a parking pass for you at the gate."

Betsy went back upstairs, and Teddy and Peter sat down in the office.

"Betsy is perfect," Peter said. "Two minutes into our conversation, she was redefining the job, and she was right. She's going to work for Ben and Hattie, too, until we need more help. We've got another room at the bungalow that you and Betsy can use as an office. I'll call Ruth and have her get some furniture in there."

"Sounds great," Teddy said. "Now let's get to work."

Stone rode back to The Arrington with his agent driver, and as they passed the Bel-Air Hotel, Stone said, "Let's stop here for a drink."

The driver ignored the instruction and continued on.

"Didn't you hear me?" Stone asked.

"You used to be a cop, didn't you?"

"Yes, for fourteen years."

"During those years, how many times did you do security details, protecting a VIP?"

Stone thought about it. "Never."

"I thought not, otherwise you wouldn't ask me to take you into a place where two people who want to kill you and know what you look like are staying. Can you see why that wouldn't be a good idea?"

Stone said nothing.

"You were hoping to get another shot, weren't you?"

"All right, I guess I was."

"You've already been involved in one shooting incident today and got off scot-free. You've got a lot to lose. Don't push your luck."

53

Stone and Mike Freeman were having an early breakfast. The kids had already left for work.

"I read the reports from yesterday," Mike said.

"Your people did well."

"Yes, they reacted well, even if one of them tiptoed along the edge of our company policies. He was reprimanded for that."

"You should be pleased to have him working for you," Stone said.

"I am, but all my people are expected to meet company standards in their behavior — that means *my* standards."

"Mike, I apologize for leading your agent even a little astray, but I came within an inch of ending this."

"Yes, and in the middle of a crowded Los Angeles avenue, with a cop watching from across the street and at least fifty potential witnesses."

"We walked away from it," Stone said.

"This time. You're going to have to alter your behavior."

"In what way?"

Mike sighed. "You're going to have to be more careful."

Stone looked at him askance. "You're not telling me to stop trying?"

"Just be more careful," Mike said. "And I will not collude with you on this."

"Understood. Do you have any advice?"

"Don't work alone," he said. "You have access to someone who is experienced at these things, much more so than you or I."

"Ah, Teddy. Or Billy. He thinks his best move is to guard Peter and take out Vlad when he comes for him."

Mike shrugged. "That's one way to work — a valid way."

"He won't go on offense because he says the Bel-Air is too secure."

"Not *that* secure," Mike said. "I think he means there are too many people around for him to get in and out alone."

"So you're telling me to work with Billy?"

"I told you, I will not collude with you in this business. However, I did send two men with Peter this morning, instead of one. They will be with him all day. That should free up Billy." He took a jotter pad from a pocket, wrote down something, and slid it across the table. "This is Billy's cell number."

Stone was sitting at poolside, reading some contracts that had been sent from New York, when the phone beside him rang. "Yes?"

"Mr. Barrington, this is the front gate. There's a Mr. Barnett to see you."

"Send him up to the house." He hung up. He had already alerted his security man.

Five minutes later, Billy Barnett was sitting next to him, sipping a Virgin Mary. "In my former existence," Billy said, "we used to call this drink a Bloody Awful."

Stone smiled. "A very good name."

"Why did you want to see me?"

"Because I'm tired of this. It's wearing us all down, waiting for Vlad to pounce. I'm sorry I missed him yesterday."

"Patience is required," Billy said.

"I'm not a patient person," Stone said. "My personal motto is *Si non nunc quandro?*"

Teddy laughed. " 'If not now, when?' I like it."

"You know your Latin."

"The product of a misspent youth," Billy said.

"You said the Bel-Air was too secure to

take it to Vlad there."

"I did. That hasn't changed."

"It would be less secure, would it not, if you were two?"

"Half as secure," Billy said. "Surely you're not contemplating joining forces?"

"I am thinking exactly that," Stone said. "In spite of my missed shot of yesterday. I am extremely angry, and taking out Majorov, too, would be a great bonus."

"I think I prefer you in the role of look-out."

"Looking out for what?"

"The Bel-Air is not a high-rise hotel with elevators and long corridors. It is a large cluster of buildings standing in a lush, tropical garden. That might make it easier to approach and enter a particular building, but the place is crawling with guests, and in particular, staff — maids, bellmen, room service waiters, valets, et cetera. However, it is possible to exclude them all from a particular suite for hours with a simple 'Do Not Disturb' sign hung on a doorknob. Unfortunately, that will not stop the other occupant of the suite."

"Quite right. I assume you have an inkling of a plan?"

"I followed the two gentlemen when they checked into their suite, so I know the number. I have since had a word with a staff member who, for an emolument, gave me two valuable pieces of information. One, every morning at seven-thirty or so, Mr. M. takes himself to the outdoor restaurant, where he consumes a large breakfast. Two, Mr. V., on the other hand, does not rise until Mr. M. returns and rousts him from his slumber. That means there is about an hour's time available to enter the suite and deal with him decisively. Perhaps both of them." He looked at his watch. "Not enough time to prepare today, but tomorrow?"

"Just tell me what you want me to do," Stone said.

"I would like you to send flowers," Billy replied, then he continued.

When Billy had finished, Stone thought about the plan and the risk to himself. "You're on," he said.

54

Teddy returned to Centurion and found Betsy at her new desk, making calls.

"Hi," she said. "Peter asked us to join them and Stone at Spago for dinner tonight. Emma Tweed is back in town, and they're taking her to dinner. She and Tessa are flying back to London tomorrow. I'm booking her ticket now."

"Book us at a separate table, but nearby. Tell the restaurant it's for security purposes."

"All right. I'll tell Peter."

"And when he goes to lunch today, I want you to come with me for an hour."

"All right."

Teddy didn't much like the idea of Peter's dining out, but with the two Strategic Services agents and himself, he thought they should be able to keep him safe.

At noon, Peter, Ben, and Hattie left for

lunch, and Teddy put Betsy in a golf cart and drove her to the armory.

"I've never asked you this, but have you ever fired a gun before?"

"I shot some skeet with a boyfriend once, but I've never fired a handgun."

"After the near miss with the Viper, I'd feel better if you were armed."

"Now that you mention it," she said, "I think I'd feel better armed, too."

He took her to the range and gave her his tiny Keltec .380 pistol, then he picked up the remote control and moved the target to ten feet. "Most gunfights are at this range or closer," he said, "so there's no point in training you to twenty-five or fifty feet." He showed her how to operate the gun. "You couldn't hit anything with this gun beyond ten feet anyway, the barrel is too short, so let's have you fire some rounds now."

He showed her the proper stance and grip. "Point it at the middle of the target," he said, "both eyes open. Pull the trigger slowly, which is called 'squeezing.' Don't jerk."

She fired the six rounds; all of them hit the target, but none in the center. "Fire more slowly," he said. "Concentrate on getting the first round in the center of the target. The rest will take care of themselves."

She fired another magazine and did better; one more and she had an eight-inch grouping.

Teddy moved the target to five feet. "From here," he said, "go for a head shot. When he's this close, you've got to stop him, and the head is the quickest way."

She fired two more magazines from that range and did well. Teddy took the little gun into the shop, cleaned and reloaded it, and gave it back to her. "Keep it in your bag, or better yet, in a pocket, if you have a pocket. Women seem never to have pockets."

"Only when wearing jeans," Betsy replied, making sure the gun was on safety before dropping it into her bag. "And they would be too tight to accommodate a gun."

They went to dinner that night, and their table was well placed. Teddy looked at the group; they seemed very happy, and he wanted the evening to end that way. The two agents were at another conveniently located table.

"Why aren't you looking at me?" Betsy asked. "It's creepy talking to someone who isn't looking at you."

"I'm looking at the people I'm protecting," he said, keeping his gaze past her. "I'm watching their backs. You watch mine."

"Okay," she said, putting her handbag on the table.

"Just watch," he said, "don't fire. If you fired six rounds in this restaurant, you'd hit four diners and me."

"But I did well today — you said so!"

"You did, but you weren't under any pressure, and you didn't have to act quickly. That's shooting we can do at another training session on the range, but not at Spago."

"Oh, all right, but if I can't shoot, why am I watching your back?"

"If you see the Viper, tell me, and I'll do the shooting."

After dinner, Teddy said, "I'll take you back to the hangar, then I want to borrow your car. I'll be out all night."

"Who is she?" Betsy asked, archly.

"Don't ask. And if anybody else asks, I slept next to you all night."

"I want to clean out the rest of our things from the apartment," she said. "Why don't I do that tonight?"

"Not tonight," Teddy said. "Tomorrow night, if we're lucky."

"Is there something you want to tell me?" she asked.

"Lots of things," he said, "but none of them tonight."

He caught Stone Barrington's eye as they waited for their cars from the valet, and they exchanged a nod. It was on.

55

Stone and Emma renewed their acquaintance in bed after dinner.

"Stone," Emma said, when they were done but still lying in each other's arms, "Tessa doesn't want to go back to London, but I'm making her. Am I doing the right thing?"

"How do you make her go back?" Stone asked. "She seems like a self-operating adult to me."

"A mother has ways."

"Guilt?"

"Guilt is very helpful with Tessa," Emma said, "but I try to rely on logic and appeal to her better nature."

"And that works?" Stone asked, surprised.

"She's a *responsible* adult."

"So, if she's so responsible, what's the problem with leaving her in L.A.?"

"She's half in love with Ben. I'm afraid they'll marry."

"Emma, you need to look into your own psyche, not into what you imagine are Tessa's inclinations. But if you want to look at marriage as a worst-case scenario, Ben Bacchetti is a very worthwhile young man. Anyway, kids live together these days, instead of marrying."

"But *Hollywood*? She could have a grand career on the London stage."

"Making Hollywood movies — good ones — is no bar to appearing on the London stage. You've got to learn to trust your daughter's judgment."

"I do, but . . ."

"It's the 'but' you've got to deal with."

"I know."

"I think the problem is not where Tessa lives, but where she lives in relation to you. Why don't you open an office out here and spend some time running it?"

"I already have a small office here."

"Enlarge it — move some of your operations here from New York. I'll bet a lot of your employees here would jump at the chance to move to the Coast."

"You really think so? New Yorkers?"

"I really think so. A lot of Londoners would, too, and you're a Londoner. It's not like you have to spend *all* your time here."

"I'll think about that."

"What time is your airplane tomorrow?"

"Two PM."

"Sleep on it, and make a decision in the morning."

She burrowed into his shoulder. "Good idea."

Stone tried to sleep but couldn't; he stared at the ceiling, tried to daydream, but the only thing he could think of was the box of flowers on the backseat of his car.

He waited until five am to go into the study to call Dino.

"You're up early," Dino said.

"I haven't been to sleep."

"I thought you were the world's champion sleeper."

"I thought so, too."

"Okay, tell me about it."

"Majorov is here, and he's brought an assassin with him from New York, a Russian."

Dino let a beat pass before he responded. "Anybody I know?"

"His name is Vladimir —"

"The Viper? Jesus!"

"That's not the worst of it. He's more interested in Peter than me."

"Then why haven't you killed him yet?"

"That's why I couldn't sleep."

"You planning to do him yourself?"

"I'm about to set him up for someone else."

"That Billy character?"

"Yes. I need your advice on this, pal. I've never been a party to murder before."

"Here's my advice," Dino said. "Don't get caught."

"That's good advice," Stone said.

"Let me know how it comes out."

"Will do."

"And good luck."

"Thanks, Dino."

"You're welcome, Stone, and for what it's worth, if it were Ben at risk, I wouldn't hesitate."

"I guess I should have known that. Bye." Stone hung up, took a deep breath, went back to the bedroom, and got dressed. Emma was snoring lightly when he left. He had crumbled an Ambien into her brandy glass at bedtime.

He had some orange juice and a cup of coffee, checking his watch regularly. Finally, he went upstairs, got into a dark golf jacket and a baseball cap and a pair of driving gloves.

He ran his pistol onto his belt, took a deep breath, and left the house by the rear door.

56

Teddy had arrived at the Bel-Air by five AM, leaving his car up Stone Canyon and walking down the hill to the rear of the hotel, wearing a black sweater over a white shirt, black trousers, black rubber-soled slippers, and latex surgical gloves. He carried his silenced pistol in a holster under the sweater and a switchblade knife in a hip pocket.

Majorov's suite was the second up the hill from the rear service road, and Teddy was through the hedge and over the wall very quickly, landing lightly on his feet. A streetlight cast some light on the suite's patio, and he moved into a shadow and waited for three or four minutes. The Viper was probably a light sleeper, and if he heard anything he would come out armed.

There were three sets of French doors, one for each bedroom and one for the living room. Teddy checked all three and in one bedroom found Majorov's bulk visible by the light of a television set that he had failed to turn off before falling asleep. He went back to the patio outside the other bedroom, half expecting to encounter the assassin on his way.

Nothing happened. Teddy carefully picked up a chair from the patio and moved it into a dark corner, then he crept to the French doors and listened for movement inside. All he heard was snoring. He stared through the glass into the room and located the bed with its sleeping lump, dimly lit by a night-light. When his eyes had adjusted better he saw, on the bedside table, a silenced pistol. Vlad was a cautious man.

He put his hand on the doorknob and tried turning it. Locked. He had expected as much, and he had come prepared. He removed a strip of sturdy but flexible plastic from his pocket and inserted it between the door and the jamb. He probed until he felt the bias-cut bolt begin to open, then he stopped, leaving the plastic strip in place.

He went to the chair in the corner and settled into it; he had a couple of hours to wait. He switched on his iPhone, turned down the backlighting a bit, then went to the *New York Times* website and began reading the front page.

■ ■ ■ ■

Stone let himself out of the house and got into Peter's Cayenne. It was parked on an incline out back, where he had left it after visiting the florist, so he let it roll for a hundred yards before starting the engine. He rolled up to a back gate, and it opened automatically at the approach of his car.

The drive to the Bel-Air took only three minutes, and the sun was up now. Twenty-five past seven. He parked the car just up the street from the rear gate of the hotel, and then he got lucky. He looked around a hedge and saw the guard on duty at the back gate leave his sentry box, presumably in search of a toilet.

Stone managed a brisk walk, without appearing to be in too much of a hurry. As he walked, he rubbed his gloved hands over the spots on the flower box where he might have left fingerprints. He turned right and climbed a few steps, passing a room service waiter carrying a tray of dirty dishes, then he saw what he needed. He walked over to a guest door and removed the DO NOT DISTURB sign, then he walked a few steps more and found the correct suite number on a door. He hung the sign on the doorknob, leaned the box against the door, took a deep breath, and repeatedly rang the doorbell, then he turned and retraced his steps to the car. The security man had still not returned.

He had seen no one but the room service waiter, and the man had carried his tray on his shoulder, so that it blocked his view of Stone as they passed. He drove back to The Arrington and punched the code into the box outside the gate. It opened slowly.

He put the car away and went back into the house, tiptoeing up the stairs to the master bedroom, then he undressed in his dressing room and got back into bed with Emma.

He worked at relaxing, until his heart rate was normal.

At six-thirty, Teddy heard a door to the patio behind him open. He froze and switched off his phone. Then he heard singing from a gruff, baritone voice. Majorov in the shower.

At seven o'clock, with the sky lightening, Teddy moved to a position that allowed him a full view of Vlad's bedroom and, through the open door, a view of the front entrance. Shortly, Majorov appeared, opened the front door, and closed it behind him. On his way to breakfast.

Teddy watched closely to see if Majorov's moving around had wakened Vlad, but the man continued to lie on his back, snoring. He waited, trying to stay relaxed, for the sound of the doorbell.

It came at the stroke of seven-thirty, then again and again. Vlad stirred, then sat up and shook his head, as if he couldn't identify the sound. Then, muttering, he put his feet over the side of the bed and walked toward the front door. As he did, the bedsheet moved back, revealing the butt of a shotgun. The man slept with a shotgun in bed!

Teddy moved quickly, now; he pressed home the plastic strip, moved the bolt back, opened the door, and stepped inside. He moved quickly to the side of the bed where the pistol rested on the bedside table, then slid behind the drawn curtain. He drew his pistol and flipped off the safety.

He heard a flower box being thrown across the room and a spate of swearing in Russian. Then Vlad stumbled back into the bedroom, muttering, and got back into bed. Shortly, he was snoring again.

Teddy peeked from behind the curtain and found not the sleeping figure he had expected, but a man sitting up in bed pointing a silenced pistol directly at him. He was still snoring, but he was smiling, too.

"Good morning, Mr. Burnett," Vlad said.

Teddy fired through the curtain at where he thought Vlad would be, then he pushed back the heavy cloth with his gun raised, ready to fire again. Vlad was gone.

Teddy ran around the bed, ready to pursue him into the living room, but he found the Russian lying faceup on the floor on the other side of the bed, his head in a growing pool of blood. He had hit the man somewhere. Vlad's body began to shake, and Teddy fired another round into his forehead. He lay still.

"Good morning, Vlad," Teddy said. He started to leave the room the way he had come in, but then he noticed a black suitcase on a stand across the room from the bed. He walked over and examined it; it was unlocked. He raised the lid and found an assassin's dream: a case of instruments of killing. There was a disassembled sniper rifle, two pistols, a silencer, four knives, and some disposable syringes with a rubber band around them. Next to the syringes was a bottle labeled POTASSIUM.

Teddy closed the case, locked it, and buckled the two straps that secured it, then went back to the patio, stepped outside, and set the case down. Then something unexpected happened: the front door opened.

"Vlad!" Majorov shouted. "Wake up!"

Teddy held the plastic strip in place as he pulled the door closed, then withdrew the strip, locking the door. He ran to the patio wall, set the case on it, stepped on a chair, and hoisted himself to the top. He dropped lightly to the other side, then jumped clear of the hedge. A moment later he was back in his car, wondering why he had not stayed to shoot Majorov, too. Never mind, he would leave the man to the police.

He was halfway back to Santa Monica Airport before it occurred to him that Majorov wasn't going to call the police.

57

Majorov took one glance into Vlad's bedroom and saw the body on the floor, covered with blood. He reached for the weapon he carried in a shoulder holster and pointed it into the bedroom, waiting for someone to appear. No one did.

He tiptoed around the suite, looking into corners and closets, and found no one. He picked up the phone and was about to dial the hotel operator, but he stopped and thought for a moment. He hung up, got out his cell phone, and called his pilot.

"Yes?" He sounded sleepy.

"We're leaving Los Angeles immediately," Majorov said. "Get to the airport as fast as you can, and file for Gander, then Moscow." He would feel safer at his dacha outside Moscow than in his Paris apartment.

"I can be ready to taxi in one hour," the pilot said.

"Have the airplane brought to the ramp

immediately. I'll wait aboard for you to arrive."

"Yes, sir."

Majorov hung up and looked at his watch: seven-forty. Vlad had room service deliver his breakfast every morning at eight. In a panic he went to his closet, got out his three cases, and began throwing things into them, then he went to the bathroom and raked his toiletries off the shelf over the sink and closed the small valise that carried them. He went back to the bedroom and called the front desk.

"Yes, Mr. Majorov?"

"Please send a bellman to my room immediately and get me a car and driver for the airport." He didn't mention which airport; if the police came too soon, they would think LAX.

"Are you checking out, sir?"

"Yes, but my companion is staying for one more day. Just put it on my bill."

"Yes, sir. I'll send a bellman right away."

Majorov hung up, then carried his four bags to the front door, opened it, and set them outside on the little entry porch. He couldn't have a bellman entering the suite. He noticed that the do not disturb sign was already on the doorknob. Had Vlad put it there? No, probably his murderer. Burnett

— it had to be Burnett.

He went back to the bedroom, put on his necktie and jacket, and returned to the living room. As an afterthought, he closed Vlad's bedroom door.

The bell rang, and he let himself out to find the bellman loading his cases onto a cart. "I'll meet you at the car," he said to the bellman, handing him a hundred-dollar bill. "Go ahead and load everything."

"Yes, sir." The man began pushing the cart away.

Majorov went back inside and checked for any of his belongings he might have left. Then, instead of taking the usual route along the hotel paths to the parking lot, he walked to the road, walked down the hill and into the lot, where he found the bellman closing the trunk of the hotel limo. He ambled, as casually as possible, to the car, where the driver held the door open, gave the valet a fifty, and got into the rear seat.

"LAX, sir?" the driver asked, as he closed his door.

"No, to Santa Monica Airport, Atlantic Aviation." The car began to move. *Good God!* he thought. *I forgot to call room service!* He checked his watch: seven-fifty. "And step on it," he said, "I'm running late."

"I think we'd better avoid the freeway if

398

you're in a hurry, sir. May I take Sunset to Bundy and go that way?"

"Fine, whatever you say." He was sweating, and he pulled the silk square from his breast pocket and dabbed at his brow, then he adjusted the air-conditioning for more flow.

Stone got out of bed and went to the bathroom. When he returned, Emma was sitting up in bed, reading *The New York Times*. "Breakfast in bed or downstairs?" he asked.

"Oh, I think in bed," she replied.

"Order me bacon and eggs, orange juice, and coffee," Stone said, getting into a robe. "I've got to give Peter his car keys."

He grabbed the keys from the dresser and walked downstairs. Peter, Hattie, and Ben were having breakfast in the dining room. He gave Peter the keys. "Don't be late for work," he said.

"Dad, we're traveling in the Strategic Services car."

"Oh, I forgot," Stone said. "Have a good day."

"Dad, how long do we have to do this security stuff?"

"Not much longer, I should think," Stone said. "I'm just guessing, of course."

"Great."

Stone went back upstairs, shed his robe, and got back into bed.

"Did you go somewhere last night?" Emma asked.

"Go somewhere?"

"I woke up at some point and you weren't in bed."

"I must have been in the bathroom," he replied. "Or maybe you were dreaming."

Majorov's car arrived at the airport and was buzzed through the security gate. The Gulfstream was just being towed to a halt on the ramp. He waited until the airplane had been chocked and the door opened, then he showed the driver where to put his luggage. Finally, he took off his jacket, hung it up, and went to his usual seat.

He reclined the seat halfway, put a pillow under his head, and closed his eyes. He needed to calm down.   •

58

Teddy arrived at Santa Monica Airport, was buzzed through the gate, and drove to the hangar. He stopped at a taxiway to check for traffic and saw Majorov's Gulfstream being towed out of a nearby hangar. So the man was not hanging around the Bel-Air to speak to the police.

He pulled into the hangar and closed the big door behind him. Tim was not at work yet, and Betsy would be upstairs. He had seen some things belonging to Livingston's pilot, but where? In the flat? No, in the pilots' lounge somewhere.

He walked quickly back to the lounge carrying Vlad's weapons case and looked around. Not in the closet where he had put the safe; in the other closet, maybe. He opened it and found a uniform jacket, a cap, and a laundry box on a shelf above them. He broke open the box and found a shirt. A moment later he was dressed as a corporate pilot.

He hoisted Vlad's case onto the table, opened it, removed one of the syringes from the bundle, filled it with potassium from the bottle, replaced the cap, and put it into an inside pocket near his holstered pistol. He put on the cap and his aviator sunglasses, left the hangar by the rear door, and walked toward the ramp. As he emerged from behind the hangar he saw a limo drive away from the Gulfstream and depart through the gate. He walked quickly toward the airplane.

As he approached, a stewardess came out of Atlantic Aviation carrying a heavy bag of ice in one hand and a caddy filled with wine bottles in the other. He caught up with her. "Let me give you a hand," he said, taking her burdens from her.

"Thank you. I'll go get the lunches — they weren't quite ready." She turned and walked back toward the FBO.

Teddy walked quickly toward the Gulfstream and up the airstair. At the top he peeked into the airplane. Cockpit, empty, but in the rear of the cabin, stretched out in a reclining seat, was Majorov, his head on a pillow, a blanket covering his lap, his eyes closed.

Teddy carefully set down the ice and the wine in the galley, stood very still for a moment, and watched the man for some sign of movement; he appeared to be sleeping, or trying to. Teddy reached into his inside pocket and retrieved the syringe, then began walking carefully down the aisle toward his quarry.

As Teddy approached, Majorov heaved a deep sigh and resettled himself in the seat, then he opened his eyes and looked at Teddy.

"Leave me," he said. "I need sleep."

"Yes, sir," Teddy said, and stood where he had stopped. He waited a full minute for Majorov to settle down, then he walked silently toward the man. When he reached his side, he uncapped the syringe, put it in his right hand, and with his left, pushed Majorov's head firmly into the pillow and held it there while he sought the carotid artery. Majorov began to struggle, but Teddy held his head down as he slipped in the needle and pushed the plunger home. Then he released Majorov.

The Russian sat up, rubbing his neck where the needle had gone in. "What have you done?" he demanded.

"Just something to help you sleep," Teddy said. "Compliments of Billy Burnett."

"You?" Majorov spat. "You are Burnett!"

"For the moment," Teddy said.

The Russian suddenly convulsed and clawed at his chest. He seemed to be having trouble breathing.

"There, there," Teddy said, pushing Majorov back into his seat and buckling his seat belt. "Just a heart attack. You'll be gone in a moment."

Majorov went limp, exhaling one last time. Teddy picked up a cocktail napkin and dabbed away a drop of blood that had escaped the needle prick, then he tucked the pillow under the man's head, turned it to the right, and pulled the blanket up to his chin. He switched off the light over the seat, closed the shade on the window beside the dead Russian, then walked back toward the cockpit, closing shades on both sides as he went. The cabin was now dark, the only light coming from the open door and the cockpit windows.

Teddy started down the airstair and met the stewardess coming the other way. He took the box lunches from her and set them in the galley. "Your passenger asked not to be disturbed," he whispered to her. "He said he needs sleep."

She nodded. "Thanks for your help, uh . . ."

"Just a neighbor. I'm in the Hawker across the ramp. Have a good flight."

As Teddy walked back toward the hangar a car was let through the security gate, and two uniformed pilots got out, set down their flight bags, and, each with a clipboard, began their walk-around and preflight inspection.

Teddy walked back to the hangar, broke the syringe into three pieces, and tossed them over the fence; then he let himself through the rear door, went to the pilot's lounge, took off the uniform, and laid it on the table. He had just gotten back into his own clothes as the big hangar door opened, and Tim Peters drove in, closing the door behind him.

Teddy found a canvas holdall in the clothes closet, then folded the uniform and put it inside with the cap on top. He carried the bag to Tim's office and rapped on the doorjamb. "Good morning," he said. "I found a uniform that apparently belongs to Livingston's pilot. Can you send it to him, please?"

"Sure," Tim replied. "I'll drop it by his place on the way home tonight." He tucked the holdall into the bottom drawer of his filing cabinet and closed it.

When Tim had left, Teddy called Stone

Barrington on his cell phone.

"Yes?"

"You recall a couple of people we spoke of?"

"I do."

"It's my understanding that they are no longer a factor."

"Your understanding?"

"My certainty."

"That is good to hear."

"I thought you might think so. Goodbye." He hung up.

Teddy went upstairs to make sure Betsy was awake. She was drinking coffee in the kitchen.

"Hey, there. How about some breakfast?" she asked.

"Stick with your coffee. I'll toast myself a muffin." He did, then sat down with her.

"You look well rested," she said. "Did you sleep well last night?"

"You should know," Teddy replied. "I was right beside you the whole night."

59

Stone was getting dressed when Emma came out of the bathroom. They had spent half the morning making love, and she seemed aglow.

"You all packed?" he asked.

"Yes, and I just got off the phone with Tessa. She's staying — oh well — in Hollywood. I made some calls to my New York office, too, and got some volunteers for a move to L.A."

"I'm happy for everybody concerned," Stone said. "What time do you want to leave for the airport?"

"In half an hour, I think. I'll have lunch in the first-class lounge."

Stone's Strategic Services driver was finishing a cup of coffee in the kitchen when Stone came down. He stood up.

"Ready to go out, Mr. Barrington?"

"Dick," Stone said, "I think I'll drive myself today — and every day from now on. You can report back to Mr. Freeman."

"As you wish, Mr. Barrington."

Stone walked into the dining room and found Peter's keys to the Cayenne on the table where Stone had left them earlier that morning.

He read the papers until Emma came down, followed by the butler carrying her bags. They got everything into the Cayenne and drove to LAX.

"How long before you'll be back?" he asked, as a porter loaded her luggage onto a cart.

"Give me a month or so to sort out the personnel changes, and I'll be back in New York with you. Or will you be here?"

"In New York, I think. It's time I let the kids get on with their lives."

"You're no longer concerned about their safety?"

"I'm told that the problem has been resolved," Stone said.

They kissed, then she followed the porter, and Stone got back in the Cayenne and headed for Centurion Studios.

Stone found everybody on the set, including Billy and Betsy. He watched as they shot a setup, then broke while the lighting was changed for the next shot.

Peter came over, and Stone handed him the keys to the Cayenne. "Okay, kiddo, you're on your own again."

"Should I go armed?"

"Unnecessary, I should think."

"That's good news," Peter said, grinning.

"I'll let your security detail know," Stone said, glancing over to where the two guards were chatting up a pretty extra. He walked over and cleared his throat to get their attention. "Fellas, I'm afraid your careers in the film business are over. You can stand down, just as soon as you've given me a lift back to The Arrington."

"As you wish, Mr. Barrington. Will Peter be needing us tomorrow?"

"No, Peter is going to be just fine on his own. We all have to let go."

As he was walking from the building, Billy Barnett caught up with him.

"Good morning," Stone said.

"Morning to you."

"Did you sleep well last night?"

"Everything went about as it should," Teddy replied.

"Both of them?"

"Vlad will get the attention of the LAPD," Teddy said. "Majorov will be attended to by the Moscow morgue, when he arrives there."

"Do I need to know anything else?"

"I don't think there's anything else you want to know," Teddy said. "And it's best to forget what you already know."

"Are you going to work for Mike Freeman at Strategic Services?"

"Probably, eventually. First I have to get your boy an instrument rating and see that he's at home in his new airplane. That will take a few weeks, and then my work here will be done, and Mike and I will talk again. You can tell him that for me."

Stone shook his hand. "Thank you for my son's life," he said, "and those of Hattie and Ben, too."

"You're very welcome," Teddy replied.

Stone left him, walked out to the car, and got into the rear seat. "Let's take a turn around the lot before we go back to the hotel," he said to his escorts.

"Yes, sir. Anything in particular you want to see?"

"Maybe the New York street. No, let's see it all. I've done some hard time in this place, and I want one more look at it before I go."

ABOUT THE AUTHOR

Stuart Woods is the author of more than fifty novels, including the *New York Times*–bestselling Stone Barrington and Holly Barker series. He is a native of Georgia and began his writing career in the advertising industry. *Chiefs,* his debut in 1981, won the Edgar Award. An avid sailor and pilot, Woods lives in New York City, Florida, and Maine.

CPSIA information can be obtained
at www.ICGtesting.com
Printed in the USA
FFOW03n2325230414
5011FF

9 781594 136955